BROOKLYN KNIGHT

BROOKLYN KNIGHT

C. J. HENDERSON

A TOM DOHERTY ASSOCIATES BOOK · NEW YORK

TOR®

BROOKLYN KNIGHT

A Tor Book
Published by Tom Doherty Associates, LLC.
175 Fifth Avenue
New York, NY 10010

www.tor-forge.com

Library of Congress Cataloging-in-Publication Data

Henderson, C. J.
Brooklyn Knight / C. J. Henderson.—1st ed.
p. cm.
"A Tom Doherty Associates book."
ISBN 978-0-7653-2083-4
1. Museum curators—Fiction. 2. Magic—Fiction.
3. Talismans—Fiction. 4. Four elements (Philosophy)—Fiction.
5. Brooklyn (New York, N.Y.)—Fiction. I. Title.
PS3558.E48244B76 2010
813'.54—dc22

2009036275

Printed in the United States of America

0 9 8 7 6 5 4 3 2

There are editors who take their jobs seriously, who can find every tiny typo you make, helping to keep you from looking like the jerk you are.

There are editors who know your moods, who like a good friend, or caring relative, work with you and for you and around you, realizing when it's time to allow you your creative angst, and when it's time to hit you on the snout with a rolled-up newspaper.

There are editors who watch for opportunities perfectly crafted for you. Who go out of their way to mold you into more than just a good writer. Who work ceaselessly in the background to make you better than you are.

And then . . .

There are those editors who do all these things, and more, and make it look easy.

This book is dedicated to one such wondrous being.

His name was Brian M. Thomsen

And he was my friend.

Submit to fate of your own free will.

—Marcus Aurelius

Perfect courage is to do without witnesses what one would be capable of doing with the world looking on.

—François, Duc de La Rochefoucauld

BROOKLYN KNIGHT

AN EXCERPT FROM:

Ruminations on the Past

A Study of the Myths, Legends, and Oral Tradition Surrounding the Euphrates River Valley

Compiled by Professor Niles Wentworth Standard

Published by Priceton & Waterbury, 1876

Even at a significant distance, such as from any of the four major hills surrounding the city, the most casual observation would reveal an overall appearance not like that of any other habitation to be found throughout the known world. There was good reason for this. Indeed, the place appeared as far more than all others for one simple, undeniable reason—it was more.

Far more.

The name of this unique metropolis was Memak'tori, and in its day and age it was the finest sanctuary ever fashioned by the hands of men. Any traveler reaching one of those four major hillocks in between which it was nestled had more than sufficient cause to pause and marvel. For, even at that initial distance of several miles, no matter their level of worldliness, or from wherever said journeyman might hail, they were certain to be amazed.

Memak'tori was an enormous and heavily populated center, one so far advanced beyond the simple grouped farms and other budding communities one could find in any of the other far-flung corners of the world men had reached that visitors to it were stunned by their first glimpse of its grandeur—they could not help themselves. To gaze upon vast Memak'tori for the first time was to stand in wonder.

The city stood in the center of a lush and rolling river valley, a well-nurtured, continually green oasis in an otherwise arid landscape. Once merely an agricultural center, the advent of merchant shipping caused it to become a center of commerce. As the decades passed and the wealth created by their fortunate location began to pile up all about them, the people of Memak'tori started to build in earnest. They constructed their city with a cunning and ingenuity unheard of elsewhere, some of its buildings arching upward into the sky to the staggering total of three, sometimes even four stories.

Far more impressive, however, was the fashion in which the metropolis' great stone towers jutted higher still, seemingly grasping at the passing clouds. The city's pennants flew above them at such unbelievable heights that men who had not seen them for themselves, who only heard tales of their awe-inspiring proportions, would often scoff in disbelief, branding those who persisted in telling of such miracles as fools or liars. Indeed, in the end, fabled Memak'tori was simply one of those places that had to be seen to be believed.

There was no denying that something had come together in that temperate corner of the world which had not yet spread to any other land. What combination of circumstances led to its existence none could say with certainty, nor were such things overly worried about in those far-gone days.

Men simply knew that if adventure, knowledge, or sophistication was that for which their heart yearned, Memak'tori was where it could be found.

For whatever reason Fate chose to bring these blessings together thus, this grand and sparkling city was the site that would mark mankind's first grand thrust upward out of barbarism and savagery. Memak'tori was far more than simply a gathering place for human beings—all other lands knew these.

Its greatness resided in something beyond it merely possessing a convenient location for merchants and farmers to interact—these also could be found in plenty elsewhere throughout the known world.

No, what made this one place so different from all others was that it had a purpose beyond the mundane. Memak'tori was the first active center of human knowledge ever created. Its streets were not so much different from those of other cities, but those who walked them were.

The people of Memak'tori knew they had been placed among the human race's elite members. Some believed they were blessed by the gods. Others thought the waters in that area gifted individuals with insights denied others. One school of thought had it that the position of the city, sitting as it did just so beneath certain of the night stars, created its favorable prosperity. The idea of what made their society the foremost one in the world was hotly debated in many a tavern and temple—and just as many of those structures stood outside the great city's boundaries as did within them.

There came a certain time, however—suddenly and without warning—when a returning traveler reaching one of the fabled metropolis' surrounding hilltops would spy something different about it. Nothing overt, or immediately noticeable, to be certain. Nothing the physical senses could pinpoint with assurance. No, it was more in the way of a mood, a feeling that the atmosphere around Memak'tori had somehow changed. As they approached its massive gates, they would then note a shocking lack of security, of even activity.

That was only the beginning.

Passing through the oddly unguarded portal—trepidation their unavoidable guiding emotion—those outsiders coming to the city at that point in its history would discover the streets strangely deserted, window curtains hanging askance, doorways filled with growing piles of encroaching dust and sand. They would find tables set for a meal, plates positioned properly, fruit and bread rotten and crumbling upon them. Mugs would be found next to the plates, their contents long since evaporated.

Most who came to Memak'tori after that time dared not tarry. No people to be found within its limits—no animals, seemingly not even insects—it was too much for them to comprehend. Some braver souls would penetrate deeper into its bowels, of course, looking for prizes to carry off. These were often handsomely rewarded for the citizens of Memak'tori might have disappeared, but they did not take their possessions with them. Like their meals, they left behind their gold and precious stones, their maps and tools, their cloth and clothes, beds and brooms—everything.

Not all such adventurers profited, however. Few did so, in fact. For most of the looters who dared pass through the city's silent gates, their fate was to never be seen again. Those who went searching for them might find a recognizable staff or cloak, but of those for whom they searched there would be no further trace. Indeed, most of those who went searching never returned to report their findings, either.

Such events cannot continue to occur for very long, though, before the news of them begins to spread. As word of Memak'tori's unexplainable fate became common knowledge—a tale confirmed by the mysterious disappearance of several of the more famous thieves who bragged they would be the one to finally loot the great ghost city—word spread across the land. Terrified words spoken in fearful whispers.

And thus Memak'tori was labeled officially as a damned place, denounced in the temples, cursed in the streets. Its people, it was assumed, certainly must have offended the gods in some manner. Many felt it was its populace's shameful hubris, their wretchedly different ideas, which had brought down such a terrible fate upon their heads.

It was not long before peoples far and wide began demanding that no such recklessly dangerous notions be imported to their own home states. Memak'tori, one day the shining light of hope for the future of humanity, became on the next a pariah to all men. Roadways leading to it were blocked, marked with signs leaving no doubt that nothing but tragedy awaited ahead.

Feared and mistrusted, the place was given a wide berth by all who heard the horrifying tales whispered about it. And, as years turned into decades and the centuries passed, the weather wore away its towers, piling the sand higher and higher, filling its halls, covering its roofs. And thus, a thousand years before such sites as Heraklion or Tartessos were erected, Memak'tori passed into the realm of legend. By the time Greece and Rome were in their glory, it was barely a memory.

Sadly, though, that would change. Millennia after its strange and curious passing, fabled Memak'tori would be rediscovered, its rooftops cleared of their layers of sand and detritus, its streets swept and opened to the world once more. Interest in the remarkable city would suddenly be renewed, on a far greater scale than ever had been reached when men first walked its streets and marveled at its glory.

And, as one might suspect, all of this, of course, was nothing more than an invitation to the disaster which had once removed the world's greatest civilization to return—this time to consume all of humanity.

PROLOGUE

"Listen to me, my good woman, this conversation is costing me per minute more than your weekly salary. If you do not mind, I would appreciate it greatly if you did not further waste any of my resources with your excuses."

The speaker was not by nature an unpleasant man.

Indeed, he was trying his best to keep from becoming one. He was also, however, famously known as being quite an excitable person.

Of course, given the reason for his phone call, anyone in his position would be understandably just as excited. Most would probably be just as unpleasant, as well, if not more so.

"So, knowing this, if you could, just find him, without any more delays, and put him on the phone—would you, *please?*"

Standing in the sands of a long-dried riverbed, a spot thousands of miles from his home, waiting to be connected to the one person who could change his mounting anticipation and eager hunger into unparalleled joy, the caller sighed as the secretary on the other end of their call promised once more to "see what I can do." With an audible sigh, one incapable of masking his growing fury, the man agreed, then began waiting once more, swallowing his burning frustration as best he could.

The beating sun ravaged his tall, thin body, stealing every spare drop of moisture it could wring from him. Despite the lightness of his wardrobe—white cotton shirt and socks, shorts cut just above the knees—the heat tore at him. Sweat leaked from his smooth forehead, dampening his close-cropped hair, stinging his brown eyes, dripping from his slightly hooked nose. Standing helplessly in the dry, arid breeze, the man found his body twitching, the muscles in his legs jumping, causing his feet to alternately tap the ground unconsciously, as if he were auditioning for the lead in *The Fred Astaire Story*.

And each passing second only rattled the caller further, making him more aware of his surroundings, and of those sharing them with him. Every ticking moment dragged the man away from his hoped-for dreams, turning him back toward reality, toward remembering, toward facing the horrible possibility that he might not be able to accomplish what he needed to through the person he was trying to reach.

This must work; it has to . . .

Of course, he knew, he was being foolish. His panic was unreasonable. Nothing more than nerves—foolishness. There was no actual reason for him to worry. He merely had to calm himself, stop worrying about the expense involved in his call, and wait. The person he was seeking would have no difficulty in delivering unto him that which he so desperately wished to acquire. That person would be happy to do so. And then considerations as vulgar as mere money would become meaningless to him.

But, he despaired, unable to stop himself, *what if I am letting desire blind me? What if he cannot do so? Or . . . what if he will not? Worse, even if he has no problem with releasing it unto me . . . after all, he most likely will want nothing more than to grant me complete access to it, but . . . the museum, they all have their bureaucracy, their red tape, the swirling nightmare of procedure—*

What if there is nothing he can do? What if someone else purchased exclusive research rights? And then, the unthinkable: *What if it is no longer within the museum?*

This frightening notion made the breath freeze within his lungs. Despite the sweltering, draining heat of the desert, the tall, thin man felt a terrible chill at the all too real possibility his fears had uncovered. Museums, research centers, universities, they all engaged in such practices anymore as a matter of routine. Ever since the late 1940s especially, the infighting, the resource bundling, favorite-son packaging—all of it nothing more than blatant excuses to tie up access to valuable data for years, decades!

"Oh my God," the man muttered, his fears gnawing through the last of the restraints his common sense had been able to provide him. Realizing how the one simple thing he needed might possibly be kept from him, he began to mutter a plaintive mantra: "Oh dear God, dear God in Heaven, oh dear God . . ."

The tangle of conflicting thoughts, rushing joy tumbling across a dozen different paranoid reasons for expecting said joy to evaporate made the caller's ever-mounting tensions grow exponentially. Unable to help himself, the man tried to force himself simply to breathe regularly as his mind continued to ricochet from one extreme to the other until finally his tapping and twitches were in danger of sending him completely out of control.

"Oh, dear God, dear God in Heaven . . ."

Mopping at the sweat pouring down his temples and the back of his neck with his handkerchief, he squeezed out the deeply stained rag, then began again. For a moment, the small torrent surprised him, distracting him from his worries. Having worked in desert settings for so many years, he could not understand from where so much moisture was coming.

Such a mild diversion could not capture his attention for long, however, and it was but a matter of seconds before his frightened nerves began him mumbling once more.

"Oh, dear God . . ."

Attempting to get hold of his runaway fears, to compel himself back to a calmer state, the wildly perspiring man broke off his frenzied mantra and closed his eyes. After forcing himself to simply stare into the darkness behind his eyelids for a moment, he then opened his eyes once more. As he purposely turned his head slowly, working at taking in all around him, a voice from the back of the caller's mind whispered to him, reminding him of how much he had already accomplished.

You will not fail in this, it whispered to him warmly. Comfortingly. *You will not . . .*

And indeed, all about him, practically as far as the eye could see, stood solid proof backing up all of its whispered words. In every direction the once barren desert was alive with a steady activity, activity for which he was entirely responsible, that he alone had created through his singular vision and efforts. Workers numbering in the hundreds labored at a score of tasks—clearing heaping mounds of dirt and sand, screening recently loosened clumps of soil, relentlessly searching for miscellaneous bits of the past. Tools, cups, pots, furnishings, musical instruments—even the smallest fragments of the same—anything that had survived, anything that could be found, was treated as what it was: a treasure of incalculable worth.

You cannot fail. . . .

And beyond the laborers lured from every local city, town, and village, as well as the prisoners delivered unto the caller by the local government, a legion of students from around the world labored as well, all of them a part of the caller's great project. The soothing words whispered by the back of his mind diverted his attention away from his near-crippling fears, focusing it instead once more upon his inspiring accomplishments.

You must not fail. . . .

He had gone against the collected wisdom of all the greatest experts in the field. His ideas had been condemned by every major Assyriologist, and most of the minor ones as well. Their words held considerable weight with Syria's Directorate General of Antiquities and Museums, but he had offered them more than words. He had poured the passion of his theories into his proposal, had presented his facts and the assumptions build upon those facts with a frenzied belief that one by one had seized the hearts and minds of every government official in his way.

Must not fail. . . .

Relaxing finally, the caller nodded as he looked upon the details of his vast and ever-unfolding accomplishment. His tired brown eyes scanning the great activity stretching all about him in every direction save upward, a certain smugness descended upon the perspiring man. A smile finding his parched lips, he suddenly relaxed, wondering;

Why? Why am I so worried? Who could possibly scoff at us at this point? At this? he thought, his free arm sweeping the vista of labor and discovery before him, *At all this?*

No one . . .

What I have uncovered here, this find, it is among the absolute greatest ever made. Archaeologically speaking, of course, it might very well be the most important discovery of all time. Tell me, in all of history, what rivals it?

Nothing . . .

Taking a deep breath of the dry desert air, the caller finally felt his usual calm descend upon him. So far, he had made not a single error. His proposal had been correct in every detail. The remains he had uncovered—the ruins to which his own, often-challenged vision had led him, despite the opposition of the supposed best minds in the field, were undoubtedly going to prove to be not only the first major city ever built but also the most fabulous the ancient world had to offer.

Nothing at all. . . .

And, as each day, as every passing hour, was proving, "ruins" was not even a word one could apply with any degree of accuracy. What he had found, that to which his pure and true vision had led him—these were not ruins. As foot after foot of earth was stripped away, every new building uncovered proved to be in the most remarkably well-preserved shape. It was as if the ever-farther-sprawling metropolis of Memak'tori had been emptied, wrapped up, and left waiting just for him.

"Hello," the American accent sounded again finally, disturbing the caller's thoughts, capturing his attention, "Dr. Ungari? Are you still there?"

"Yes, yes," he answered with near-paralyzing excitement, his heart rate jumping, "I am here. I am. Do you have him? Let me speak to Professor Knight."

"I'm sorry; he isn't here at the moment, Doctor."

"What?!" The single word was a half-screamed, half-strangled noise, a burning thing of confused hatred so overwhelmingly intense it literally frightened the woman half a world away to the point where she nearly dropped her phone.

Before Ungari could add anything further, though, the secretary blurted;

"Please, sir. He isn't in the museum right now, but I was given permission to release his cell phone number to you. That's what took me so long. I apologize, but—"

"No, no," Ungari cut the woman off, his voice dropping to a far more pleasant tone, the terrible pressure that had seized his chest dissipating. "Forgive me, please. I am most terribly sorry. I do not know what came over me."

As the woman made her own polite noises, the doctor scrambled through his vest pockets, searching out the pad and pencil he always kept on his person. Then, as the woman gave him the number she had found for him, Dr. Ashur Ungari smiled. Nothing, he knew—

You will not fail. . . .

—could stop him now.

CHAPTER ONE

"All right, my dear, finally, to begin our little introduction," the man standing ever-so-proudly on the observation deck of the Empire State Building instructed, "look in that direction. Take it all in."

As he pointed, the young woman with him stared off over the side of the building. Before and below her stood quite a few skyscrapers along with numerous smaller buildings, all leading to the water's edge nearly a mile away. Pressing as closely to the restraining fencing as she could to enhance her view, her simply cut shoulder-length red hair rippled in the crisp breeze. The color of her wavy tresses screamed out that they were dyed, but none of the men present on the observation platform seemed to mind the fact. For that matter, none of them seemed to be spending all that much time staring at her hair, either.

"Now, of course, understand that all that you can see before you, every building and warehouse, every street and lane and alley, indeed, every inch from here to the water's edge, all of that is New York City, or as we here humbly, but correctly, like to call it, the greatest city in the world."

"And what's the land on the other side of the water?"

"Oh, that's Jersey. That's unimportant."

The young woman smiled. Even though originally from Montana, she got the joke. Also, coming from such a mountainous, underdeveloped state, she was quite accustomed to both heights and the wide-open spaces they could reveal. Nor, despite her rural upbringing, was she completely what one might label a "small-town girl." She had begun her studies in the west coast's Portland, completed them in Chicago, and in her junior year had even taken a road trip with two girlfriends to Las Vegas, with a stopover in Denver. Thus she possessed more than a touch of familiarity with what her relatives back home would call big cities.

"That's a lot of city, all right," she admitted in a tone that implied she believed her tour was over. Grabbing her wrist, her companion gave her a gentle tug, shouting;

"Come on now; as I said, this is just the beginning."

The man was tall enough, over six feet, but by no more than an inch, possibly two. His hair was longer than his companion's, but cut so that when pulled back it appeared quite conservative. It was for the most part extremely dark, but run through in several spots with streaks so blond they looked to be as unnatural as his companion's shade of red. Closer examination revealed numerous ebony strands mixed in with the straw-colored ones, however, leaving most women envying his distinctive mane. Throwing in the seductive shade of blue Nature had granted his eyes did not help very much in negating such jealousies.

"Now, this side, again, as far as the eye can see," the man pointed toward the south of Manhattan Island this time, "here as well, everything stretched out before you, this is also our beloved New York City."

"All the way to the water?" she asked with surprise. After a moment's consideration, she added, "Why, that must be miles away."

"Oh, it is," the man responded, grinning. Delighting in showing off his city to a newcomer, he added in a playfully casual tone, "Oh, and that rather formidably large landmass out there beyond the water?"

"Yes . . . ?"

"That's Staten Island. That's part of the city as well."

"I have heard of it."

"As well you should," admonished the professor. "Onetime home to famed photographer Alice Austen, as well as Antonio Meucci, the actual inventor of the telephone, and, of course, still home to Fresh Kills, although now closed, still the largest landfill in the world."

As the young woman's eyes went round as the proverbial saucers, Knight asked quietly;

"Do you know how Staten Island got its name?" When she answered that she did not, he told her;

"It was the early sixteen forties when the Dutch first settled in this area. As their first ship came into sight of the continent, all the crew marveled at the great size of the land they'd found. Then, just as I have here, one sailor pointed, asking the captain if he had noticed the island. To which, we're told, he replied, 'Zat's an island?' "

Bridget grimaced at the professor's horrible pun, but her amazement was hardly dented. What he was showing her, despite the movies she had seen, some of the camera angles having been shot exactly from where she was standing, it was still so much—too much.

After all, it was one thing to view something so massive, so all-encompassing, from the safety of a movie house, a place designed for fantasy—one where routinely she also watched talking mice, werewolves, alien creatures, dinosaurs, and song-filled pirates. It was, however, quite another to see it in person, to watch the concrete canyons roll on mile after mile. After mile.

It's unbelievable, she thought, the voice in her mind small and awed, practically frightened. *It's so, so . . .*

The redhead had been maintaining the cool demeanor for which she felt the situation called, but that was quickly being eroded by her companion's utter exuberance, as well as her own desire to give in to it. Yes, she thought, she had known heights in Montana, but they looked down on endless forests and serene lakes. They were nothing like what she was being shown.

Before her, in every direction, was human life unbound—unrestrained. How many buildings twenty, thirty, forty stories tall and more had she seen? All of them filled to overflowing with people. And the streets, miles of them—scores of miles of them—all filled with traffic, with thousands of people. Hundreds of thousands.

The turmoil of it, the intoxication, the unrestrained energy of every inch before the young woman, was overwhelming, making her giddy, smashing aside her thin veneer of sophistication as easily as an excited dog's tail might scatter unbound straw.

Not giving her mind a chance to question him or even to begin to recover, the tall-enough man took her wrist once more, gently leading his companion back the way they had come. He walked them slowly, pointing out the cruise ships and the aircraft carrier docked in the Hudson. Then, rounding the far corner, he pointed to the north, telling her;

"And that, once more, as far as the eye can see, all you survey, my dear, is also New York City."

This time, the view extended far beyond what she had found to the west or the south. As she tried to take it all in, the never-ending buildings extending all the way to the distant horizon, she found herself utterly lost—unable to grasp all she was being shown. It was staggering; it was colossal. Indeed, it took the young woman several moments before she even realized that there was a quite massive stretch of greenery in the middle of it all.

"That's Central Park," she said in an amazement-filled whisper. "My God, Professor Knight, look at it. It's got to be like . . . what? A mile long? Two miles long?"

"At least."

"That's, that's . . . ," she stammered, pausing to gulp, "dear Lord, that's longer than my hometown. You *could*—you could fit my hometown, all of it, everything, you could just sink it and lose it, in that park."

"And what a park. It commands such attention, one can almost miss some of its neighbors." Pointing toward one imposing, multiple-blocks-long structure, he added, "Such as the magnificent Museum of Natural History there. No real rival to where you shall be working, of course," he teased, "but a competent place to take schoolchildren on a rainy Saturday, to be certain."

As the redhead simply stared, the professor caught her attention with the selfsame finger, shifting it slightly to point out another landmark.

"And there you have the both notorious and somewhat creepy Dakota Apartments, where boy director Roman Polanski shot his breakout thriller *Rosemary's Baby*, and where self-absorbed musician John Lennon was murdered for reasons which even today are barely fathomable."

"Stop," insisted Bridget, laughing as she did so. "If you keep it up we'll be here all day. I mean, it's like every brick in this town has a history."

"Well, Ms. Elkins," answered the man, one side of his mouth curling into half a smile, one just a shade short of patronizing, "you did ask, you know."

The young woman's mind jumped back an hour. She had been

surprised when Professor Knight himself had met her flight at New Jersey's Newark Airport. Yes, she had been told someone would pick her up at the airport. But when she had been lucky enough to capture the paid internship allowing her to spend the summer as the assistant to one of the directors of the Brooklyn Museum, it had never occurred to her that said director would end up doubling as her personal chauffeur. Instantly the fact set off a familiar debate within her mind.

In Montana she would not have thought twice about such a thing. But as most everyone she knew there had warned her, New York City was nothing like home. People were shot down in the streets, raped in their churches, robbed and stabbed and beaten to death in their own homes—victimized and terrorized in ways the good folks of tiny, fit-inside-a-park Wolfbend, Montana, could scarcely comprehend.

Had Knight seen a picture of her beforehand, she wondered. Was the director putting "the moves" on her? Worse—could that be how she had gotten her internship in the first place?

Bridget Elkins was a stunningly attractive girl, one so beautiful there was no vanity in the fact that she knew it. Long before her first days on campus in Portland, or at the University of Chicago, her amazing good looks had forced her to learn to deal with boys and men of all ages—often harshly, sometimes with violence. Tall, with a tapered waist but plenty of curves, at the age of twenty-two she had been fending off unwanted masculine attention for nearly half her life.

"So now, Bridget," Knight had told her in a conspiratorial tone as they claimed her luggage, "I'm going to let you in on a little secret."

"A secret?"

"Well, it's not a very closely guarded fact, but it is a frightfully important bit of information you'll need to know for your work, so it's best I tell you immediately."

"And that secret is . . . ?"

Leaning close, his eyes as sincere as he could make them, the professor whispered;

"I probably know far more about everything than anyone else you've ever met."

"Oh, really?"

"Yes, quite true." The man gave his companion this assertion with a nod and a look so comically smug he accomplished two goals at once. The first thing he did was to put her conscious mind at instant ease. Anyone in a position of authority willing to appear that silly, she knew from long experience, was not working to seduce her. The second thing he did was make her subconscious suspect that everything he was telling her was the truth—truth merely shrouded in humor to make it more palpable.

"I tell you this because as my assistant this summer," he said with a trace of a smile, "you're going to need to know that I am absolutely infallible. That everything I say is correct and that you must always obey my commands exactly as given. Do you understand?"

Delighted to find that her superior could be so wonderfully playful, Bridget Elkins raised her hand quickly to her forehead, saluting Knight, responding;

"Aye, aye, sir. Message understood, sir."

"Ah, excellent—bless all the tiny monkeys."

The professor had slapped his hands together then, his blue eyes flashing with a devilish mischief. Bridget remembered, she had giggled at the sight, as well as his bizarre little catchphrase, feeling far more like a high school student preparing to cut class than a recent college graduate meeting her new boss. And that was, indeed, when it had happened.

"All right, since you understand, I now give you your big chance to consult the oracle. You get one question. Ask anything, any secret mystery you would like explained. Test the limits of my vast and mighty knowledge. You have sixty seconds."

Taking only five, she posed her query:

"Okay—I have a question for you. Everyone always acts like New York is the biggest city in the world, like it's the size of the moon or something. Tell me, what is it that makes New Yorkers think their city is so great?"

Shaking his head ruefully, as if she had passed by all the lost treasures of fabled Cathay for a fast-food burger, Knight had promised her an answer, then led her to his car. An hour later, atop the largest building in New York, on all the eastern seaboard of the American continents, he had delivered on his promise.

"And again—"

Taking her wrist one last time, she ran along with him to the east, needing no coaxing. Then, coming around the last corner the observation deck of the Empire State Building had to offer, Knight released the young woman, extending his hands before him as if offering the view before them as a present.

"As far as my eyes can take me," Bridget interrupted, "all I can see is wondrous New York City."

"You are correct, fair damsel," the professor agreed. "But not counting lumpy, only-good-for-taking-up-the-overflow Queens out there in the background, in the grand tradition of saving the best for last what you now behold is the finest, most wondrous and magical part of New York City—"

"Or," she said, playfully echoing his words, "as we like to call it, the greatest city in the world."

"Indeed," Knight agreed, chuckling slightly. Taking a moment, the tall-enough man looked at his new assistant with a calculating eye. Her enthusiasm, her joy at their little tour—he struggled for the right word, then thought;

Zest. That's what she has, and I must admit, I think I like it.

"Oh, Professor," said the redhead, still staring out at the city before her, "it's all so . . . intoxicating. It reminds me of something I read; what was it? Oh, I remember, Moss Hart: 'The only credential the city asked was the boldness to dream. For those who did, it unlocked its gates and its treasures, not caring who they were or where they came from.' "

"A loftier description than most would grant her," responded Knight, "but accurate enough, I suppose. Especially when you consider that all that which is laid out before you now is our most magnificent metropolis' crown jewel, that wondrous home to happiness, Kings County, otherwise known in sonnets and ballads as Brooklyn. The center of all things great and good."

It was truly an inspiring sight for the young woman.

Unlike the mostly flat expanses of endless cement she had seen in the other directions, Brooklyn had hills and turns, valleys and folds promising all manner of mystery. The professor stepped back to allow her a moment to soak in all she had seen, and that she had yet to see. He understood the awe and unbridled excitement his city generated in the first-time viewer, and like anyone else sharing one of their favorite experiences with another, he was having more fun than his companion simply by watching her face as she reacted to all he placed before her.

She'll see the gray and black and the ugly New York has to offer soon enough, he thought. *Let her build herself a shield now against the crap that will descend later.*

And then Knight's cell phone rang, and although he did not know it, at that exact moment the most monstrous depths of the gray and black and the ugly the universe had to offer began rushing forward at both of them from every possible direction.

CHAPTER TWO

"Where are you, Professor," asked the voice coming from Knight's phone. "The reception is wonderful. It's like you're standing next to me."

"High in the sky, Ashur, old friend. Atop the Empire State Building, actually. It's so good to hear from you. Are you back in the country finally?"

"Oh, heavens no, I am still in Syria."

Knight blinked in disbelief. Annoyed at first, part of his brain furiously attempting to calculate the cell charges for accepting a daytime call from the other side of the world, the rest of his mind worked at an equal speed, shoving such considerations aside, jumping to the obvious fact that something desperately urgent must be afoot. When he inquired as to the reason for his call, Ungari told him;

"You know about our discovery—you must certainly remember Memak'tori. And if you do not, your museum does. They have, after all, already made quite handsome offers for anything the Syrians will allow to be taken out of the country. You know of all this—yes?"

"Please, are you joking? A find like yours? I'm the one who sent the board in your direction. You must know I've always had faith in this project, Ashur."

"I know you have, which is why I promised them the first exhibit-worthy materials to leave the country would most certainly go to the great and wonderful museum of Brooklyn, provided the proper settlement can be reached with the Assads, of course."

"Of course," agreed Knight.

The professor did so without rancor, knowing that there was nothing in Ungari's words implying anything of the opportunistic. The doctor was merely a scholar hungering after knowledge. The Assads, however, were the ruling family of Syria. Nothing was done anywhere within their country without their intense oversight and complete approval—without all the correct palms being sufficiently greased. From government appointments to any business deals made between corporations outside Syria as well as all those within, and especially to the release of any artifacts from their cultural sites, the Assads kept all that went on within their borders under a most careful scrutiny. Not that anyone involved found anything unusual in the arrangement. Kickbacks and payoffs were simply the long-understood reality of the Middle East.

"Piers, my friend," Ungari started, "you must know now that there is most assuredly more going on here than you could ever have imagined. I have something to tell you, that I will tell you, which I need for you to brace yourself most resolutely. Is that decadent Western heart of yours ready for some true and most glorious excitement?"

"I've quite a hearty constitution these days," Knight responded, a hopeful smile crossing his face. "I think I might possibly stand the strain."

"Be certain now—"

"Ashur, would you please just tell me what's so exciting you couldn't simply send me an e-mail and not cost us a thousand dollars apiece?"

"Memak'tori, old friend. It is *it!* It is the site—*the* site. It is, unquestionably—and I say this after months of telling myself I could not possibly be correct—it is the unmistakable, undeniable birthplace of true civilization."

Knight listened, his entire mind kicking over into its completely professional mode. His assistant forgotten, his location dismissed, cell phone charges suddenly insignificant—all his attention focused intently on the voice speaking within his ear. He recognized the tone behind Ungari's words, had heard it uncounted times in the past when the speaker was absolutely convinced they were utterly and absolutely correct.

"Your carbon dating—verified? Double-checked?"

"Triple. And done by myself. No one else would I trust—who could I trust? My idiot assistant, Hamid? The man is a simpleton. If it were not for the Syrians, forcing that spider of a man upon me—"

"Ah, Ashur," interrupted Knight, more interested in his colleague's findings than the shortcomings of his staff, "you were telling me about the dig?"

"Oh my goodness—yes. I am saying it to you now, Piers, my old dog, such playgrounds as Sumer, Mesopotamia, veritable children, no older than the Romans. This site, this truly magnificent site, this may not only be the birthplace of the ever-mysterious Arcadians; my wonderful Memak'tori may actually *predate* them!"

Professor Piers Knight blinked.

His ears were sharp ones, his hearing a match for that of any other and better than most. And yet, for the briefest of instants he did something he almost never did—he doubted himself. Nothing, it was most firmly believed, could predate the Arcadians. Indeed, there were as many schools of thought that would stake their reputations on the idea that no such place as Arcadia had ever existed as would do so—probably more. To claim to find something older, to have the proof—

Proof?

"Ashur," Knight managed the single word, speech practically failing him, caution reining in the ability, forcing him to double-check anything he might say, "are you certain of this? Are you really *sure*!?"

The professor listened while his colleague half a world away indulged himself in a knowing chuckle. It was not the laughter of the self-righteous, although it did border slightly on the smug. Moreover, it was a joyous thing, a bit of uncontrollable, childlike giddiness Ungari simply could not contain. Gaining control over himself once more, however, the Egyptian doctor of archaeology cleared his throat, and then, in a slightly embarrassed tone, whispered into his phone;

"We are most certain, my old friend. Memak'tori grades out at an absolute minimum of ninety-two hundred years. Unmistakable. If some readings prove true, possibly even as much as ninety-five hundred."

Knight was stunned. It was amazing, unbelievable. If true, it doubled the time man had been a creature capable of creating more than the simplest structures, of grasping any purpose beyond gathering enough to eat for the day. And, if he was responsible for maneuvering his own Brooklyn Museum to the head of the line to receive any outside exhibits, then it was a coup beyond measure.

"You will not even begin to comprehend it all until you behold it for yourself. There is no way to describe it so that you truly see it, my friend, even someone like yourself. The city, my most wonderful Memak'tori, it has proved to be laid out on an amazingly massive scale. I tell you, it rivals Ankor, not only shrouded in an equal amount of mystery, but in a rivalry that extends also to size, the mathematical precision of its centrally planned layout, and its buildings, my goodness, oh, Piers, my God. . . ."

Ungari paused, the sudden jumbling of his words causing him to sound almost out of control. Knight did not judge him too harshly. If his colleague was correct, the man had every right to be flustered.

"The reason," the doctor began again, "I originally thought the site would prove to be only a small find, was that what we had uncovered back then were only the uppermost sections of the tallest buildings. How can I . . ." Ungari paused for a moment, then continued, saying, "You just told me that you are at the top of your Empire State Building, yes?" After the professor agreed, Ungari continued once more, telling him;

"Imagine your New York City covered by the sands of time. Some future archaeologist discovers the summit of the Empire State Building. He has found a building, and of course he is confident he will find a neighbor to it somewhere close by. But think, Piers—how long would it be, how far would he have to dig, before he realized what he had truly found?"

"You mean . . ."

"I mean, those first structures we discovered five years ago, they were merely the tower tops of what proved to be three- and four-story buildings. Prehistorics, building to such heights. Can you believe it? And these people, these wonderful, wondrous people, they had the cornerstone; they developed the keystone. These people, they were builders—they understood arches, bracing, municipal planning. And more. . . ."

"More?"

"Oh, far more." His voice falling into a whisper centered firmly within the conspiratorial range, the doctor said, "You know as well as I that obviously no city structure of such dimensions could exist without a written language."

"Obviously. . . ."

"They had one. There was no mention earlier because there were no traces in those upper stories we first uncovered. It has only been in the past, oh, no more than, say fifteen months that we finally began to uncover fragments of text. But so little of it was in a form that could stand up to the elements. We had traces, bits and pieces—"

Knight understood the frustration of such events extremely well. The professor could sympathize with his former colleague all too easily. He also had endured the tantalizing hope offered by scraps of information one prayed would come together into something conclusive but which in the end rarely actually did so. As he listened to Ungari's voice, however, Knight began to realize the doctor was headed toward the extraordinary, where hope turned to realization. Thus he asked;

"I'm thinking, Ashur, you're telling me that this is not one of those times when nothing comes from years of research and prayers, eh?"

"That is indeed what I am not telling you," agreed the doctor, laughter in his voice. "Not in the least. We have reached the foundation of the city, the main streets, and there is writing everywhere. Engraved in stone. Permanent, perfectly preserved. Ready to be translated."

And as Ungari finished his sentence, the excitement in his voice triggered a realization within the professor's brain. This was the reason for the frantic call. This was the purpose so important, so immediate, it could not be delayed. Believing he understood what he was being told, Knight asked;

"This language you've found, this isn't a new thing, is it? You've seen it before, haven't you?"

"Yes I have," answered the doctor. He gave Knight a moment to soak in the idea, then added his kicker. "And, so have you, Piers, old dog."

"I have?"

"You remember the Language of Dreams, do you not?"

And in that moment, Professor Piers Knight suddenly understood his colleague's excitement, and why mere considerations like propriety or expense had been rendered inconsequential. For if Dr. Ashur Ungari was correct, all of history was about to be rewritten from the ground up. Both men realized the fact, and for a single moment they shared the utter ecstasy of both unbridled joy and pride.

It was the last they would ever know.

INTERLUDE

"How did you get this number?"

The question was not simply put. There was no anger in the voice of the one posing it. Sitting at a console in a somberly lit room, a windowless affair filled with rows of high-powered computers, the speaker waited patiently for his answer.

"Is that really important?"

"It is most assuredly important," came the answer. Without pause, the voice continued, adding, "I believe that you actually cannot imagine how important."

The two voices dueled across the airwaves. The first was not even a true voice. What the second was hearing was a highly sophisticated, electronic distortion of the speaker's voice. For all the caller knew, the voice on the other end of the phone was of a woman, a man, a toddler with an exceptional vocabulary, or even an amazingly talented dog. Indeed, the intonations coming out of the second party's receiver were so heavily masked, he would not even be able to tell if more than one person was answering him.

"You will not believe my answer," responded the caller, prompting the voice to inform him;

"I will also not speak with you further unless you tell me something. So, my advice to you is that you might as well try. Go ahead—give me something to believe."

"Very well. . . ."

The caller paused, the back of his brain revealing to him just how absurd his position was about to become. What he was attempting was not only illegal, but it was also the type of crime one only witnessed in movies focusing on international criminals. He, a part of their mind noted, was in no way a mastermind of such a magnitude.

Then again, a separate whisper came to the caller from the back of his mind, *is that not exactly what we are about to attempt—to become a mastermind? To engineer the fate of the world according to our own whims?*

"I have a particular need," the caller began, speaking slowly. "I must obtain a certain something . . . at any cost. By any means. But I will admit to you that this is not the kind of situation in which I normally find myself."

"Yes—"

"I, on my own . . . I did not know how to do such a thing, to . . . go about this. . . ."

"Just tell them," the voice came to the caller once more. Strong. Determined, its confidence working him subtly, becoming his own. Relaxing slightly, pulling a deep breath in through his nostrils, the caller said;

"So . . . I decided to sleep on the problem."

"Ahhhh," the electronic voice responded. "I believe I begin to see. Now let us return to my original question. If you please, tell me, how did you get this number?"

Tell them—

"It came to me in a dream."

"Very well," the distorted voice replied, seemingly mollified. "Now, tell me, what is it you need, when do you need it, and do you possibly believe you can afford our services?"

CHAPTER THREE

"This is just wonderful, Professor," said Bridget, proclaiming her approval over not only the morsel she had just consumed but their entire meal as well.

Of course, she definitely had good reason to do so, one that had little to do with their restaurant's atmosphere or waitstaff.

Not that they were not also things worthy of appreciation. The mood created by the soft music, muted lighting, and attentive personnel would be enough to attract and please many a New Yorker.

But not Piers Knight.

No, the professor only frequented one type of eatery—the kind known for good food.

Decor, music, the clothes worn by the workers—even the prices—such things meant nothing to him.

All that did matter to Knight, from the finest restaurant to the lowest hash house, was the quality of the meal he could expect to find behind its doors.

"Glad you're enjoying yourself."

Tucked away on 78th between Second and Third Avenues, Iron Sushi was one of those "unknown" spots—the kind Knight adored, one where the owners always managed to find a table for him somewhere no matter when he might arrive. That night, arriving at the height of the evening rush, he and his new assistant had, with great apology, been relegated to the back corner near the lavatory. Still, the restaurant's single restroom was hidden behind a curtain and the excellence of their meal was more than compensatory.

The pair had started with the standard vegetarian spring roll appetizer, remarkably light and crisp treats of which Knight had grown quite fond and which he now insisted on introducing to everyone he took to the establishment. Bridget's use of mere soy sauce on hers caused the professor to frown, but her pure delight over the Rock Shrimp Tempura Bites, batter-fried baby shrimp served in a sweet orange sauce, sprinkled with but the merest dash of fiery pepper, more than made up for her culinary faux paus.

"I have to admit," the young woman continued, "we don't have anything like this back in Wolfbend."

From there on, the young woman's palate had been nothing but overwhelmed. She appreciated the miso soup, and the edamame, green pods one popped into their mouth, then dragged through their teeth to extract the beans within, delighted her to no end. She also bravely tried her first calamari, both the crisply fried rings as well as the Ika Maru Yaki, a broiled squid marinated to give it a particular smokey taste. The first she merely enjoyed; the second made her eyes roll in delight.

Knight teased his new intern over the fact that she found his favorite Japanese restaurant to be better only than those that might be found in her hometown, but he knew the truth. He had watched her make her way through the near-overwhelming amount of various dishes he had ordered, and had even allowed her stealing of the entire portion of snow crab salad, one of his personal favorites.

But it was the arrival of a single plate containing but two lone morsels that truly overwhelmed her. These were called Plum Kisses, large delicately-prepared whole scallops, surrounded by rolls of grilled salmon. The pair of delights sat in a seductive pool of plum sauce, were glazed with an equally intriguing orange sauce and then generously sprinkled with caviar.

They were a treat beyond compare, so delicious, and of such a that-makes-the-meal-complete quality that when Bridget was shown a dessert menu she thought surely the waiter had taken leave of his senses.

"No." The young redhead dropped her head somewhat shyly, smiling as she did so. "I was just teasing. I've never had anything like this anywhere—ever. Trust me." The professor nodded, accepting her recantation. He also accepted her next question, finding it more than a little refreshing that she had the courage to both ask it and do so without looking for anything in his answer but the truth.

"Professor," she started, the slightest trepidation in her voice, "may I ask you a question?"

"Anyone who poses such a query using 'may' instead of 'can' will not only receive my blessing in the asking but will most probably even receive an answer as well."

"Picking me up at the airport, your little tour guide bit, now bringing me here. I know I'm going to sound as if I'm pretty full of myself, and I'll apologize for that if need be. . . ." As the young woman paused, Knight prodded her gently, asking;

"Yes?"

"I just have to ask . . . is this what you would normally do for a new assistant, or . . . or only for a . . . female assistant?"

"A female assistant," asked the professor, "say, with great legs and a stunning shape? One with features so finely chiseled one is forced to wonder why she didn't choose a career in modeling, acting, or some such thing?"

Bridget stared at Knight for a moment, not certain how to respond to his answer. Where the professor's words sounded like the beginnings of some patented "come-on" line, nothing in the man's attitude or tone suggested that was his motive. Having given the redhead a moment to realize such, Knight spoke again, his voice soft and understanding.

"Listen, in my defense, as well as to save the museum the expense of a sexual harassment charge, I would remind you that at the airport I did have to attract your attention with that sign with your name on it."

"Which you misspelled."

"Oh my, yes," he admitted, sighing. "How kind of you to remember." As she giggled despite the seriousness of the moment, he continued, telling her;

"That aside, yes, I knew you were female, and I did expect you to be on the young side since I was informed you were a recent college graduate, but if your feminist sensibilities can tolerate my saying so, the rest was merely a delightful surprise. The truth be known, I do simply like to get out of the museum on occasion, and more to the point, I greatly enjoy getting to know the people I'm going to be overworking unmercifully. I also will admit, my dear, to using sexist terms of endearment because I sometimes suspect the back of my mind wishes I lived in a black-and-white movie."

"Thank you," answered Bridget, her tone filled with an honest reassurance, "and truthfully, sir, I don't mind a 'my dear' or two at all. Really, to be big-sky honest, it makes me feel like I'm back home. But I saw the menu. Maybe I am kind of a hick, but these prices . . . my mama always said a man doesn't pull out his wallet without knowing what he's buying. And I—"

Allowing a sigh to escape his lips, a thing sounding as if it came from a grandfather trying to train an especially beloved pet, the professor cut the young woman off with a gentle wave of his hand.

"Montana's own Bridget Elkins, allow me to be perfectly frank with you." His half smile returning, Knight continued, saying;

"Although you are indeed an ingenue, I am no Broadway producer, and dust-laden museum archives are not the place for casting couches." Then, his eyes filled with sympathy, he moved both his hands toward each other slightly to focus Bridget's attention, as he told her softly;

"Look, you really are an adorably sweet girl, and once you get to know me, I think things will go quite smoothly between us. To facilitate that, let me address your concerns. First off, yes, besides being sweet, which frankly I think is your finest natural asset, you are a wonderfully attractive female, and having you as an assistant will only give the other directors one more thing to envy about me."

"The other things being . . . ?"

"Why, my good looks, enormous intellect, and quite natty fashion sense, of course."

"And your humility?"

"Oh, good God, no. Barely have an once of it. No, I don't think anyone's ever envied me that."

Bridget giggled quietly once more, despite the seriousness of the conversation, a great part of her relaxing as the professor spoke. She had found everything about him charming and interesting so far, and would have hated to discover that any of it had been a sham, the tacky first move in some ridiculous game for which she had no desire.

"As for dinner, my dear, well, quite honestly I simply like to eat. Also, I am blessed with a marvelous metabolism—another thing many envy about me, to be certain—one that lets me consume morning to night and not gain much more than a pound or two, which I then seem to burn off without much effort."

"I could envy that myself," admitted Bridget, "considering how hard I have to work to look this way. All 'wonderfully attractive,' as you said."

"I understand. You have my complete and utter sympathy. If ever I were to start gaining weight more in line with my ability to consume that which creates it, I think I would be heartbroken. Crestfallen. I do so enjoy stuffing myself with the best food I can find—" Looking around the room, he then added, "I also like doing it in places where they know me and cater to my whims, and I enjoy most of all doing it with other people who enjoy eating, which, I must admit, you certainly seem to do."

Blushing, his companion answered him quietly, "It's true. Daddy loved to take us out to every new steak house and rib joint in or anywhere near town. I've got a pretty healthy appetite, but like I said, I do have to work to keep it off. I'll be looking for a gym to join once I get settled in."

"Then," said Knight, staring directly into Bridget's warm and trusting eyes, "do we understand each other?"

"Yes, sir," she answered, smiling brightly—honestly. "I think we're going to get along just fine."

"Of course we are," he insisted. "You're young and eager to learn, and as I told you before, knowing pretty much everything, and being infallible, I'm the absolute perfect person to mold you into the unconditionally first-rate museum director I think you're capable of becoming."

"Thank you, good sir."

"Don't thank me," Knight insisted. "I wouldn't say so if I didn't think it true. Which now leads us to your first decision as an official employee of the Brooklyn Museum."

"Yes, sir?"

"Your choice, do we go back to the museum tonight to dig out and prepare the Dream Stone for Dr. Ungari, or do we have dessert instead?" Bridget thought for only a moment, then responded in mock seriousness;

"Why don't we have dessert, then go to the museum? I mean, why go to work simply full when we can stagger in like bloated pigs?"

"Bridget, my girl," announced Knight loudly, his eyes twinkling, laughing as he clapped his hands together, "I like the cut of your jib." Then, turning to one of the waiters, he shouted;

"Hurry, man—we need two Toppa Caffes, and your largest Exotic Bombas. And make it quick; the world of scientific inquiry needs us desperately!"

If Bridget had chosen to only have dessert or to go directly to the museum, they would have avoided what would happen to them next. And with that one simple error was the entire world thrown down the path to the almost irresistibly inevitable destruction of the human race.

CHAPTER FOUR

"And here, as the large green sign announced so clearly, is the fabled Brooklyn Bridge, your gateway to paradise."

Bridget smiled, at both the professor's seemingly endless parade of facts about New York City and the sign he had just mentioned. More amusing, however, was the sign they found at the other end of the bridge. It was a standard municipal welcoming announcement, but its full wording:

Welcome to Brooklyn
How Sweet It Is

delighted her to no end. Brooklyn, the redhead thought, might just live up to her new boss' ever so favorable opinion of it. She admired his enthusiasm for his hometown, not having tiring of his continual, spontaneous lectures even after a full day of them. Knowing a fact about the bridge herself, she said;

"It's over a hundred and twenty-five years old, isn't it?"

"Indeed," answered Knight. "Designed by visionary engineer John Roebling. Took him ten years to get his designs approved, and after all that struggle, when he was scouting for the site for the Brooklyn tower his foot was crushed by an incoming ferry. Never recovered from the accident. His son Washington had to take over."

"Died from a crushed foot?"

"Oh, the Gray Lady took a score of lives before she was through. Young Roebling himself was nearly done in by her. Left paralyzed by caisson disease. Had to work through his wife." As the professor maneuvered his car onto the off-ramp for downtown Brooklyn, making the practiced illegal turn over the multiple white lines forbidding such an action all New York drivers made without a second thought, he added;

"Emily Roebling, remarkable woman, really. Rather than let the project slip from her husband's hands, she had him tutor her relentlessly in mathematics and bridge engineering. She delivered his instructions on a daily basis, taking over his on-site responsibilities."

Heading up Camden, Knight continued chattering about the Brooklyn Bridge. After ten more minutes of driving, even as he began to slow, scouting for a parking place, he told his assistant, "First steel cables ever to be used in a suspension bridge. Only reason she's lasted this long. Roebling called steel 'the metal of the future.' "

All conversation ceased, however, as he sighted a legal spot. Racing forward, Knight threw all his attention into sliding his vehicle into the space. Then, as he and Bridget disembarked from his car, the redhead asked;

"I know you didn't want to talk shop at dinner, but we're here now. So could you tell me, please, just what is this Dream Rock?"

"The Dream Stone," corrected Knight while he helped his aging seat belt to roll itself up. Tossing the lock switch, the professor finally shut his door and then turned back to his companion, directing her around the corner and up the great front stairs of the Brooklyn Museum as he explained;

"It was, in its time, the much-hoped-for Rosetta Stone of the ancients of ancients. My great-great-grandfather, who was, I will have you know, father to one of the very first directors of this hallowed museum, he uncovered it in the region of Jordan, back in 1855, '56, somewhere around then."

"And it resembles the Rosetta Stone in what manner?"

"Quite simply, where the Rosetta had a complete list of the Greek alphabet carved alongside those pesky Egyptian hieroglyphics everyone had been having such trouble deciphering, allowing the scholars of the early eighteen hundreds to finally crack the mysteries of the pharaohs, the Dream Stone contained three distinct alphabets. Ancient Phoenician, Attic Greek—"

"Those are the early Greeks, right," asked Bridget. "Sort of their Dark Ages?"

"Yes, very good," answered Knight. As the pair drew close to the front doors, he headed them to the far left where the one door employees could use at any time was situated—if, that is, they were important enough to not need to circle around to the back entrance everyone was supposed to use. Pulling out his keys as they continued forward, he went on, telling her;

"And, obviously, there was a third language. One no one recognized at the time. Indeed, one no one has ever found another trace or even the slightest hint of to this very day."

"And exactly why is it called the Dream Stone?"

"My ancestor, I'm afraid, was a full-blown romantic. Upon discovery of the comparative chart, he contacted every authority in the world searching for any clue that would explain the mystery of this unknown alphabet. When it proved to be a completely unknown set of letters, he dubbed it 'the Language of Dreams.' The name stuck, and the slab of rock in which it was inscribed to this day has been known as the Dream Stone."

"It's such a romantic story," said Bridget. "Ummmm, the romance of archaeology, you know what I mean. Dedicated scholar makes incredible find, works feverishly to uncover its meaning, dies without ever learning the truth." As Bridget let out a whimsical sigh, one that charmed Knight while also reminding him of just how young she was, he said;

"Yes, that was Great-great-granddad."

"So, tell me, the way people in our field love to mythologize the slightest of matters, why is it I've never heard of the Dream Stone before?"

"Oh, it's like so many things, I imagine," said the professor as he removed his key from the lock. Both pushing the door inward and then holding it open so his assistant could enter, he offered, "After a few score years, people stopped looking for an answer, simply forgot about it."

"Really?"

"Yes—the way of things, I suppose. But, in all honesty I doubt there's a textbook with a mention of it these days. There hasn't been a request to examine it in all the years I've been here. Sadly, I doubt there's even a single copy of its text still in existence outside of our own files."

"That's kind of sad."

"Well," answered Knight, trying to be magnanimous, "that's fate for you. The Brooklyn Museum has one of the largest collections in the world, over a million and a half pieces—with over a half-million square feet in which to display them."

"That's a lot of room."

"Ohhhhh," Knight answered, his voice going quiet, wistful, "but there should have been so much more. The original design was a thing of magnificence. The architects, McKim, Mead, and White, I believe, their vision, if realized, would have created the largest single museum structure in the world."

"Didn't the merger of Brooklyn with Manhattan interfere with that?"

A great sadness collecting in the professor's eyes, his voice dropped even lower as he answered, "Yes. Suddenly the money that had been allocated tightened, disappearing down some rat hole or into some back pocket." His tone growing ragged, his voice began to ratchet upward in volume as he continued, saying;

"She was meant to hold the most glorious displays in the world. A comprehensive collection of not just world art, but of natural history as well. Scientific objects, research and education projects of every stripe and caliber . . ."

As Knight paused, his assistant attempted to cheer him by reminding him of how large the museum still was. Snorting, his contempt still aimed at the long dead politicians and backroom deal makers who had scaled back Brooklyn's original dreams of greatness, he said wistfully;

"True enough, and yet, even with what seems like a great deal of room, there are literally thousands of things stored in the various collections here that haven't seen the light of day in decades. And not even for the obvious reasons one might first assume, like political correctness, or the current fad of deemphasization of Western culture . . . it's just . . ."

Bridget wondered at the professor's curious pause.

Having spent the better part of the day with him, if there was one thing she was certain she knew about Professor Piers Knight, it was that he had an inexhaustible set of opinions and a finely tuned vocabulary with which to express them. As the idea continued to take root in the young woman's mind, she realized this was the first moment she had seen the professor at a loss for words over anything. A further examination of his face, however, led her closer to the truth of the matter.

Knight was not struggling for a path down which to take their conversation.

He had abandoned it completely.

Although looking forward into the gloom-shrouded lobby of the Brooklyn Museum, he was not focused on anything within range of their vision. This worried the redhead slightly. Although she could not imagine what might have captured the director's attention, Bridget Elkins was no fool. From the tilt of his head to the set of his shoulders, the way his fingers seemed to have frozen in mid-air, everything about the professor's body language was screaming to her that something beyond her immediate comprehension was seriously wrong.

What it was that had captured Knight's attention she could not say. Staring inside through the glass doors, scanning the building's vast main pavilion and lobby, she saw nothing amiss. Dark as the area was, she still had a clear view of the entire area all the way to the visitor center and the first of the galleries. Nothing seemed out of place in the least.

At that point most people, even those with some sense of self-control, would have begun to blather, throwing useless questions out such as, "What is it?" "What's wrong?" "What's going on?" Time-wasting chatter that accomplished nothing more than making the speaker feel less inadequate.

Much to her credit, Bridget knew better. She had gone hunting with her father and two older brothers often enough to recognize the look that had come over Knight.

It was obvious to her that something was going on of which she had no clue—something about which the professor himself seemed to have no solid ideas. As his tension grew, she asked quietly, "What can I do?"

Without shifting his eyes from the shadows hanging throughout the front entrance's massive foyer, Knight handed his assistant his cell phone along with a card he pulled from his wallet, whispering to her, "Take this; the number on the card is the direct number to the desk officer at the Seven One—that's the local precinct house. Ask for a Detective Sergeant Dollins—"

"If he's not there?"

Knight was not the kind of man who took kindly to interruption, but he realized Bridget was correct. Considering it far more likely Dollins might not be in the station, despite his self-centered assumption the detective would have to be there simply because he wished him to be there, the professor corrected himself, answering;

"As I was saying, ask for Dollins. No Dollins, ask for LaRaja. If you can't find either of them, take whatever detective you can get. Tell whomever you get who you are, that I prompted you to call, and that there is something wrong in the museum. Do so while you walk back out to the plaza. Once the police are on their way, find a cab; get in it—leave."

And then, Knight moved forward into the massive lobby, not giving Bridget the slightest glance. His attention was completely focused on the poorly lit interior before him, almost as if he were listening for something rather than looking for it. The professor stepped cautiously, moving from one display sculpture to another, not allowing his shoes to make a sound, even careful that, as he rounded one marble piece after another, he did not slide his hand across the stone too harshly. He knew even the slightest squeak could give away his position. To whom, he had no idea. But that there was someone inside his museum—someone who did not belong there—of that much he was certain.

All right, he asked tersely within his mind as he moved across the wide lobby, *where are you?*

As quickly as possible, Knight made his way to the main security desk. The fact that no museum personnel were to be seen at the post was the first thing that had aroused his curiosity. Of course, the desk was not manned every second of the day—sometimes those on duty were simply called away.

More important . . .

People were also human beings, he knew, not robots. They had to stretch, had to get an occasional drink of water, had to go to where they could relieve themselves of all their drinks of water—

Who are you?

But, the fact had caught his attention, prompting the professor to turn all his senses up to their full capacity. When he had done so, Knight instantly realized that he was hearing none of the usual background sounds of the nighttime museum. The tread of security rounds being made, the soft noise of the cleaning crew's plastic wheels, the electric clatter of their radios, chatter of any other late-night employees—

And most important of all, just what in hell are you doing in my museum?

Of course, he realized, security could be in another part of the vast museum complex simply making their rounds. The cleaning crew might already be finished for the evening and on their way home. As for additional staff, perhaps no one other than himself had need to be in the building quite so late. Any of these explanations were possibilities. But not each and every one of them. In all its days as far as he knew, at no time had the Brooklyn Museum ever been completely empty.

And, thought the professor as a sound finally came to his highly sensitive ears, *it seems it's not all that empty tonight, either.*

Listening intently, he quickly identified the sounds he was hearing. Gum-soled shoes—quiet, nearly completely silent. Four sets of them. Moving together.

No, he thought. *Not quite in unison. Two sets of two. One scouting—the first clearing the way, opening doors. The last one following, watching the group's back. And the central two, their attention is focused on something else. Those two, they're going slower, moving with caution—* And then he snapped his fingers, suddenly not caring about the noise as he muttered;

"They're carrying something—something heavy."

Knight's brow wrinkled at the thought—there were thieves in his museum. Focusing on the sounds he was sensing more than hearing, the professor determined that the quartet for whom he was searching were making their way up from the basement area. Checking his pockets, making certain he had at least one of the objects he was hoping would make the task before him easier, he headed directly for the back corridor that would take him to the stairs leading upward from Antiquities Storage.

Where everyone was, he had no idea.

How these intruders had managed to get inside the museum without setting off any alarms, or being noticed by either some member of the institution's personnel, or any of the building's hundreds of cameras and motion sensors, he also had no idea. Nor did he care.

At that moment, Professor Piers Knight had only two concerns. What was it that was being stolen and, could he stop the thieves without damaging their prize?

If he had known what they were taking, and why, however, instead of trying to stop the intruders, he would have done everything in his power to make certain that they got away with it.

CHAPTER FIVE

The first person Knight discovered was Jerome Dribben, a fifty-three-year-old security guard who had performed that function for the museum for twenty-two of his fifty-plus years. The professor liked Jerome, for the man had proved countless times that he knew three things—every inch of the building complex, the contents of all of its vast collections, and, most important, his job. When the professor came across the guard, however, the man was crumpled in an awkward heap, sprawled out on the floor, sleeping peacefully.

There was no doubt in Knight's mind the man was uninjured. Not only could the professor neither see nor smell any traces of blood, but also Jerome was snoring too loudly and too contentedly to be in any way damaged. Kneeling at the guard's side, Knight first shook the man to see if he could be awakened. When he could not, the professor bent close to Jerome's face, sniffing around his nostrils. Catching a distinctive scent Knight had not noted in the air anywhere in the building so far, he began piecing together what must have happened.

Chloroform, he thought as he arranged the guard's body a bit more comfortably. *Too light a dose to have been forced on him. Besides, his clothing shows no signs of a struggle. His hair's still combed.*

Remaining at Jerome's side for the moment, Knight puzzled over exactly how the man had been rendered unconscious. Thinking for a moment that the intruders might have employed something on the order of a water gun, Knight felt the guard's face. There was no moisture to be found there, none trapped in the man's less-than-well-trimmed moustache. Rubbing his fingers together, the professor felt not even a trace of residue. An uncomfortable look crossing his face, Knight bent low over Jerome once more, taking a second set of sniffs around the man's nostrils.

Damn, he thought grimly, feeling the fool for not having noticed the faint trace before.

Ozone. . . .

The slight burning scent, he knew, one ever so minutely different from any most people would ever encounter within their lifetimes, had come from an electrical spark generated in only one damnable fashion—magic.

Ozone. Oh, damn all the fools who plague me so. . . .

A thin chill ran the length of the professor's spine. It was not the gelid fingers of fear; Piers Knight knew too much of the beyond realms to find terror in the news that some unknown force was toying with the arcane arts, aiming them toward his person, if even indirectly. He had studied both the white and black disciplines of hundreds of cultures. Indeed, when he had checked his pockets earlier, it was to make certain several of the various magical items he sometimes made use of were on his person.

His only discomfort came from the realization that those he

was hunting might be as familiar with such disciplines as himself. He had been counting on that knowledge as his edge. Now he felt somewhat less confident about confronting the intruders—uncertain.

What damn bunch of idiots is it this time, he wondered, *that think they've got the goods to confront me in my own fortress?*

Knight was not actually as confident as the confrontational thoughts flashing through his mind might have suggested, however. His rapidly growing problem resided in the fact that the professor had been assuming the few items he was carrying would make his task of stopping the intruders a simple one. His sending of Bridget to summon the police had merely been his way of not only getting her to safety but also of removing her from the premises where her continued presence would have hindered his freedom to use his abilities.

That, however, had been before our little discovery that our opponents are magic users themselves.

And, if his guess was correct, fairly competent ones. The ease of their entrance, the fact that they had most assuredly taken out everyone in the building with a hunter spell—an incantation designed to track down each individual within an area and render them unconscious without polluting the atmosphere its casters themselves were about to enter—these were people who knew what they were doing.

Then again, he wondered, *do these fellows use magic themselves, or did they simply purchase their entrance?*

Knight sighed in frustration, knowing he had no actual way of gauging what kind of power levels he would soon be facing. Assault spells or assault weapons? Maybe both. Sighing once more, knowing there was nothing more he could do for the security guard, and that his own time was running out as well, the professor stood once more, his eyes lifted slightly upward as he muttered quietly;

"For once, Lord, couldn't things be easy? Just once?"

Not waiting for an answer, Knight pulled a round metal disc from the inside breast pocket of his suit coat and began making his way once more toward the sounds of the intruders. He could tell the quartet was drawing closer, their footsteps almost to the top of the stairwell from which he knew they would soon emerge. As the professor continued moving to intercept the foursome, he found himself silently applauding their professionalism. Despite the apparent weight of their prize, they had taken the stairs rather than risk the cameras in the elevators. Judging the amount of time he had to prepare for the arrival of the thieves, Knight gave himself no more than thirty-five seconds before the door at the end of the hall would open.

No idea of their power levels, he thought. *Any one of them, possibly all of them, could be full-fledged practitioners.* Then, he dismissed his cautious approach, the other side of his brain snapping, *Doubtful. For one thing, top-drawer talent doesn't lug booty. They don't do scout work, either. They don't creep—their kind stride. The four walking up the stairs, they might be competent, and they certainly might be dangerous, but ultimately they're just somebody else's muscle.*

And then, as the doorknob began to turn, Knight's mind focused on the one word he had thought, but of which he had not recognized the true significance—

Walking—

As the door opened, the first of the scouts exited the stairwell and moved cautiously out into the dark hall beyond. If the professor was correct, everyone within the museum had been rendered unconscious by a casting—one that would have targeted every living being, surrounding their heads with a cloud of chloroform. This would have dropped any- and everyone who could have been of any interference, acted as a witness, called the police, et cetera.

If this was timed correctly, Knight was assuming the intruders made their move at the evening security change. That meant they could have entered with any of the night shift, which meant no breaking and entering. No assault charges.

They didn't avoid the elevators because of the cameras, thought the professor as he watched the first man make his way out into the shadows of the hallway. *They've dampened the building's electrical systems. The elevators aren't working, because they wanted to take out all the cameras. The motion detectors, the laser alarms . . .*

And yet, the designer of the invasion had known the museum's systems well enough to not interfere with the few lights for which any passing patrol car would be looking. That told Knight volumes about the magical abilities of his opponents. With the museum's security routed through both the city's primary electrical utility and the building's own backup generators, if select lights controlled by both power sources had been dampened while others were still functioning, those moving into the hall had to possess controlling abilities of things not only natural but mechanical as well.

This, old man, both sides of his mind warned the professor, *is not going to be easy.*

In the handful of seconds it took for the first thief to ascertain that the hallway was clear and to signal his compatriots to follow him, Knight had realized he was up against something far more than any simple band of brigands. Holding back, he continued to study them from a distance. As he did, his respect for the intruders he had listened to for the last few minutes as they made their way up from the basement continued to grow. No matter who they were, or what they were after, they were part of something extraordinarily sophisticated. Their assault was well planned and certainly seemed to be working thus far without a hitch.

Looking the scout over, the professor noted his garb—soft boots, pant legs tucked in, pants and pullovers loose enough to allow movement but tight enough to minimize snagging or noise. His hands gloved, head masked, even his eyes covered by goggles. Impossible to identify if seen, equally unlikely he would be leaving behind much in the way of forensic evidence, either.

More disturbing than any of that, however, was the filled holster the professor could see hanging from the man's belt. He also spotted fitted pouches for spare ammunition, and what he thought might be others for grenades. As the two thieves carrying the quartet's prize began to emerge from the stairwell, Knight's anger grew exponentially. That his museum was being robbed was enough to anger him by itself. But, the men doing so had brought both guns and explosives with them.

That they would risk any of the irreplaceable artifacts within his museum—*his* museum—among all of its priceless statues, the paintings, the ancient cups and pieces of jewelry, the tapestries, the tablets, all of it, *any* of it . . .

The thought of bullets streaming through his beloved corridors was upsetting enough. The added notion that those looting his museum might be willing to hurl about shrapnel weapons within range of any of its treasures was more than he could tolerate. As the fourth man, the one watching their retreat, emerged into the hallway, the professor admitted to himself that he had the quartet in the best possible place to contain them. They were in a hallway where no art, no curios or trinkets of any kind, was on display.

"I do believe it's now or never, Piers."

And, so saying, the professor returned the disc of levitation he had extracted a moment earlier to its place within his suit jacket's inside pocket. With the disc removed from the atmosphere, its effects began to dissipate, and Knight drifted from his vantage point on the ceiling down toward the rear guard. His plan was simple.

With surprise on his side, he would take down the last man, he hoped quietly enough that he would be able to also take out one of the pair carrying off their prize before the others were alerted. Only two yards away from his intended target, the professor was preparing himself for his assault when suddenly the hallway was filled with a blinding light as a voice from the stairwell shouted;

"Four—above you!"

Below him, Knight could just make out the barest outline of the rear guard pulling his automatic free. Then, the overwhelming illumination stole what little was left of the professor's vision, leaving him helpless.

CHAPTER SIX

"Kill him!"

Once more the order came from behind the blinded Knight. Not wasting time with worrying over how anyone else could possibly be present, the professor instead hurriedly jammed his hand back inside his suit coat, once more pulling free his disc of levitation. The mental commands needed to activate it screaming through his brain, Knight shot toward the ceiling even as the invader identified simply as "Four" opened fire. The man emptied his weapon, laying down a blanket pattern in a crisscrossing direction, then ejected his spent clip. As he pulled free a fresh replacement with professional detachment, slipping the empty inside his belt, the voice from the stairwell screamed at him;

"Did you get the son of a bitch?"

"Can't tell."

"And why not?!" The voice roared once more, demanding its answer, screaming to be heard over the still-echoing ring of the previous gunfire. Uncowed, Four bellowed in return;

"Because I'm half-blind despite the goggles, you moron. You're supposed to warn people before you illuminate. Before you—"

"Enough." The stairwell voice screamed the single word. Continuing as loudly as possible, it commanded, "Four, One, find that bastard and eliminate him. Two, Three—keep going. We've got to get that damn hunk of rock out of here!"

"Relax," growled the man designated as "Two." Hefting his end of their prize, he added reassuringly, "This thing's no problem. It's actually lighter than it looks."

As the no-longer-shining fifth member of the band of thieves finally entered the hallway, from his vantage point in the shadows high above Professor Knight cursed himself, thinking;

And so much for your "knowing more about everything than anyone else" crap. Miserable fool, I've warned you about your damned arrogant lack of caution—

Not so busy castigating himself was the professor, however, that he was not able to also continue paying attention to those below. His eyes finally readjusting to the gloom, he suddenly discovered why he had not taken note of the fifth man earlier when he had heard the others. As he exited the stairwell, the new figure did not walk as did the rest of the thieves. Instead, he glided forth. The same as Knight, the intruder was levitating. Finding his foes to be possessed of further extraordinary abilities did not so much fill the professor with fear, but it did make him wonder;

So he wasn't giving off any footfalls for me to hear. Still, he has to breathe; his body had to rub against the passing air; everyone burps or farts sooner or later. Why— And then, suddenly all was revealed. As the fifth intruder continued floating forward, he passed too close to Four. There was no collision of the pair, however, except in the most technical sense of the word, for the levitating man's arm passed through Four's shoulder without making actual contact.

Well, now there's a news flash, marveled Knight. *My new playmate's not physically, not* really *here.*

The professor grimaced at the knowledge. Realistically, he knew he had but seconds in which to act—but what actions should he take? The leader of the intruders was untouchable. Whether holographic or some form of astral projection, Knight was well aware he himself was armed with absolutely nothing that could affect a phantasm. Yes, there were certain relics within the museum that might afford him some ability to combat the intruder he had designated within his own mind as "Five," but such pieces were all locked away on other levels. And with the thieves less than a hundred yards from their chosen exit, he could reach none of those other pieces quickly enough to utilize them in any helpful fashion.

More to the point, two armed professionals were actively searching for him, men who had no compunction over using brute force, nor who seemed surprised by his own use of magic in the slightest. They might not be magicians themselves, but they were obviously no strangers to the arts—were comfortable around their use, and evidently not frightened by them. Hidden within the shadow-draped folds of a ceiling tapestry large enough to envelop his entire body, the various sections of Knight's mind went to war once more.

He could easily ascertain that Four and One below were not hunting him actively, despite Five's rabid bellowing. With the cold calculation of longtime mercenaries, they were certainly watching for him, both with guns drawn and ready. But the pair were backing their way to the door, more covering the team's escape than worrying overly about murdering Knight.

And why not? After all, the professor mused, it was not as if he was going to make much in the way of a useful witness. The thieves were all of equal height, more or less, and completely masked by their uniform outfits. Adding murder to their list of crimes would do the intruders no good—escaping without further incident would. Watching their carefully guarded retreat, Knight had no doubt that if he simply did not interfere further with the quintet below him that he could remain quite safely hidden until they made their exit.

But then, he thought, grinning as he did so, *where's the fun in that?*

The part of his brain urging cautious withdrawal shrugged in defeat but also refused to allow him to simply rush forward and further risk his life without running one last inventory on everything in his possession. Having no actual weapons, Knight gave in to the preserving thought, forcing himself to go through his pockets once more. The Disc of the Winds was still firmly in his left hand. With his right, he quickly felt through all his pockets, finding the usual accessories of modern life—his keys, wallet, some spare change. His baton was, of course, in its especially designed holster within his jacket where it should be.

Wait—

Suddenly, as he checked his vest more carefully, his fingers brushed against something small caught in a mass of loose threads in the corner of one pocket. Smiling, he pulled the blue stone circlet free of its snare and slipped it onto his finger, beginning his final descent with the complete approval of all his brain's formerly warring factions.

MOVING ACROSS THE WIDE LOBBY AS QUICKLY AS THEY MIGHT, considering the weight of their prize, the five intruders had almost begun to relax. Whoever the would-be hero was who had tried to stop them, the fundamental bluntness of hot lead seemed to have severely decreased his interest in any further heroics. Still, those comprising the quintet were professionals, and none of them were about to relax their vigilance so close to the conclusion of their evening's endeavor.

"Haste still makes waste, gentlemen," said Five, his tone surprisingly lighter, almost joking. "Let's wrap this operation up, carefully, but let's do move on."

The group progressed boldly toward the central doors of the museum's front entrance. It was where they had entered, and their plan called for them to exit the same way. Knight had been wrong in his assumption of the band having followed personnel into the building. Such would have called for luck or chance, and this particular set of intruders was not in the habit of counting on either. These were professionals keeping to a strict timetable, one that was close to running out.

Still, none of the quintet was overly worried. The four corporeal thieves knew they were not trapped. When they reached the doors, their ghostlike companion would simply drift through the metal and glass before them, the electrical charge of its form disrupting the locks as it did when they entered. Once outside, they would allow the door to close, their astral leader would pass a wraithing appendage through the locks, sealing the mechanisms once more, and that would be that.

None would know what had happened or be able to explain how any of it had been accomplished. The meddler who had tried for a moment to stop them would have some idea, of course, but he would say nothing to anyone. Of that they were most certain. Magic users needed to maintain a certain anonymity. It might no longer be the Dark Ages, when magicians and witches were burned and hung on a regular basis. But still, mankind's primal fears had not changed all that greatly. Certainly not to the point where any real practitioners of the arts would dare expose themselves to even the slightest hint of publicity. To do so was understood by all, no matter what their orientation, to be taking the first step toward their ultimate destruction.

No, the four men walking across the lobby were smugly confident they had seen the last of their unexpected, and, indeed, unexplainable, assailant. Considering the spells used on the museum that evening, they should not have encountered even the slightest interference. Then again, they were not the types to rely solely on necromancy to see them through an operation. That was why they had all come well armed, was it not?

Thus it was that, thinking themselves as close to success as possible, only a scant three yards from the front doors of the Brooklyn Museum, the band of thieves received the last great shock of their lives.

"I GIVE YOU MEN ONE WARNING ONLY—PUT DOWN THAT WHICH you are attempting to steal and leave this place at once."

"I don't believe it."

The words spoken by One were understood and felt by all his fellow intruders. Unexpectedly—unbelievably, for that matter—Knight had returned. Hanging in the air above the group, the professor drifted down to take up a position before them, between them and the outside world. As his feet touched the bare floor, he stood casually but prepared for action. His eyes were alert, his mouth a thin line curled in the barest of smiles at one end only.

"Fly away, little bird," said Two, "or we will simply put you down—understood?"

"I take your meaning," answered Knight, his tone meant to imply he might actually be considering their offer, the accent he suddenly began using letting them know he was not, "but, this being Brooklyn, what can I say but, well, you know, youze gotta do what'chu gotta do; I gotta do what I gotta do—youze know what I'm sayin'?"

Without hesitation, Four and One swung around their sidearms. As they did, Five uttered a pair of nonsense words that the professor took for a private signal. As Two and Three began lowering their burden to the floor, Five blazed once more into full illumination. As he did so, the two scouts, this time warned and squinting their eyes tightly, were able to target Knight clearly. Without hesitation the pair let loose a pair of full-auto barrages directly on-target. Eighteen bullets sped toward the professor who appeared to be in no hurry to move out of their way. Not willing to assume victory, Three and Two also pulled their sidearms, preparing to add more lead to the attack if necessary just as the first bullets fired found flesh.

To their surprise, however, none of the flesh torn into belonged to Knight. As Five diminished his brilliance, the wraith was shocked to see all of his accomplices either falling to the floor or grasping various sections of their bodies. All four were bleeding. All four were cursing—screaming in pain. A satisfied look on his face, the professor pulled forth the cigar-sized baton from inside his suit coat. Giving it a quick snap, he released the inner sections, which slid outward from both ends, increasing the weapon's size from roughly five inches to twenty-five.

"Now, gentlemen," he said, raising the weapon above his head, "is there anyone who doesn't want to have a seat?"

Knight found it fairly easy to beat the quartet into submission. Five wasted breath bellowing various threats, but the professor ignored them, not bothering to comment until the sight of flashing police lights closing in on the museum's entrance came into view. Having kicked away all of the intruders' weapons, feeling fairly confident they would not go to the trouble to set off any of their explosives with themselves in the blast area, Knight turned to the wraith, asking;

"So, my noisy friend, are you going to continue to hang there and jabber until the authorities arrive, which, by the by, I would prefer—having your ghostly presence here will make explanations so much simpler—or are you finally going to do everyone a favor by simply shutting up and disappearing?"

Seeing both uniformed and plainclothes officers moving up the stairs toward the front of the building, Five suddenly went serenely calm. Locking eyes with the professor, he answered;

"You are one smug, supercilious bastard, whoever you are—but you have no idea with what you are dealing. Nor now, I suppose, will you ever."

And with those words, the astral presence extended his right arm, pointing it toward his accomplices. That accomplished, he mouthed an apology in their direction, after which he murmured a few words in ancient Latin, then winked out of existence as the spell he had cast detonated the grenades the others had been carrying, blowing out the front doors and tearing the four intruders into the tiniest of pieces.

INTERLUDE

"I'm thinking this is not a call filled with news I very much wish to hear, is it?" The speaker sat at a table, nervously drumming his fingers. As suspicion and dread swirled within his mind, the voice on the other end of the line told him;

"I regret to admit you are correct, sir."

He knew it. The electronically masked words stung him, filling him with an exasperating frustration. Deep within himself he had somehow known since the entire operation had begun that things would go wrong.

"And what is it that makes me correct when I so very much wish not to be so?"

"Our team failed to acquire the object you requested. Their failure was actually something quite unexpected. What should have been a simple retrieval, a thing of minimal effort, somehow has gone terribly wrong."

"How wrong?"

"Four of our people are dead. Another was forced to

cause himself serious injury simply to escape the authorities as well as to cover our tracks. These matters are, of course, sir, not your concern. Our organization in no way is attempting to hold you responsible. Nor are we looking to alter the terms of our agreement. We are, at this time, merely informing you that it appears we simply were not prepared for all contingencies."

"This is what you are telling me. Fine. I am told. Now, what is it you are actually suggesting?"

The electronic voice asked for a moment to confer with its colleagues. After that the line went quiet as the voice on the phone went into muffled conference with others equally disguised. Their discussion consumed only a handful of seconds, ones taken up with what seemed to the party on the other end, not so much any kind of debate rather than a discussion concerning whether or not everyone he was listening to was in agreement. Finding they were, the distorted voice returned to the line once more, ready to make an offer.

"You must understand, sir, we pride ourselves on delivering on any contract. We have a reputation, after all, as the best in this business."

"And so, your offer . . . ?"

"You have a choice. We will either refund your deposit, even that interest earned on it while in our possession . . ."

"Very generous. Or—"

"Or, we will make a second attempt. You must understand, however. Unlike our previous foray, the piece you have shown an interest in is no longer sitting waiting in a museum basement. It has been moved to a police station. Also, our sources say that intense examination of it is to begin tomorrow. I hope this will not interfere with your own plans."

Tell them to get it, the voice in the back of his mind was snarling—raging. *Tell them nothing else matters.*

"The fools can study it all they like; they are gibbons clambering over an algebra textbook. Are you saying you can still get the piece for me by the date mentioned?"

"It will call upon a far greater output of resources," answered the disembodied voice. "But again, that is our concern. We have our reputation to consider. If you will allow it, we will put our second attempt into immediate action."

Tell them!

"Do it," answered the man, still drumming his fingers. "The money is of no concern. I simply must have the piece."

"So it is said," responded the voice, its dead electronic hum coming across as almost joyous, "so it is done. You shall have the object of your desire, even if we have to wipe its prison from the face of the Earth."

"Whatever it takes," answered the man, his fingers drumming, moving faster than ever. "*Whatever* it takes."

CHAPTER SEVEN

"I still can't believe it."

The words came from Detective Sergeant Jimmy Dollins. Just approaching middle age, the detective was a massive bear of a man, one gone somewhat soft around the middle, but still dangerous looking enough so that only his best friends would dare mention the fact without fearing retribution. His uncombed mane of tangled brown hair and the four days' growth of his beard did little to make him appear as if he might be looking for any new friends.

Across the table from him, his partner, Denny LaRaja, a smaller, immaculately groomed, soft-spoken man, added;

"Oh, indeed, I mean, really, Knight, it doesn't add up. Even for you—it just doesn't make any sense."

Between the two detectives sat a tired and more than impatient Professor Knight. His clothing was rumpled, the back of his jacket scorched, its stitching splitting up the middle. Off to the side sat Bridget Elkins. The four were at the local police precinct house, an innocuous-looking stone and brick building, slotted in the center of a row of such structures. Like so many of the city's police stations, it strove for a certain invisibility, to blend in with its urban surroundings.

It was an idea implemented decades earlier, the foolishly idealistic notion that disguising authority would render it more palatable to those who wished it removed. It was one of the city's numerous bits of nonsense concerning law enforcement. Knight's favorite had always been the repainting of all squad cars to white, because their former color frightened people, and you certainly could not have people frightened of the police.

Of course, he had thought as they entered, the endless line of police vehicles up and down the entire block outside the station house, most of them pulled up onto the sidewalk—whether they were painted white or not, whether the precinct building looked like a fort or a library—people's reactions to authority are completely gauged by their respect for the law and nothing else.

Looking about himself, glancing at Bridget, then Dollins, then LaRaja, the professor wondered briefly what the law had planned for him that night. The detectives had sequestered him and his assistant in one of the building's four interrogation chambers. The room was a sullen thing, a depressing gray box with nothing in the way of amenities save the obvious two-way mirror made a cliché by so many hundreds of movies and television shows.

The two police officers, both longtime acquaintances of Knight's, had assured him that no one was observing them. The professor did not care whether someone was listening or not. Considering what had really happened in the lobby, he had no plans on revealing what had actually transpired between himself and the intruders to anyone. From the way the detectives were urging him to "level with us and tell us what really happened," Knight knew the pair had their doubts about his version of what had transpired.

Still, knowing he had no real choice in the matter, the professor maintained his well-rehearsed stance as a sedentary curator and repeated his story again, once more giving the officers the same greatly reduced version of the actual events.

"Fellows, I repeat, Ms. Elkins and I went back to the museum after dinner so I could handle a matter I had agreed would be taken care of earlier that day. When we arrived, I saw that no one was at the guard desk and grew suspicious. I sent Ms. Elkins to call you, while I went inside to investigate." When Bridget spoke up, agreeing that such was what had happened, Dollins grunted at her that when they wanted to hear from the redhead they would direct their questions toward her.

The young woman steamed, not taking kindly to being dismissed so brusquely. Having the good sense to realize that she had no cards to play in that situation, however, she accepted the detective's rebuke and sat back in silence. At the same time, noting that the well-oiled pair knew their parts well, that while his partner had addressed Knight's assistant, LaRaja's eyes had never left him, the professor also held his tongue from letting slip any of the somewhat frosty comments he really wanted to say. Continuing on meekly, instead, he told the pair;

"Anyway, as I was saying, when I did so, enter the museum, I mean, I discovered four men exiting from the lower levels carrying a burden. They began arguing in the lobby, and then drew their weapons and gunned each other down. Somehow this must have set off some sort of explosives they were carrying." As the two detectives continued to stare, Knight merely shrugged and added; "What? What more do you want?"

LaRaja, his usually gentle eyes narrowing, focusing to hard points, leaned forward from his chair. With two fingers of his left hand, he brushed his neat, graying moustache first one way, then the other. After that he leaned in even closer, asking quietly;

"Piers, Piers—really; what is it with you? Why are you always doing things like this to us? Don't you like us? Aren't we your friends anymore?"

"Why, whatever do you mean, Denny? I like both you fellows considerably. You've always been very good to the museum, not to mention the way you've always—"

"Oh, cut it—Knight." Dollins' voice roared up out of him like a geyser rushing to the surface. Spewing it at the professor, he shouted, "Do not think you can get away playin' us! I'm warning you—do not do it. Do not try. We're talkin' four goddamned dead bodies. Blown to mother-humpin' little gooey bits! They're jelly, for Christ's sake. Your cleaning staff's gonna be Four-oh-nining that lobby for the rest of the week."

"It was quite a mess," admitted the professor.

"A mess?" Dollins rubbed a beefy hand over his face. "There's man-meat blown up, down, and around in every direction possible. You've got intestines festoonin' the front stairs and eyeballs embedded in your ceiling. That's more than just a goddamned mess, Knight!"

"Well yes," answered the professor softly, "I do agree with you, of course. But I don't understand your meaning."

"I think what we're trying to get at here, Piers," LaRaja interjected in his softer, scalpel of a voice, "is how you could be so close to the explosion to be singed as you were, but to have nothing else happen to you. I mean, honestly now, it does seem at least a little bit amazing—doesn't it?"

Knight spread his hands apart before him, presenting his body language as meek and uncertain, his face carefully set into an imploring map of confusion. His look crafted to give him as innocent an appearance as possible, using a voice calculated to ring with a desperate need to both please and find understanding, the professor answered;

"Gentlemen, I assure you, the only thing I know about my survival is that I'm overwhelmingly grateful to whatever force from beyond or accident of physics spared me any injury."

"Spare us another evening of your ten-dollar vocabulary."

"Jimmy, please," answered Knight, forcing his tone to convey the sense that he was in some kind of shock, "try to understand. I was almost killed. I'm lucky to be alive." The professor gave the large man a moment to let his words sink in, then added;

"I mean, did you question it two years ago when those men were shooting at you down in Red Hook? Do you remember that? How many rounds did they expend in your direction? Wasn't it over a hundred? And yet you came through it without a scratch?"

"What's that—"

"Can you explain your survival that day with anything outside of 'luck'?"

"Don't change the subject. . . ."

"I'm not changing the subject." Wearily, the professor inhaled sharply, then let it out in a sad, slow drizzle. Closing his eyes against the harsh lighting in the gray interrogation room, he said, "I'm trying to defend myself by using an example from your life to try and explain this moment in mine. I mean, tell me, do you actually think I shot those men?"

"No—"

"Am I under suspicion of having tried to blow up my own museum?"

"No," LaRaja took over. "Not yet."

The professor's head snapped back slightly. Thinking he had gained control of the conversation, he was surprised by the shorter detective's response. Knowing he was being manipulated into asking his next question, still Knight could see that he had no choice other than to do so.

" 'Not yet'? Bless all the tiny monkeys—not yet? And just what in Heaven does that mean?"

"It means," Dollins took over smoothly from his partner, "that there was an explosion in a public space. That this is the age of terrorism. It means that you can expect to find the feds in 'your museum' when you get there tomorrow. And, lastly, it means that as the only witness to, or at least, the only survivor of, the blast, I'm sure they'll have a few questions they'd like to ask."

"I know one I'd like to ask," LaRaja cut in. His manner shifting, it was evident to Knight he was about to change the current line of questioning. Picking up the pen near the pad he had been waiting to use, he asked, "Tell us, just what was that slab those fellows were trying to make off with?"

"It's known as the Dream Stone," answered the professor with relief, hoping things were finally going to start moving forward. Shifting easily into academic mode, he said, "It contains, inscribed upon its face, three distinct alphabets. Ancient Phoenician, Attic Greek, and one completely unknown to mankind. The tablet was discovered somewhere in the region of Jordan, back in 1855, '56. I don't recall the date exactly, but—"

"That's fine," answered LaRaja, cutting Knight off in an attempt to keep him focused. "Doesn't sound like anything much to a layman like me, though. So, tell us, Professor, why would anyone want it? Can we assume that it's valuable?"

"Sounds hard to fence," Dollins threw in. "Me bein' an ignorant cop and all, I'm sure I shouldn't even make any guesses. But if I were to, I think I'd say this sure sounds like a one-of-a-kind type'a thing—right?" When Knight nodded in agreement, the detective asked;

"Could it be somethin' outta *Indiana Jones*? Some kind of map to an ancient treasure or whatever?"

The professor began to dismiss the notion mechanically. He

could be excused doing so. The hour was late, he was tired, and ever since its discovery well over a hundred years earlier, the Dream Stone had decreased in value until it had been relegated to a back, forgotten corner of the museum's basement. Of so little interest it was considered undisplayable, it had almost been relegated to serve as one of the museum's outdoor garden displays. The only reason it had not was that it had been decided it would be simply too uninteresting to the public to be worth the bother.

But then, before Knight could dismiss Dollins' words out of hand, the facts of the phone call he had taken atop the Empire State Building that afternoon came rushing back to him. His eyes lighting wide, even as a part of his mind cursed himself for not thinking of the fact earlier, the professor answered;

"My dear Detective Sergeant Dollins, you know, in light of recent events, you just might be onto something."

CHAPTER EIGHT

Although it took him almost another hour, Knight finally managed to relate the entire story of the Dream Stone to the two detectives. Along with Bridget's help—starting with the facts of its discovery—he brought them through the years up to his conversation with Ungari. He also informed them about the probable staggering importance to archaeology of the doctor's find in Syria as it related to the possible role the Dream Stone might play in eventually unraveling the mystery of Memak'tori.

The professor also chided himself.

Not your finest moment, Knight, he thought. *I mean, there you are, returning to the museum after hours to inspect the very piece that was at that same moment the center of attention of a highly sophisticated group of thieves and you could not connect the dots? You're getting too old, my friend.*

Indeed, with Dollins eyeing him suspiciously, while LaRaja inquired aloud as to how the professor could not have made such a patently evident connection sooner, Knight merely shrugged. Taking a deep breath, he looked at the pair of detectives sheepishly, holding his hands up open before him as he explained;

"What can I tell you, fellows? I'm a museum curator, not Sherlock Holmes. I admit the whole thing is leaving me looking somewhat less than brilliant—"

"Yeah," growled Dollins. "Somewhat."

"But, I would also think," Knight added, his voice taking on a defensive tone, "that you'd take into consideration the fact I'm still a trifle shaken. I'm not used to seeing human beings gunned down, let alone blown apart, you know. I do feel much the fool for not making the connection earlier, but I also feel I certainly have the semblance of an excuse."

"Hard to believe, Professor, smart guy like you, that you wouldn't be thinkin' on that hunk'a rock after you saw that was what they'd been takin'."

"Oh heavens, Detective Dollins, I freely admit I've been thinking about the Dream Stone ever since I realized that was what was being stolen, but honestly, it's your job to look at why they were stealing it. I was mainly worrying about how much damage it might have sustained."

"Damage . . . ?"

As Dollins asked his one-word question, Bridget chimed in;

"You're right, Professor. After all these years of everyone thinking it's useless, if it was to be ruined now, now when it could finally—oh my God, what *did* happen to it, sir? Is it all right? Are the engravings all still intact? What if the stone itself suffered some internal damage from the explosion? Or a hairline crack—one that could fracture if it were even jolted too severely."

"I don't know," answered Knight, his tone one of anxious concern. "I was never given a chance to examine it. The police arrived right after the explosion, and I was rushed out of the museum so—" Breaking off, the professor cursed under his breath, then added;

"I mean, those idiots, they dropped it, then set off their damnable explosives somehow—"

Knight stopped speaking so abruptly both Dollins and LaRaja leaned closer involuntarily, waiting for whatever revelation had just occurred to him. As quickly as he went silent, though, the professor turned from one detective to the other just as sharply, posing them a question that actually frightened him.

"Good Lord," he blurted, his eyes going slightly wide, their usual deep blue draining somewhat pale. "Do you think . . . could they have been trying to destroy the Dream Stone?"

"Why would they?"

"I, well . . . it was just a thought—if they couldn't have it, making certain no one else could . . . oh, I really don't know." His voice as sincere as humanly possible, he added, "But, my word, could the stone still be in danger?"

"You'd know more about that than we would, Piers," answered LaRaja softly. "You, or this Dr. Ungari. Do you think we could get in touch with him now?"

"Well, maybe not at this moment," the professor told the detectives. "Soon, though—I'm certain. He was most eager to get his hands on the Dream Stone. I don't know his exact itinerary. How long it would take him to book a flight, reach an airport even. He was in the middle of the desert when I spoke to him. I couldn't tell you where he is right now."

"But he's coming to New York?"

"Yes," Knight assured the officers. "It was his intention. He most likely is en route here right now. As I said, he was in a tremendous hurry to see the stone."

"And why is that, Piers?" When the professor turned to LaRaja, the smaller man's soft eyes went incisive once more as he asked,

"I mean, if all he needs is to use this thing as a translator, couldn't you just send him a photograph?"

"Christ, yeah," added Dollins, his tone one of revelation. "If that's all he wants, if he just needs the damned thing as a translator, and he's in such a hurry and all, why blow all the money and time it takes to come here to look at it? Why would he bother? What sense does that make?"

And suddenly the thought that had been nagging at the back of the professor's mind all day came roaring to the forefront. In the age of computers, of scanners and e-mail, why *did* Ungari feel the need to leave the multiple sites he was overseeing, wasting time and running up unwarranted expenses in a world of limited funds, to fly halfway around the planet to make a personal inspection of the Dream Stone?

"I, I don't know," answered Knight honestly. Silently staring at his hands for a moment, the professor remained lost in thought, then finally continued, asking, "Now that I think about it, it actually doesn't make a great deal of sense—does it?"

"Professor . . . ?" All three men turned at the sound of Bridget's voice. As the trio stared, she asked, "Wouldn't the same thing apply to the thieves?"

"I'm not certain I understand," Knight admitted. "What exactly do you mean, my dear?"

"I was thinking . . . if the Dream Stone doesn't have any intrinsic value, then why steal it? Like the detectives said, those men could have just taken a photograph of it, or made a rubbing of the characters. But they didn't."

"But what's your point, miss?" asked LaRaja.

"Maybe we're looking at this the wrong way. The professor and I, we think of the Dream Stone as an archaeological treasure. You're thinking of it that way because we're your only source of information on it this far."

"So, what're you thinkin' now?"

"I'm thinking, Detective Dollins . . . if they were willing to destroy it all along, then why not just copy it, destroy it, and leave? They could certainly have gotten away faster if they hadn't been carrying a hundred pounds of rock—right?"

And, thought Knight, *that was exactly it*. Looking at his assistant with a degree of respect he would have thought it would have taken her far longer to coax out of him, he pursed his lips, nodding unconsciously, then said;

"Out of the mouths of babes . . ."

"What'dya mean, Professor?"

"You as well, Jimmy. You're both correct. Can't you see it? For some reason I freely admit I cannot fathom as of yet, the Dream Stone itself, not the characters engraved upon it, must have some worth previously unsuspected."

"But how could that be," asked LaRaja. "Didn't you just get done telling us that you and your boys at the museum have been studying the thing for over a hundred years?"

"The piece, because of its resemblance to the Rosetta Stone, was studied as if it were another Rosetta Stone. What I mean is, if you find something that looks like a car, and performs the functions of a car, you think of it as a car. You don't expect it to be a sponge, or a toaster oven. But—"

Once again Knight stopped in mid-sentence, much to the annoyance of the two detectives.

Both men knew the professor from previous dealings between the museum and the police. They respected him as a scholar and had come to expect the stereotypical kinds of behavior the world had grown used to seeing in academic types. Still, the hour was late, and they had yet to gain any information either of them saw as useful in solving the case they were actually concerned with—the reason there were four fresh bags of meat and bones in the city morgue.

Both detectives realized that men often died over priceless objects—especially thieves. But, these thieves had killed one another at the moment of their triumph, and in a somewhat ridiculous manner. That was not what was frustrating Dollins and LaRaja at that moment, however. Rather, it was the fact that both detectives were quite certain Knight was concealing something from them. A police officer reached the rank of detective sergeant through one of three means: long, hard work, extreme luck, or political connections. Neither Dollins nor LaRaja had ever considered themselves either very lucky or well connected. They had both been on the job for dozens of years, had worked thousands of cases, interviewing witnesses and suspects from every walk of life, men and women of every color and religion in, at last count, some forty-three different languages.

It was the kind of work that developed certain instincts in a man. Both detectives knew the professor was cooperating with them . . . but they also knew he was not telling them everything. Thus, in their minds, his most recent pause could be signaling that he had just had some sort of revelation or that he was once more stopping himself from saying the first thing that had entered his mind until he could edit it properly.

Finally, Knight broke his self-imposed silence. His eyes coming back into focus once more, with a snap of his fingers he said;

"I really probably should examine the Dream Stone . . . now, I mean. Immediately."

"What are you thinking, Professor?"

"I'm thinking, Detective LaRaja, that I and the rest of my kind have obviously missed something extremely important about what we all thought up until now was nothing more than a worthless hunk of rock. One man is traveling from the other side of the world to inspect it when he simply could have made use of it from photos. Four other men are dead, and as best we can tell for much the same reason." Rubbing his eyes, Knight took in a deep breath, let it out, then added;

"Yes, I really do think I should inspect it now. If there's some problem, tell your superiors I insisted on the grounds that I wanted to check it for damage—which, actually, I wouldn't mind doing as well." Standing from his chair as if all had been decided and agreed upon, he stretched his shoulders a bit, cracked his neck, then asked;

"I know the Dream Stone was brought along as evidence. So, where do you gentlemen have it right now?"

"It's been checked into the property room."

"Well, why don't we head there, eh?"

But then, before either detective could answer the question, a piercing siren slashed its way through the gray interrogation room, echoing throughout every other room, hallway, and stairwell in the building as well. The men all recognized it as a standard New York City fire alarm.

They were also all quite certain they knew, considering the way their evening had been going so far, from exactly where the alarm must have been set off.

CHAPTER NINE

"Denny," barked Dollins, throwing his massive body up and out of his chair, "get Bridget outta here—move!"

No one argued. As partners, both detectives knew they were responsible for the safety of any civilians in their charge. Bridget had to be their first concern. Dollins, younger than LaRaja, single where his partner was married, took the riskier of the two immediate jobs from which both men knew they had to choose. At one time LaRaja would argue such choices vehemently. After a stern lecture where his wife ganged up on him with Dollins, however, he learned to live with the inevitable.

"Knight," the large man bellowed as he grabbed up his coffee cup, "you're with me—let's go!"

Any other time—under normal circumstances—both detectives would have been exiting the building, working to get those under their protection to safety. That night, however, was different. Though none of them had any proof, there was no doubt in the minds of any of the three men that something—somehow—had gone wrong in the property room. Though none of them had the slightest proof, they were all certain that if the building truly was in flames, the fire must have started there—and that no matter what was the actual reason for the blaring alarm, for some reason they could not fathom, the Dream Stone was behind it.

"Lead on, Detective," answered Knight, making a flourish with his right arm. "It's your building."

And the damnable piece of rock was the only reason Dollins was willing to take a civilian into danger. As far as he was concerned, there was something suspicious about everything that had gone down that night. On every occasion the Brooklyn Museum had needed the cooperation of the police for anything, his brain reminded him, Knight had always been in the middle of it. And, the detective had always walked away from each situation, from every one of their encounters, feeling that he had been in some manner played—never told the entire truth.

"This way."

As the two men reached the door directly behind LaRaja and Bridget, the professor called out to the older detective, admonishing him;

"Take care of her." As Knight's eyes locked with Bridget's for a moment, he gave her a grin meant to bolster her courage, adding, "After all, she has quite a great deal of work to do in the morning."

"I'll certainly see what I can do, Doc," answered LaRaja, a wry smile crossing his face despite their situation. It was but an instant's respite, however. Once out in the hallway, the older detective directed the redhead toward the front door and kept her moving until the pair disappeared into the crowd heading in that direction. Dollins and Knight forced their way in the opposite direction, against the current, moving into the first stairwell they could reach.

Conversation had ceased between the pair as they fought their way through both the crowd and the growing smoke. Preparing to open a door to the basement, Dollins was slightly startled when three uniformed officers burst through from the other side. Half-blind and gagging, they stumbled into the first-floor hallway, gasping for air. Grabbing one man by the shoulder, as much to keep him steady on his feet as well as to capture his attention, the large detective asked;

"Phillips—what's goin' on down there? Couldn't you guys lay some fire extinguisher action on it or somethin'?"

"Property room," the man answered weakly. Coughing violently, he forced his voice back under his control, then added, "Didn't see what started it. Couldn't get near it, really. Smoke, everywhere. All of a sudden like, out of nowhere. Bitter, makes you gag . . . had to run. . . ."

Dollins and Knight looked at each other for an instant, simply staring. The professor gave his head the slightest of nods, which was apparently good enough for the larger man. Moving into the stairwell, the detective stopped the pair for a moment at the top of the stairs. Popping the plastic lid off his coffee cup, Dollins told his companion to hold still. As the professor complied, the detective poured coffee across the top of his own sport coat with half its contents. The other half he splashed on the lapel of Knight's suit coat. Throwing away his cup, the detective grabbed the edge of his jacket, moved it up to where it could cover his mouth, then directed the professor to breathe through the wet material of his own coat.

"It's no gas mask, but it'll filter a lotta the shit we otherwise would end up breathin'. Ain't no tellin' what's burnin', but from what Phillips said I'm thinkin' maybe we don't want all that much of it gettin' in our lungs."

Knight did as instructed, giving the big man a grateful nod.

The detective accepted the acknowledgment, then started down the stairs, taking them two and three at a time, even as he made a slight prayer that the lights would not cut out on them. The smoke had already thickened within the stairwell to the point where it made Dollins more than a bit apprehensive. The professor was also feeling an extreme touch of apprehension himself, but for a completely different reason.

Knight respected Dollins' abilities.

Three times their paths had crossed over the previous few years in an official manner. The last had been in Red Hook, when Dollins had miraculously escaped death despite scores of rounds being fired at him from nearly point-blank range. He had been decorated for his valor when the shooting ceased, but despite the fact that he had willingly smiled for the television cameras and happily accepted his upgrade to sergeant, the incident had continued to gnaw at him.

Although the detective knew there was no rational reason for him to think so, Dollins believed the professor had somehow kept him from being murdered that day. It was an absurd notion, he had told himself then—continued to tell himself. Knight had been behind him, face to the ground. There was nothing he could have done. The detective knew this, knew as certainly as he knew anything, that there was no way the professor could have possibly interceded with Fate on his behalf.

"He's not God," Dollins had told himself over and over, "no matter how much he acts like it."

But, despite all logical approaches to the incident, the big man knew in his heart that he should not have lived through that evening. There was absolutely no reason for him to still be alive, outside of something on the order of Heavenly intervention—and angels had not been reported as being sighted anywhere near Red Hook that evening. He had checked.

"Dollins," Knight shouted through his lapel. "I believe there's something wrong here, something no one has taken into consideration." By that point the pair had reached the bottom of the stairs. Directing the larger man's attention to the base of the door before them, the professor said;

"The smoke coming under the door. The smell of it, the color—doesn't it seem a bit suspicious to you?"

"What'dya mean?"

"Besides the fact this building is one big block of concrete, that there shouldn't be all that much about it that could burn, I don't think this smoke is coming from a fire." Taking a deep breath through his jacket, allowing himself to capture a sense of the reeking billow, Dollins answered;

"I'm thinkin' you may have somethin' there." Taking an extra sniff of the air, studying it for a second, the detective added, "Yeah, that don't smell electrical. And it sure don't smell like wood, neither."

"Trust me when I tell you I have no idea what's happening here, Detective," said Knight, his eyes beginning to sting. Wiping at them, trying not to cough, he added, "But after what I've been through so far tonight, I really do believe you should draw your weapon before we go through that door."

"You what . . . ?"

Dollins gave the professor a long, hard look, his mind splitting in a number of directions. A half-dozen voices all barked at the detective, urging him to as many different courses of action. Yes, he did not trust the professor, but to what extent? On the one hand, he knew in his bones the man was hiding something from him. Almost certainly far more than one thing. But on the other hand, he also firmly believed that it was Knight who was responsible for his not dying in Red Hook.

If he was really up to something, the part of Dollins' brain he relied upon the most whispered to him, *if he was actually one of the bad guys, then why bother saving some cop he knows doesn't trust him?* Dismissing the other factions warring within his mind, Dollins growled through his coat's lapel;

"Stay behind me."

Pulling his service revolver, he gingerly touched both the doorknob and the door itself with the barest ends of his fingertips, testing for heat. Finding them both relatively cool, he started to open the door. Hesitating, however, the detective bent over instead, fumbling at his ankle. When he stood up again, Knight could see the large man had removed a second weapon from his backup holster.

"You open the door," he ordered the professor. "Then I'm through first."

Knight nodded, moving forward. On a nod from Dollins the professor pulled open the door. Then, both men plunged into the thick smoke on the other side and rushed headlong into madness.

CHAPTER TEN

"Christ," cursed Dollins softly, trying not to breathe deeply as he did so, "I can hardly see a thing."

The hallway the two men entered swirled with a deep, gray smoke, one containing hints of an oddly light, bluish haze. As on the other side of the doorway, neither man felt anything much in the way of undue heat coming toward them as they moved outward into the basement. Both continued attempting to breathe through their jackets as best they could, but the sparse amount of coffee Dollins had splashed them with was rapidly drying out.

"My God," said Knight harshly, coughing as he did so, "doesn't this building have sprinklers down here?"

The oddly colored smoke stinging their eyes, the pair continued to fumble their way forward, their senses straining to understand what was happening. Rather than answer verbally, Dollins instead pointed toward an alcove ahead of them. As the two men entered, the professor saw what the detective was leading them toward—a watercooler.

Understanding what was expected of him, Knight immediately set to filling cups of cold water.

"Yeah, you'd think they woulda run some kinda sprinklers down here by now," growled Dollins. "That's the way'a things, though—building's just too old. Budget keeps going toward luncheons for the top brass. Us grunts're probably lucky we even got the damn smoke alarms."

"I guess so." The professor mumbled his answer as he splashed the detective and then himself in the face to relieve the growing pain in their eyes. After that he doused both their heads and then their jackets. Dollins did not even look in the professor's direction, his focus aimed down the hall, as were the weapons he held in each hand.

Pointin' guns at a fire, thought the detective. *They might as well call the men in the white coats to get their nets and come on over.*

Despite his attempt at humor, however, Dollins kept both his weapons pointed down the smoke-filled hallway. Though it made no sense and would be considered insane by any reasonable person, something within him, some primal section bound deep within his soul, refused to let him waver. Something was being hidden by the oddly colored, strange-tasting fumes. Something terrible enough to set off all the alarms within his mind at full alert.

As he kept his eyes focused dead ahead, Knight held a cup to the big man's lips so he could take a drink.

Dollins gulped the first half deeply, then used the second half to gargle before he swallowed, realizing that would be the last relief he would know. Diverting his attention for the briefest of moments to his companion, he saw that the professor had taken his own drink. Not seeing any reason to hesitate further, Dollins started them down the hallway once more.

The two men encountered no one else as they continued

making their way steadily forward. With the fire alert siren still blaring they could hear nothing else, either—could barely understand even each other. So loudly did the alarm echo in the narrow corridors of the underground section of the precinct house that when it suddenly ceased being broadcast it was actually several seconds before either Dollins or Knight realized the thing had gone silent. Both men stopped moving, pausing to listen to their surroundings.

Fire, each of them knew from bitter experience, possessed a very distinctive sound. They were also listening for any other possible noises, such as any others who might still be in the basement area—friendlies who might be trapped somehow or intruders who might have been the reason the alarm had been set off in the first place. Able to detect nothing out of the ordinary, the pair continued their cautious forward movement. Once they turned the last corner between them and the property room, however, the sounds reaching them changed.

Dollins turned to the professor, moving close to ask him if he might be hearing the same thing the detective was. Before the larger man could speak, however, Knight gave his head a sharp nod, making his eyes go wide so as to indicate that he was as suspicious of the sounds reaching his ears as was Dollins. Both of them understood the need for silence as they continued onward as cautiously as possible.

Once they were within ten feet of the heavy steel door to the property room, Knight caught hold of the detective's arm. Pulling on it hard enough to signal he wished the big man to stop, the professor drew Dollins close, then whispered to him;

"That sound, that hissing sound—do you recognize it?"

The detective gave over a few seconds to intent listening, then whispered back;

"I know it's somethin' I've heard before, but I don't know what. What're you thinkin'?"

"It reminds me of a campfire," answered Knight. "But, not when there are flames. I'm talking about when it's at its hottest, when it's all coals, that burning sound heat makes as it dries the very moisture out of the air around it."

Dollins' eyes went wide. He recognized the sound immediately, knowing the professor's deduction was correct . . . but how could that be? Unlike some of the rooms on the station's upper floors, which still retained much of their wood from the old days, the basement rooms were mostly stone, brick, and poured concrete. The property room was lined with nothing but metal shelves and cabinets. There simply was not enough flammable material within it to feed a fire of such intensity.

All right, let's say you're right about that, Jimmy, the detective's mind responded to him. *Fine—it's impossible. But if that is the case, then just what the hell do you think that is that you're hearin'?*

Before Dollins' brain could offer him anything in the way of an answer, however, suddenly both men began to notice the one thing they had been dreading since they began their descent. At first each of them had believed or at least sincerely hoped that the sensation they were detecting was only a result of nerves on their part. Taking another few steps forward, they both knew such was nothing more than wishful thinking.

"It's starting to get warmer," hissed Knight. "Too warm. There has to be something on fire in there."

"Any ideas what?"

"What do you mean?"

Dollins turned to stare the professor square in the eye. Something was not right about their situation; of that the detective was certain—the same kind of something that had been off-kilter every time he and Knight had ended up in the same place. During each of those occurrences things had gotten just a bit stranger, just a little more twisted. This time, however, as far as Dollins was concerned, he had stumbled into the Twilight Zone, and he had dragged his own personal Rod Serling along with him.

His eyes locking with Knight's, his years of on-the-job experience watching for any attempt to mislead him, the big man snarled, "You and me, we ain't got no more time for shittin' around. Now tell me, straight-out and honest—just what the goddamned hell is in there?"

The professor was taken aback a trifle by the question. It was not, after all, his job to be there. He had accompanied Dollins out of concern for the Dream Stone. Knight would have done so even if he possessed no other relation to it outside of the fact that it was the property of the Brooklyn Museum. Considering his family connection to the piece, however, let alone Ungari's revelations of its sudden, possibly history-shattering importance, and then its attempted theft, Knight simply had to know what was happening to the antiquity that, less than twenty-four hours previous, was considered utterly worthless.

Knight found the detective's question, coming at the moment it did, not so much a request for help, but a challenge bordering on accusation. Dollins did not fully trust him, but then, considering the fact he was hiding a great number of things from not only the officer but the world in general, Knight could not very well take offense. Indeed, over the years he had grown used to such things. Although, like most of those who dabbled in magic, he strove to appear merely a harmless eccentric, the pose was no longer working with the detective.

Sweat had begun to bead on the professor's forehead. It was nothing compared to the soak matting Dollins' thinning hair to his skull, but it was reminder enough that things were escalating at a fantastic rate there in the basement. Also, knowing their time was certain to be running out, Knight went on the offensive, snarling back at the detective;

"And just how am I supposed to know what in hell is in there until we open the door?"

His face going a deep red, from both the heat as well as frustration, Dollins took a step toward the professor, bringing their faces only inches apart as he growled;

"This is not over, wise guy."

Then Dollins turned abruptly, moving on the door to the property room. Still carrying a weapon in each hand, the detective was just about to shove one into a pocket so he could safely open the door when he stopped—transfixed. Closing with him, a worried Knight caught sight of what the officer had seen and stopped moving himself. Both men blinked involuntarily, Dollins shaking his head violently, as if the motion might change the image before him.

It did not, however, and there in the silent, smoke-filled basement the center of the steel property room door continued to glow, a harsh electrical steam fizzing away from it as the thick metal of it began to melt.

CHAPTER ELEVEN

"Back up—move. Hurry!" shouted Knight, coughing as his sudden exclamation caused him to breathe in far more of the acrid smoke swirling in the hallway than his lungs could handle. The taste of the smoke frightened him, its increasingly bitter tang telling him far more than he wished to know. Pushing at Dollins, trying to force the far larger man into moving even while still choking, the professor barely managed to add, "Now!"

"Why?" The detective snapped the word defiantly, as if whatever response he received to that question might answer many others. Grabbing Knight's arm, he demanded, "What's in there? Just what in hell is in there?!"

"Something that can melt its way through steel, you idiot!" Pointing at the growing spot in the center of the door, the academic focused the large man's attention on the streaks of fiery liquid metal beginning to ooze downward from the glistening core. Then, shaking off Dollins' grasp, the professor began backing down the hallway, forcing words out in between coughs;

"I don't possess . . . any means to combat that . . . whatever *that* is. We've got to get—get out of here!"

Free from the detective's formidable grip, Knight took two more rapid steps backward. Working hard to control his breathing, desperate to stop coughing, to clear his eyes of the terrible burning sensation gnawing its way into them, the professor knew with an unshakable certainty that whatever was coming through the door could not be stopped by two mere mortals.

Because of the growing taste of copper in the air, Knight believed he might have some slight idea as to what might be melting the door. But, he also knew that if he was correct, he and the detective would be lucky to escape the building, and then only if they turned and ran—immediately.

"You know what it is that's in there," insisted Dollins. Following the retreating professor down the hall, he growled, "I *know* you do. Fer Christ's sake, tell me what it is—what we need to do to put it down!"

Stopping for a moment, the last time he planned to do so before he reached the street, Knight placed his hand atop his head, wiping the remaining water in his hair down into his eyes. Then, placing his still-wet hand over his mouth and nose, he dragged down as deep a breath as he could through his fingers, then told the detective;

"Listen to me. Believe me when I tell you this. Yes—I might have some idea what it is that's breaching that door, but even if my guess is correct, that doesn't mean that we can stop it. Do you understand me—we can't. We can . . . not . . . *stop it*!"

"Then what do we do?"

"There's nothing we can do. I'm thinking the same thing you

are, that this all must be tied to the Dream Stone. It must be—*has* to be. And you have to believe me, if something was sent here to destroy it, to keep it out of the hands of others, then it's surely a thing of great power. Far greater than we can deal with on our own."

The large man looked deep into Knight's eyes, then turned to stare back toward the property room. The door was glowing even more fiercely, giving off molten shimmers of orange and scarlet. Fiery slag was rolling down the softening steel, dripping from above, sending a scattering of dazzling sparks in all directions. And, as Dollins stared closely, he felt his heart stop beating for a split second. Blinking hard, he looked forward once more to determine if what he thought he had just seen was actually there. Leaning toward him, the professor whispered in a voice made small by fear;

"Yes. Those are *hands*!"

Slender and tapered, two glimmering, bestial sets of fingers were crammed inside the oozing, ever-widening circle forming in the door, tearing at it, scraping away the softening metal one mushing lump after another. Dollins' eyes fixed on the horrifying sight, freezing his limbs, rooting him to the spot.

When the professor once again pulled on the detective's arm to start him moving, the big man did not resist, too mesmerized by the lunatic scene playing out before him to make any conscious decisions of his own. Finally, however, when Knight had moved him practically the entire way back to the stairwell, Dollins muttered;

"No . . . stop."

"We can't stop. We don't dare," hissed the professor, reaching for the door to the stairs. "We've got to keep moving."

"No."

As Knight's fingers reached the doorknob, Dollins stepped away from him, slipping his backup weapon into his sport coat's pocket while he moved toward a small cabinet built into the opposite wall. Throwing open its rectangular glass door, he reached inside the compact space, pulling out the fire extinguisher stored within it. Checking the heft of it, making certain it was fully charged, he told the professor;

"Go on—take off. I'll stop this thing."

"Don't be a fool—you can't stop it with that," insisted Knight. Reaching for the detective once more, the professor insisted, "For God's sake, man, it'll roast you alive!"

"Gotta try." Swallowing hard, Dollins added, "No one else did nuthin' . . . just ran. Someone's gotta do somethin'."

Knight's hand stopped short of the detective's arm. Making any further attempts to get him to flee obviously would be futile. The professor was almost certain he knew why no other officers had made a stand against the horror just beyond. He recognized the aroma of a planted repulsion there in the harsh atmosphere of the basement. Whoever had sent the thing in the property room had first charmed it with a fear caster—not an overly long or powerful one, just enough to allow the thing to form and be about its business. No unprotected human could resist the urge to retreat in its presence. It was no wonder the area had been vacated so quickly and without question.

"Go on," ordered Dollins, pointing with his weapon toward the door to the stairwell. "This ain't your fault and it ain't your fight. So, do it—go!"

The professor nodded, turning toward the door once more, then suddenly stopped. Touching the detective's arm to catch his attention, Knight began removing the blue stone ring from his hand as he said;

"Last year, in Red Hook, when you survived the shooting . . . you remember, I was there. I was wearing this at the time. It's . . . it's lucky."

The two men locked eyes one last time. Sliding the ring onto his left pinkie, the only finger he possessed small enough to accept it, Dollins said simply, "Thanks," then turned and moved back toward the property room. Knight, knowing he had done everything he could, fled into the stairwell. Taking one final glance, the professor could tell from the amount of black sparks coming from around the corner ahead that the collapsing door would soon be no barrier at all to that which was behind it. Throwing Dollins a heartfelt salute, Knight then did the only thing he could, and retreated to the surface.

Alone in the smokey hallway, the detective started once more for the property room. He did so slowly but resolutely, walking with the heavy-duty fire extinguisher held high in both hands, waiting for the inevitable. In the last moments he had spent talking with Knight, the temperature had risen more than ten degrees. With each step taken toward the corner before him, sweat rolling off his head, down his back, into his eyes, Dollins could feel the wildly increasing heat—knew what it meant.

"All right, you bastard," he sneered as he reached the corner. "Show yourself."

With a sudden increase of light flooding the area, the detective knew the property room door had finally collapsed—that whatever had been restrained by it had freed itself at last. Swallowing hard, the large man took the final step needed to where he could view the situation for himself. And at that moment, suddenly there it was before him.

"Jesus, Mary, and Joseph . . ."

Tall it was, a willowy, vaguely humanoid frame, but one constructed out of bones cast from lava wrapped in fascia created of flame.

Seeing the entire thing at one time, Dollins understood why it had needed to melt its way through the door. The demonic shape's fingers were an illusion, a distortion caused by both the heat and the detective's intense desire to understand, to assign comprehension to that upon which he was looking. The fiery imitation of a human form standing before him was not something that could turn knobs or press buttons. It was a gathered mass of elemental fury, forged into an approximation of being sent out to accomplish a task. Staring at the blazing shambler, struggling desperately to make his brain function once more, Dollins swallowed hard, then snapped;

"Okay, I guess you got your job and I got mine." Flipping the restraining safety catch on the fire extinguisher, as the very plaster in the walls and ceiling began to liquify, dribbling all about him, the detective pulled hard on the trigger, screaming, "Drink up, Shirley!"

Frigid carbon dioxide blasted forth from the canister's release nozzle, the streaming cloud of it splashing against the creature's torso in violent reaction. Lungless, brainless, the thing made no verbal response as it reared back, the language of its movements suggesting Dollins had actually managed to wound it to some extent. Holding back from emptying the extinguisher, the large man moved his hand still holding his service automatic and fired, emptying the entire clip into the monstrous shape before him.

Every bullet fired entered the burning mass drawing toward him, but Dollins could see no effect. Dropping his weapon—discarding it as if knowing he would never need it again—he hoisted the fire extinguisher to his chest once more, pulling the trigger and releasing all the frozen ammunition he had left to him. Again the horror was staggered, but in nothing one might consider a hope-giving amount. Perhaps if there had been forty or fifty men all armed with such weapons, the detective thought, there might have been a chance of stopping it.

"But that, of course," he growled, "would be too easy."

Knowing the ring Knight had given him was somehow protecting him and that without it he would have burst into flames long ago, James Albert Dollins hefted the now-empty metal cylinder in his hands like a club. Hunched over, breathing hard from the heat, he pulled forth all he had within himself, throwing himself erect. Then, screaming in defiance, the detective sergeant raced forward, battering with all his strength at the slice of Hell trying to set foot in his world.

INTERLUDE

"I regret to inform you, sir, that the object you commissioned us to obtain for you has apparently been destroyed."

Of course it has, the man thought, drumming his fingers against his leg with increasing violence. Within his mind, a dozen voices seethed, writhing in confused anger, pushing at him, screeching—but the rage of one in particular, the new one, the only one that mattered, was beyond description. Its fury was about to boil over, to explode.

"We have our own code of procedure for such regrettable occurrences," the electronic voice said. Despite its heavy masking, the sound of it seemed one of genuine regret, leaning far more toward sincere apology rather than indifference. "And we are ready to render unto you full and unconditional recompense. But we do have a few questions."

"Questions?" The man on the other end of the line choked out the word in a tone situated roughly halfway in between laughter and a snarl, threw it out to the caller as if the thought were beyond his comprehension.

"Yes. First," answered the electronic voice, seemingly unaware of the level of distress present on the other end of the line, "the obvious thing we need to know is whether or not you truly needed to possess the article, or if, perhaps, your need was to keep it out of the hands of others?"

The fingers of the man listening to the electronic voice stopped beating against his leg. Instead, clawlike, they began to dig harshly into his flesh, unnoticed, as if of their own volition. Staring off into space, his eyes unable to focus on anything within his surroundings, the man's head began to vibrate, shaking uncontrollably. While the distorted voice continued to speak into his ear, the man closed his eyes, unable to bear the sight of the real world around him to any greater extent than that found within his eyelids. His teeth clamped together, a twisted, feral growl began to grow deep within his throat.

Cheated, lied to, betrayed—

The voice from the back of his mind was hissing now, the words of it like steaming fangs within his brain, chewing upon his memories, tearing at them, consuming vast portions of the man, bending him into its willing vessel.

"Sir," the electronic voice droned somewhere in the distance, attempting to make its case, "we understand you must be feeling a certain sense of loss. We here cannot stress how much we regret this. Our organization is not used to having to report such failure. If you could but—"

"Silence, animal—"

The distorted voice broke off, somewhat alarmed. The familiar tone it had come to know, the person it had been conversing with over the past day, was somehow suddenly gone. Something the speaker on the other end of the line could not fathom had transpired. In the business of making his firm's rather exotic clientele happy, the owner of the electronic voice pushed past any concerns for himself, asking;

"Sir . . . ?"

"I said *silence*!"

And then, a crackling burst of energy surged from within the speaker's mind, flashing into his cell phone, following the transmission back to its source. At the speed of light it arrived in the spot halfway around the world where those who had attempted to arrange the theft of the Dream Stone dwelt. Its unexpected arrival spelled the end for everyone there.

The shock wave erupted violently through the receiver on the other end, flooding the room, and then flashed throughout the entire building. Impossibly, it grew exponentially, killing everyone within—more than killing them. It consumed them, obliterating each person within reach from their innermost core outward, swallowing their spirits, devouring their souls. So violent was the attack, it burst the bodies open, splattering their blood across the walls, superheating it so that in many instances the sizzling liquid melted the plaster where it struck.

In an instant the deed was accomplished. Those who had failed were destroyed, their essence stolen and delivered to what up until that moment had merely been a whisper in the back of the caller's mind. Now, however, it was more. Those who had failed it had paid the price for disappointing it with their lives.

Disgusting fools—

Destroying those who had failed it, however, in no way lightened the sinister voice's foul mood. The darkly growing thing in no way felt compensated—it could not. The Dream Stone held too major a spot within its plans.

But, what was done was done.

Releasing the vessel of which it had taken command's grip on its own leg, the invader immersed itself within the energies it had just stolen, then recessed to the back of the man's mind once more. It had gained a great deal of power and it could see that more would be just as easily obtained. Further, as it studied its newfound freedom, even while concealing it away within the folds of its host's subconscious, it knew its actions were still undetected. Satisfied, the voice that had traveled so far pushed aside its remaining regrets over the Dream Stone. There were other ways to accomplish its goals. Settling its essence, it basked in the warmth of its newly stolen energies, delighted in their taste. Looked forward to more.

"This place," it whispered, its grease-drenched words oozing their way into the furthest corner of the man's mind, "it is so incredibly rich. So invitingly full of life—

"It is so wonderfully good to be back."

CHAPTER TWELVE

"It's been a long night," suggested LaRaja, his voice tense, sounding close to snapping. Raising one hand, moving his index finger back and forth between himself and Knight, he told the professor, "Everyone's wrung out and, as at least you and I know, there isn't anyone here that has the slightest clue as to what's been going on. So, why don't you stop getting in our way and take this poor kid out of here? I can always start harassing you again in the morning."

"Thank you," answered the professor. "And of course, I am assuming there was nothing in the way of humor in that. . . ."

"You assume real good, Piers."

Knight nodded, grateful for the detective's reprieve, as well as his candor. Still, the professor was concerned enough about his assistant to worry about LaRaja and whatever further questions the police might have later. For the moment, he had to admit that LaRaja was correct about one thing—Bridget Elkins had been within the city limits of New York for not even half a day and already her mind was pulsing toward overload. Knight himself had completely overwhelmed her sense of size and order in the world immediately upon her arrival with their little trip to the top of the Empire State Building.

He had meant to do so, had done so partly for his own amusement but also, he knew, ultimately for her own good. One of the Big Apple's specialties was knocking people for a loop. The quicker she caught on to that fact, he felt—the faster she took that rocket ride to the top and followed it up with the inevitable, crashing disappointment the city always eventually provided—then the better off she would be. But from there on, things had progressed at a far more rapid pace than he could have ever predicted.

Hell, thought Knight, allowing himself a faint touch of self-pity, *she'd better have been overwhelmed by it all. I'm feeling fairly overwhelmed myself right now.*

The professor did not bother to chastise himself for taking his new assistant to the museum that night. She was young and full of energy. To see the fabled Brooklyn Museum, the art of Africa and the Pacific, of ancient Egypt and the modern Islamic world, to walk its corridors overflowing with seven hundred years of European painting, it was paradise for any who understood the joys of a repository experience. And that was the regular, render-your-donation-and-enter-with-the-public experience.

To see it as she would have, after hours, to walk its beautifully laid out, well-appointed stone hallways, to view its seemingly limitless treasures in private—especially in the dark, with its wonderful ability to make anything seem forbidden—their work then would have been the icing on a slice of cake the flavor of which she would have remembered fondly for all her days. Possessed of a few of his own cherished remembrances, he had meant it as a gift.

"Instead of a happy memory, however, the poor child ends up traumatized."

Knight wanted to curse the luck of it, but had no direction in which to sling the abuse he so desperately wanted to hurl away from himself. Who, after all, could he blame? Ungari? The thieves or the police? Maybe himself, he thought. Maybe he could find nowhere else to hurl it because none deserved it more than he did.

Fie, it's all or none, the back of his mind snapped, to which another voice within his brain responded, *But then, isn't it always?*

When they had first driven to the precinct house, Knight had been allowed to take his own car. He had driven Bridget there as well, since the detectives had insisted on her coming to be questioned. New to town or not, the young woman was a witness, after all, and the professor knew the police were offering both himself and his new assistant quite a grand amount of consideration by allowing them to travel both together and without an escort.

If there had been even the slightest substantial suspicion that either of them might be responsible for the deaths in the museum that night, of course, such would never have been allowed. It did not pay to give suspects the chance to get their stories straight between themselves before questioning them.

But Dollins and LaRaja both were seasoned professionals. They could tell from every movement of Bridget's body language, from every glance she offered them and the tone of every word she spoke, that there was nothing of the criminal about her. If she was hiding anything from them, LaRaja had actually commented to his partner at one point, she was damn good enough to keep it hidden.

The large man had agreed, smiling as he did so.

As he offered his hand to the redhead, helped her up from the hard wooden bench upon which she had fallen asleep, Knight could not help but think of Dollins and his incredible sacrifice. No one, not even himself, he was quite certain, would ever know exactly what had happened to the detective. But the professor was also certain his guess would be far more accurate than that of anyone else.

The big man had not been one to quit. With the protection of Knight's ring, Dollins would have been able to approach the elemental sent to the property room. When bullets failed him, the detective would have gone for the direct approach.

"You were never one to give up," the professor mused to himself while waiting for Bridget to stretch out the cramps that had invaded her muscles while she dozed on the uncomfortable slats. "Not that it did you very much good in the end."

Dollins' remains had been brought up out of the basement in several bags, all three of them giving off a reeking steam. When questioned by LaRaja, the firemen explained that the body had been so charred it had crumbled when first they attempted to move it. In a whisper that Knight had caught only because he could read lips, the fireman stopped by the precinct house's captain admitted the only way he and his men could gather up the detective's remains had been with a shovel.

Within hearing distance of the conversation, LaRaja had nodded his understanding, simply staring at the men carrying away his partner as if they were moving out nothing of any more consequence than lumps of kitchen trash. Knight watched the detective's face carefully, however, witnessed the subtle hardening of the older man's eyes, the bursting of capillaries within them from the strain of holding back his tears. He also noted the slight draining of the policeman's usually far brighter spirit.

The changes did not encourage the museum director.

LaRaja was in his fifties, old for a police detective. He had his twenty years in, could have retired at any time over the preceding six years. He continually put off those who questioned him over the fact by saying he wanted a larger piece of the retirement pie, that he would "laugh all the way to the bank" once he made his thirty.

The truth was he had always enjoyed the work, and once partnered with Dollins had enjoyed it even more.

But now the big man was gone, burned to death by a thing barely aware of the fact that it had taken the detective's life. Knight was certain the monstrosity's tally would have been far higher if Dollins had not confronted it. Calling on the powers that had granted the creature its momentary existence came at a price. Once its task was completed, it was understood the demonic presence would be free to spill as much blood as it could in whatever amount of time it had remaining to it. Dollins had sacrificed himself to contain the horror—to keep it surrounded by brick and concrete.

How, Jimmy? Knight wondered, his mind unable to find even the beginnings of a theory. *How did you manage to contain such a thing?*

The professor's unspoken question was not unreasonable.

He had recognized the odor and color of the creature sent to the property room. He knew the standard list of demons, knew of what they were capable. Even if the thing sent against them had been the most minor of its species, still Dollins should not have been able to contain it. It was a creature of mindless needs. Once it had procured the Dream Stone, done as requested of it, then it should have been freed to follow its own desires.

Thousands should have died.

Why they had not was a complete and utter mystery to the professor.

"My God," he muttered, "if that thing had managed to reach the surface . . ."

"What thing?"

Knight's eyes went wide with mild surprise as he realized he had spoken aloud, at least, loud enough for his assistant to hear him. The pair had just reached the front doors of the precinct house, the professor's fingers around the handle, ready to usher them out to the street. Caught somewhat off-guard, Knight stalled, responding as if he had not heard Bridget's question. When she repeated it, he offered;

"Oh, forgive me. I was just thinking of the fire—thinking out loud, I suppose. Sorry."

"That's okay." Her tone soft, sympathetic, she stifled a yawn, then added, "It really must have been pretty intense to do what it did to that detective, though."

"Oh," answered the professor, again slightly surprised. "I didn't realize you saw, ah, heard. . . ."

The two stared absently at each other for a moment, neither knowing what to say next. Silently agreeing that perhaps they should avoid the subject for the present, the pair passed through the station house doors and into the darkness of early morning.

Leading the way back to his car, Knight said, "You know, it's actually just dawned on me, I still have your luggage in my trunk. We never dropped it . . . ," and then, the professor finally realized just how intense a whirlwind he had made of the redhead's first day in New York City. His mouth hanging slightly open, he apologized;

"Oh, bless all the tiny monkeys, I'm so sorry—I just realized . . . we never got around to . . . oh my, I am embarrassed. I was having such a grand time escorting you about . . . I never had the good sense to ask where you were staying, did I? Or what arrangements you had made. And now . . ." Knight's voice trailed off for a moment as he struggled to regain his composure. Searching to find the best thing to do, he asked, "Is there someone waiting up for you? Waiting to hear from you? I mean, it is the middle of the night, but—"

"It's all right, Professor," Bridget answered. Taking a moment to stifle a more aggressive yawn, she then continued, saying, "I actually have a sorority sister who lives in Queens—Stephanie Buddenhagen. I was going to be staying with her and her roommate until I could find a place closer to the museum."

"Is it too late? Can I take you there now? Anything—"

"Relax, please, sir," the redhead cut Knight off, a trace of humor in her voice. "I called her hours ago, told her what had happened. I also told her to go to bed and that I would get back to her in the morning."

"But, ah . . ." Knight paused, uncertain what exactly to say next. Slightly amused at his discomfort, the redhead continued, telling him;

"I figured if I didn't end up spending the night in jail I would impose on you and bunk on your couch tonight. You do own a couch, don't you?"

"Yes, I . . . I mean . . ."

"Listen," said Bridget, her tone going a trifle shy, but retaining a sense that she was certain of what it was implying, "I'll be honest. After all we've been through, I just want to get some sleep."

"But, Bridget, your family—won't they be worried?"

"I called home after I called Stephie," answered the young woman. "And don't worry; I didn't tell them anything to get worried over. You know how families can be. And really, I don't want to spend the rest of the night answering a lot of questions—especially ones I don't know the answers to. That'll just make them crazy."

"Yes," mused Knight absently. "That's certainly one of the ways families can be."

"Right. I told them all the things they wanted to hear—how excited I was, how wonderful my new boss was, how big New York City is . . . blahblahblah . . ." The redhead's voice trailed off for a moment. Then, finding it once more, she added, "And not only did I not want to get into any kind of long discussion, let alone an argument; I also . . ." She paused for a moment, then said, "I didn't want them to know that I don't want to be alone." Staring at the professor, her voice went softer as she said;

"I know it's an imposition . . . but I'd really just like to spend the night under your roof. I, I know it's ridiculous, that there's no sane reason for it, but . . . I think I'll just *feel* safer there than anywhere else."

Knight was certain there was nothing untoward or sexual in the nature of Bridget's request. She had been through a tremendous ordeal, was in a strange city, a vastly larger, as well as colder and more impersonal, one than she had ever known. And although, like any man, he did not relish admitting uncomfortable truths to himself, the professor was fairly certain that at that moment young and beautiful Bridget Elkins most likely saw him more as a father figure than anything else.

"Of course you may stay in my humble home," he said, surrendering to the proper and making his tone as parental as possible. "It happens that I have a quite excellent couch, for the purpose of napping, that is. Trust me, it's been very well tested. I'm certain I can scare up a spare pillow or two and even a blanket."

"Thank you, kind sir," Bridget answered as they got into the car. Closing her door, the young woman began strapping herself in. Then, just before Knight could actually begin driving, she added;

"And, once we get there, while you're making me a cup of hot tea, or whatever you serve to traumatized young ladies to help them regain their sanity, or at least their composure, you can explain to me how it is you can fly."

CHAPTER THIRTEEN

Knight had not answered his assistant immediately.

Backing out of his parking place, he had quickly moved into the light, but still present as usual, 3:00 A.M. traffic and driven off. At the first red light, one in the Grand Army Plaza traffic circle that the professor never seemed to catch when it was green, he explained that they had returned to the area of the museum because he lived close by and that he would be more than willing to have such a discussion as she had proposed once they reached his home. Nervous enough about having blindsided her new boss, Bridget was more than willing to put off their talk as well.

Knight's home proved to be an inauspicious brownstone building in the Park Slope neighborhood of Brooklyn, even closer to the museum than the young redhead thought it might be. Bridget found her curiosity about the professor's home thwarted by both the darkness and the street's lack of adequate lighting. Attached on both sides to similar structures, it seemed simply another building among many.

"So, you own your own brownstone?"

"It came available when the market was right." As Knight slid his car into line with his garage's entrance, he asked his assistant, "Tell me, do you know why they were called 'brownstones' way back when?"

"I'll bite—why?"

"Because they're made out of brown stones, of course. Well, a reddish brown sandstone to be precise. Very popular building material, back in the day, as they say."

On the one hand, Bridget grimaced at being caught by such an obvious word puzzle. On the other hand, having heard from several different sources before coming to New York that parking came at a high premium in the city, she was suitably impressed when the brownstone turned out to come with its own garage. As Knight pressed a button on a small remote control attached to his sun visor that began the opening of his garage door, the young woman commented;

"A New Yorker with his own private parking spot. Pretty ritzy. I mean, something on this order makes you officially one of the elite—yes?"

"A rather knowledgeable, local-color comment for someone who claims to be from Montana."

"I do read," answered Bridget.

"Yes," replied Knight, fatigue allowing his voice to grow just the slightest bit testy. "Those lovely green eyes of yours get put to all sorts of purposes, don't they?" As they pulled into the darkness of the garage, the comment caught the young woman somewhat off-guard. If the professor's tone had been even a touch harsher, the redhead could have easily slid from nervous to frightened. Realizing he had no right to take his mistake out on her, however, as the garage's automatic lights came on, he quickly added;

"Forgive me. If I should have learned anything over the years, it's that the past is the past, and that there isn't a blessed thing one can do about it."

Shutting down his car's engine, the professor hit his remote once more, returning his garage's door to its closed and locked position. As its mechanism slid quietly into place, he turned once more to his assistant, telling her, "Come, let's see if I don't have the right blend of tea to regain your sanity for you—or at least your composure. Then we can talk of ships and shoes and sealing wax . . . and other flights of fancy."

SOME FIFTEEN MINUTES LATER THE PAIR HAD MADE THEIR WAY FROM Knight's garage to the main hallway of his first floor, which led through his living room and finally to the kitchen. All along the way Bridget had made note of the craftsmanship to be found in every aspect of the professor's home, as well as the abundance of fine pieces that graced all its nooks and corners. His well-cared-for furnishings seemed to be completely made up of antiques. Every shelf held at least one statue, fossil, or bronze casting, every wall at least one painting, print, or mural.

"It's like being in a wing of the museum," Bridget commented as Knight put a pot of water on to boil. As she studied a small carved-ivory figure of obvious Chinese origin she found on its own small shelf over the kitchen table, she asked with a trace of humor, "You haven't been taking any pieces out 'on loan,' have you?"

"Ah, your priceless wit must have kept the livestock in stitches," the professor tossed back at her. Rummaging through his cabinet, he offered, "Lipton, or something made out of bits of fruit rather than tea?"

"Really?" Blinking hard to fight the fatigue tearing at her, she asked somewhat in surprise, "Lipton? You don't have a cupboard filled with little tins of exotic dried leaves gathered from a score of ethnic marketplaces from around the city? Some *tana* leaves filched from the Imhotep exhibit? I think I'm disappointed."

"However will I bear the crushing burden of not living up to the expectations of another?" Moving his head from around the cabinet door, Knight added, "Lipton is a fine tea—I know it must be, for it's what my Asian friends all drink when no one is looking. Will that be good enough for you, or should I dispatch a runner to the British East India Company?"

Bridget was about to throw out another wry comment, then stopped herself. A sudden flash of inspiration revealing to her why the two of them were verging on antagonism, she pulled back, accepting the offered tea, while adding an apology.

"Let's not get brittle with each other. I know this is my fault. You told me to walk away and not look back. I tried—I swear—but I couldn't find a cab. Maybe I walked the wrong way, or maybe I just had to know what was going on, but whatever it was, I got scared. It was dark and you were all ominous, and . . ."

"And you came back to the museum because," Knight said, finishing her thought, "even if there might be some kind of danger there, it was the only place you knew, and the only person you knew in town was inside it." As the redhead nodded sheepishly, Knight continued, suggesting;

"All right, let's do this. Tell me what you saw."

The professor was fairly dismayed when Bridget revealed that she had observed pretty much everything of her employer's second confrontation with the intruders. She had seen him float down from the ceiling, had witnessed his turning back of the thieves' barrage of bullets. She had also taken note of the fact that one of the intruders had not been a thing of flesh and blood.

"My, my," he said quietly. "And here I thought I was kidding. But those big green eyes of yours, they really do see a lot, don't they?"

"More than they should have?" As the professor's teapot suddenly erupted, filling the kitchen with its steaming whistle, the curator shut down the gas, telling the girl;

"Well, it depends on whether or not you actually saw what you think you saw or, in other words, on the way your mind interpreted the information. For instance, you said you saw me flying. But was it really flying, something that when said brings to mind images of Superman streaking through the sky, or was it merely levitating . . . an ability well documented in Eastern cultures?"

"Vampires and werewolves are well documented in some cultures, too, but—" Turning with teakettle in one hand, the professor held up his other hand in an interrupting gesture. Smiling at the redhead, he told her;

"Yes, they are. And there are many in this world who do all they can to cast doubt on such things. Many because they are true skeptics, and others because they are believers."

"You mean, Area Fifty-one kind of stuff, or the stories of the Russians and the CIA doing research into telekinesis? Homeland Security . . . ?"

"Let's just say, my dear," Knight answered softly, "that during World War Two, the Allies kept the Manhattan Project, the development of the atomic bomb, a secret for a reason." Hoisting his teapot, the professor filled the waiting cup with water, leaving enough room for whatever extras Bridget might desire. She asked for sweetener only, which he provided. After that, he pointed the way back to the living room. Directing the redhead to a seat, Knight stepped over to the corner of the room, which held its only modern conveniences.

Powering up his CD player, the professor simply set the last disc to which he had been listening to playing once more.

That his new assistant recognized it as the music of Hildegard von Bingen pleased him to no end.

Knowing he could put things off no further, comfortably ensconced within his living room, Bridget on the couch, Knight in his favorite overstuffed chair, he said;

"Well, let's get down to the facts. As for the abundance of knickknacks within these walls, this building is what you might call the ancestral home of the grand and wonderful Knight clan. Great-great-grandfather moved in before the turn of the century; that's actually two 'turns of' back now, I suppose. It's been passed down ever since, along with its ever-expanding collection of treasures, or dust-collecting junk, depending on my mood, I suppose. The bulk of the notable pieces did come from Great-great- and Great-grandfather's time, and Grandfather's, I suppose, back when people didn't care that much about Western looting of sacred Eastern places."

Bridget sipped her tea, nodding quietly.

"As for what happened to the intruders, I warned them not to fire upon me, but while I was in effect warning them of what was coming, I will admit that, yes, I was goading them into doing such. When they did attempt to gun me down, their bullets were turned back upon them, as I knew they would be, by a ring I was wearing at the time. It's several thousand years old, and according to legend has served many masters."

"How?"

"The story of it is that it is capable of turning harm and force back upon those who employ such things. Rasputin was the last owner who could be verified, and he did manage to survive all manner of difficulties."

"You're not wearing it now, though," said Bridget, commenting on his naked fingers.

"No, I . . . I gave it to Detective Dollins before I ran off, leaving him to go to his doom." Bitter reproachment seeped from Knight's voice as he chastised himself once more for the officer's death. When Bridget offered the rationale that such could not be his fault, he snapped at her, saying;

"I know that. He was the police officer, the trained professional, the one paid to go out and take the risks for us, the grateful, helpless citizenry. But, knowing the truth of that doesn't keep me from knowing the other truth, that I knew what he was going to face, and that I knew there was no way he was going to win against it."

"Then why didn't you tell him?"

"I . . ." The professor paused, the horrible scene in the basement flashing through his brain once more, then said, "I did. But he didn't, wouldn't listen."

"Why didn't you try to convince him?"

"Because . . ." Knight practically shouted the single word, then stopped himself from continuing. Dropping his head slightly, half-closing his eyes, he froze his anger, pushing it away from himself. Feeling it dissolving, he took a deep breath, shutting his eyes completely for a moment. And, after the moment had been exhausted he finally exhaled, then continued quietly, saying;

"Because he wasn't the kind of man who quits. If I had told him in exacting detail what he was about to face, if I had managed to convince him of the truth of my knowledge, all I would have done was frighten him. And then maybe he wouldn't have saved the, well . . . God only knows how many lives he saved."

The two sat quietly in the shadow-filled living room, Bridget sipping occasionally at her tea, Knight hanging his head in deep recrimination. Within his mind, conflicting ways to tell his new assistant any more of what happened screamed back and forth, parts of him begging to share some of the secrets he had carried around within himself for so long, others barking down any such foolish notions. Finally deciding he had sat before her in silence long enough, he looked up, ready to continue their discussion.

"Bridget, let me say . . ."

And then, the professor went silent. Bridget Elkins had slumped over sideways during their brief respite and fallen into what appeared to be a deep sleep. Rising from his chair, Knight pulled a quilt from a nearby stand and spread it over the sleeping girl. Instinct taking over, the redhead pulled the cover up over her shoulder, her body understanding all too well that it was time to rest. As her well-formed legs automatically found their way up onto the couch and under the quilt, the professor crossed the room to the hallway that led upstairs. Staring at his houseguest for a moment, he said;

"Sleep peacefully, oh, so young Bridget Elkins. I'll reveal a few more of my secrets to you in the morning."

And then Knight shut down the small light still on in the living room. He would leave the light on in the hallway, just in case she awoke in the night needing the bathroom, or something from the kitchen, or for whatever other reason one might awaken in the middle of the night.

The professor thought about turning off the music as well, but then considered that the softly sung Latin hymns of the twelfth century's most famous abbess would probably be more comforting for his guest than the police car, fire truck, and ambulance sirens that made up the background noise of the typical Brooklyn night. Giving the girl a second glance, he nodded unconsciously, confirming he had done all he could for her for the moment. And, so deciding, he exited the living room, heading up the stairs to his own bedroom.

Yes, he thought, *that's all I have to do in the morning, reveal more of my secrets. And, of course, explain to the board about the break-in, and the destruction of a useless artifact which had just become one of the most valuable pieces the museum had ever owned. And, of course, what I was doing with an intern in the museum in the middle of the night, and what the police had to do with it, oh, let's not forget all the blood and bone fragments decorating the main lobby, and . . .*

"Oh," he told himself aloud as he reached the top of the stairs, "just shut up and go to bed. It's not as if everything won't still be just as bad when you get up."

CHAPTER FOURTEEN

"So, my bright and delightful houseguest, how do you like your eggs?"

Bridget stood in the doorway to Knight's kitchen, eyes shut lightly, hair an unbrushed rat's nest, her mouth looming open in a prodigiously wide and vocal yawn. She finally moved a hand to cover her mouth a split second before her yawn ended, realizing the uselessness of the motion even as she made it. Her other hand scratching at the side of her head, working its way through the tangle of her hair, she tried to respond only to find her voice garbled by her need to yawn once more. Sitting down at the kitchen table, she finally asked in a tired voice;

"Eggs?"

"Yes, eggs. You know—hen slugs, cackle fruit. Small, white, oval-shaped, those things they recommend you don't put all in one basket—"

"I know what eggs are."

"Ah, then we do have a basis for communication this morning, don't we?"

The young woman tried to focus her eyes on the professor for a moment, then gave up and simply shut them once more. She had only arisen because the noise coming from the kitchen had invaded her sleep.

It was not that Knight was in any way an overly noisy chef. If Bridget's slumber had been restful the redhead would have never stirred. But the truth was her sleep had been plagued by discomforting dreams, nightmares confusing and frightening enough to force her mind to search for any reason to escape back to the waking world. Coupling that with the fact that she had slept with her contact lenses in all night, one could readily understand why she might not be in the sunniest of moods.

"You always this obnoxiously chipper in the morning?" The young woman asked the question while focusing one eye on Knight. Her voice beginning to clear from use, she added, "Especially mornings after nights like the one we just had."

"Well, to be perfectly honest," the professor replied, one eye on the three large squares of butter melting in his skillet, "I have no way of gauging the level of my chipperness, as it were. There's never anyone here to comment one way or the other." Hoisting an egg into cracking position, he asked;

"Now again—eggs?"

"Scrambled?"

"A time-honored method of fixing the venerable, delectable egg," he replied. "One heartily approved from the tables at Junior's just down the road, all the way back to the court of Constantine the First. And who knows, perhaps further." Quickly breaking open a half dozen one after another with one hand, he added, "The bacon is on that plate, there on the table, under those paper towels—"

"Bacon?"

"Yes, you know, pork—beloved by man and dogs, food of the gods, the other white meat . . ."

Bridget groaned as if being physically assaulted. As Knight tended his skillet of eggs, dashing pepper, stirring and flipping, the redhead sent a hand clawing across the table toward the aforementioned platter. As she lifted the edge of the paper covering with her index finger, the scent of warm bacon slithered outward toward the helpless young woman.

"Oh God, you're evil—"

"Moi?"

Caught in its siren spell of fatty goodness, Bridget hesitated for a moment, then finally pulled forth a piece, part of her mind assuring her that the resulting damage to her health and figure would be all the professor's fault while another, more straightforward segment of her brain crowed with joy over the fact that the bacon was both thickly cut and not overly crispy. The young woman devoured the first piece and was pulling two more free when Knight approached the table, a plate in each hand. As he slid one in front of her, eyeing the buttered toast next to her eggs, Bridget swallowed, then asked;

"Do you eat like this all the time?" When the professor assured his assistant that he did, she added, "Then how do you stay so slim? Are you, what—like in the gym thirty, forty hours a week?"

Knight shook his head, driving a fork into his own eggs with one hand while gathering a handful of bacon with the other. Depositing the strips atop his eggs, he attacked the mass with knife and fork, cutting it all into sections, which he then started shoveling into his mouth with lip-smacking gusto. After his third bite, he started in on a piece of heavily buttered whole wheat toast, talking in between bites.

"No, no time to waste on gyms. I do a lot of walking, however. Here in New York we walk everywhere. One does all their shopping within their own neighborhood."

"Really?"

"Any place you go in the city, within ten blocks you should be able to find anything you need—bakeries, hardware stores, plumbing supplies, groceries, coffee shops, automotive centers, oh yes. The faces may change, Irish, Italian, Jamaican, one ethnic bundle unrolling over the last, waiting for their turn to be displaced."

Knight took another staggering mouthful of everything on his plate, leaking noises of enjoyment from the corners of his mouth. Finally, after he managed to swallow the lot, the professor moved away from the tangent he had begun, saying;

"Anyway, it could be the walking, or as I told you yesterday, I am blessed with an exceedingly indulgent metabolism."

"Along with the superpowers?"

Bridget's comment brought a hammer down on the china plate of their conversation. The question did not shock Knight, did not catch him off-guard or even give him pause. He had been expecting it. He was not, however, about to stop chewing his mouthful of bacon, eggs, and toast to rush into an answer. Finally swallowing, however, the professor dropped a forkful of eggs onto the remaining bit of his first piece of toast, saying;

"I don't have any superpowers, lovely Bridget. And, before you begin to protest, allow me to explain."

The redhead sat back against her chair, unconsciously moving her body straighter. Her eyes wide open, she stared at her superior intently, as if doing so could in some way verify his veracity. Her attention focused upon him to the exclusion of everything else, she did not notice herself planting her feet firmly against the floor, or the fact of her fingers balling into fists, pressing into the flesh of her legs. Barely able to breathe, she simply stared, waiting for the promised explanation.

"I'm a scholar, as you know, of antiquities. I've been on digs around the world, have studied in, oh, I don't even remember how many universities at this point . . ."

Knight paused for a moment, his eyes taking on a faraway look. Absently picking up a piece of bacon, he held it between two fingers, moving it back and forth in a languid pattern. His voice slower, more thoughtful, he began speaking once more, his eyes still locked on some spot beyond the kitchen.

"I've also met my share of outsiders in my time, alchemists, black priests, Wiccans, all manner of both fraudulent and legitimate occult characters, users of magicks black and white . . . and I've, well . . . I don't know how else to put it . . . I've learned a few tricks along the way."

"Tricks?"

"You know the kinds of things I mean, slowing the heart rate until it stops, snake charming, hearing thoughts, dream casting, card reading—"

"And the flying . . ."

Knight paused once more. The young woman across the table from him could read the hesitation in his eyes, sense the tension mounting throughout the muscles of his neck and shoulders, down his arms. Even his jaw seemed tighter. Then, much to Bridget's surprise, suddenly he seemed to completely relax. Half his mouth curling into a smile, the professor raised the piece of bacon he had been toying with to his mouth and bit it in half. Chewing the delicious strip, he popped the other half into his mouth as well, then wiped his fingers on his napkin, talking around his bacon while he chewed:

"In the eastern Andes of Peru, in the Urubamba Valley, one finds the ancient city of Machu Picchu. It was built by the Incas at the height of their civilization, a remarkable centrally planned metropolis carved out of a mountainside a mile and a half up in the sky. It was found by modern man in 1911, after it had apparently lain dormant and unused for over four hundred years." The professor swallowed his half mouthful, unconsciously smacking his lips before he went on, saying;

"It has always been believed that when the Spanish tore through the New World they somehow missed the rich splendor of Machu Picchu and its sister cities. Such is not the case. They found it, all right, and in the early fifteen hundreds they marched up the mountain determined to slaughter and plunder that amazing city as they had so many others. But, when they reached the summit and came roaring in, they found the inhabitants of Machu Picchu all together in the center of town.

"The soldiers, crude and brutish, laughed as they prepared to wipe out yet another civilized population, but their greedy joy turned quickly to fear. The Incas they had surrounded there, eight thousand feet up in the clouds, managed to evade their guns and lances. All of them—every single man, woman, and child—escaped death that day by doing something that so frightened the invaders they reportedly ran all the way back to the floor of the valley without stopping."

"They flew away?"

Knight let the other side of his mouth curl as well to create a complete smile. He liked his new assistant. She was intelligent, had grit enough not to fold into weeping hysterics after all she had been through, and did not shy away from pork products and all their nitrate-soaked goodness. The tone in her voice held nothing of sarcasm. She was offering her thoughts on the subject, showing an ability to step beyond that which most people were incapable of achieving.

Tell her! a voice from the back of his mind shouted. *For Christ's sake, just tell her—*

Reaching into his pant pocket, the professor pulled forth the Disc of the Winds. Handing it to Bridget, he said;

"Yes—that's exactly what each one of them did . . . with one of these."

CHAPTER FIFTEEN

"Professor Knight," the security guard at the front desk hissed, waving the director frantically over to his station. A rail-thin young black man of average height, he continued in his conspiratorial tone, saying, "If you think alla this is bad," his hand indicating the score of forensic types working in the lobby, as well as the mob of various media types being held outside the museum, "I got some more bad news for you."

"Do tell. . . ."

"Upstairs," answered the man, shifting his eyebrows upward, "there's a buncha cops and like worse than that waiting for you in your office—they didn't none of 'em look like the happiest of dudes, neither. Maybe you might want to be thinking about turning around—sliding back out the door." Turning his head pointedly away from the professor, he added;

"I can tell 'em straight—I haven't seen you."

Putting his hand to his forehead, Knight gave the

guard a short salute. "It's all right, Dix," he told the younger man, somewhat amused by the fact that he knew his casualness about the matter was in no way what the guard had expected. Feeling he owed Dix an explanation, he added, "Don't sweat it overly, my friend. I had anticipated as much. Although," he added as an afterthought, "it will probably be a bit disconcerting to my new assistant. Please keep an eye out for her; take care of her for me."

Dix promised to do so, asking the professor for a description. As the guard's eyes went slightly wide and his mouth began to reveal a gleaming grin, Knight added, "I'd also appreciate it if you didn't start in with one of your patented pickup attacks. She's a nice girl, one I'd like to get a full summer's work out of before someone like you crushes all the sweetness out of her."

The guard made a feeble show of protesting such a description, then suddenly laughed, confessing he could not keep a straight face. After adding that he would be on his best behavior, he then said, "Must be something to do with what all went down here last night, huh?"

"That would be my guess," Knight responded. Then, lifting his eyebrows playfully, the professor put his hand to his mouth to disguise his words, adding in a mock sinister whisper, "If not, then I suppose they finally found out about my cocaine-smuggling operation. I have it sent up from Colombia hidden in statues for the museum, you know. And here I thought I was being so clever."

Dix's eyes went wide for a split second at such an admission. Then, when he realized Knight was merely having sport with him, the guard pointed an index finger at the professor, chuckling out loud as he said;

"You one crazy white man."

"That is what they keep telling me."

As the guard wished Knight "good luck," the professor accepted the sentiment both graciously and honestly, then walked off toward the elevator bank which would take him to his office, his mouth curling into his familiar one-sided smile. His hand pressing the button to summon his ride, Knight let his mind slip back to the question of his new assistant.

Despite the fact that the redhead had been at least seemingly quite open about her past when they had chatted the day before, Knight knew how clever people could be about hiding those aspects of themselves they did not want known to the world. She had suddenly learned a great deal about him—far more than most ever learned.

What, he wondered, *if she's not all she seems?*

Although he hardly thought it possible, there was nothing to say that the young woman was some innocent babe in the woods. She had done her undergraduate work in two different, major cities, after all. There was no avoiding such things. If she had never smoked a single joint, never once gotten falling-down drunk, never snorted a powder or popped a pill, et cetera, she would be a rare young American, indeed.

I suppose you think she's still a virgin, too.

Knight found no quick answer coming into his brain to answer the snide thought, one that made him feel a trifle embarrassed. Who was he, he asked himself, to be wondering about such things? After all, the professor reminded the leering side of his brain, there were such people to be found in every corner of the world. Even in the United States they numbered in the tens of millions. After so many years in a place like New York City, however, Knight had to admit that perhaps he had become more than a trifle jaded.

Waiting for the elevator, the professor found himself hoping that Bridget might be one of those non–New Yorkers. He had gotten something of that sense from her. The professor felt he was fairly good at spotting those who were hiding something, especially those hiding things from themselves.

Bridget had displayed none of the signals he was used to finding in such people. And, of course, part of his reasoning behind picking her up at the airport, for entertaining her all day and then bringing her to the museum at night, was to test her. Not once did his new assistant show anything but eager interest. If she was addicted to anything, if she was any kind of indolent slacker, she had a will of tempered steel when it came to not revealing it. No, as best Knight could tell, she was simply a sweet young woman, intelligent and observant, and eager to learn everything there was to know about working in a museum.

Which was why he had left her in his home.

She needed more rest, the chance to take a shower, get in touch with her family for longer than a cell phone call from a police station could have afforded her, and basically, as he believed the young folks still said, "get her head on straight." The professor had known the police would be waiting for him—as well as the rest of the board. If there was anything young Bridget did not need, he felt, it was more intrusive questioning.

Oh, they would get around to her again—Knight knew that. Such was simply unavoidable. But, if he was to tackle them first, to give them their chance with him, to turn him inside out with their never-ending barrage of uselessness, he felt he could most likely give them enough answers so that when her turn came they might not be all that brutally relentless in their browbeating.

And, with that thought, the elevator's muted arrival bell chimed, letting the professor know he could finally proceed to his waiting interrogation. Watching the doors begin to slide open, he thought;

Well, here we go. I left Bridget at home so she could regain her composure, and so that I could take a try at defusing the barking dogs before they start in yapping at her. After all, I believe she will certainly try not to reveal what she saw last night, but oh, those two words, "try" and "succeed." How different they are.

And with that unsettling notion rolling through his brain, Knight stepped into the elevator. As he did, of course, the pessimistic side of his personality offered;

Now, if she sticks to sleeping and showering and using the phone, and doesn't start rummaging around where she shouldn't, well, everything will just be perfect.

With a sigh, the professor watched the doors slide shut once more. " 'If' and 'perfect,' " he mused. *Two more words that did not always work so well together.* That thought in mind, Knight allowed himself a second sigh.

It was simply going to be one of those days.

CHAPTER SIXTEEN

Bridget did not, as Knight momentarily had feared, start rummaging around where she should not. She was, of course, human, and such thoughts did cross her mind.

As she was soaping away the grime of the preceding twenty-four hours in the shower, the idea of roaming through the various floors and rooms of the professor's home, searching for secret doors and hidden chambers and the such, did nag at her, teasing her toward the inappropriate, but she firmly rejected doing so in the end. She did not make her decision out of any sense of fear over being caught. Nor did she resist the temptation because of any overwhelming sense of priority. Rather, she chose to follow a warning the back of her mind passed on to her.

I think, all in all, it told her, *that we'd better leave such ideas alone for now. I mean, if he's got his hands on things that will allow people to fly, God knows what else is around here.*

Giving herself the example of the toddler who decides they want to play with the stove, the redhead decided that "better-safe-than-sorry" would be her best possible anthem for the day. So deciding, Bridget finished her shower, then dressed in the room Knight had provided for her. As she did so, smoothing the wrinkles from the set of clothes she had packed to be her first-day-on-the-job outfit, she wondered for a moment why the professor had not shown her to that room the night before.

Yes, of course, she had fallen asleep on the couch, but why didn't he wake her up? Again, she had been the one to mention wanting to sleep on his couch, but still, her mind pouted, he could have offered the room. Or, did he want her on a different floor from him, did he not want her to have a lock to put between them, did he—

Staring at herself in the mirror, Bridget was just finishing buttoning her blouse when she let escape a throaty growl of frustration.

Disappointment mixing with anger, both aimed at her own paranoia, Bridget tried to shove the thoughts from her mind. Yes, she admitted, she had known more than her share of creeps and losers. Drooling high school and college boys, inappropriate teachers and professors, friends of her family, even an uncle—one sorely beaten by her father when he heard her shouts of protest—so many others.

But, she reminded herself sternly, she had known good, kind, decent men as well. And, she was certain, Professor Piers Knight simply had to be one of them. Everything about him said so. She had never felt so comfortable with any man so quickly, with any*one*—had never been put so at ease by someone she had just met in all her life. And yet, despite every warm and kind thing she could think to say about Knight, still the professor left her with a sense that he was continuing to hide things from her.

"Like what?"

Oh, she told herself, she was not making sense and she knew it. *But,* she asked herself, *just what did make sense anymore?*

Only a day and a half previous, things had made complete and reasonable sense in her world. For one thing, if nothing else, a day and a half previous, no one she knew could levitate. No, to the best of her knowledge, they all stayed on the ground. Where they belonged. Gravity had still prevailed.

"But not anymore."

The confused young woman whispered the words as she continued looking at herself in the mirror attached to the back of the room's dresser. The image disturbed her, seeing her reflection only confirming the distressing news. Instead of turning away from the sight, however, she continued to stare at herself. Still only in her underwear, clutching at her half-buttoned blouse. She took note of her posture, pulled in and shrunken. She saw her hands, trembling, the edges of the cream white blouse vibrating in her fingers. And then, finally, she dared to look directly into her own eyes—unblinking.

As she expected, she found nothing but fear.

Bridget Elkins had left home only a day and a half earlier, ready to embark upon the adventure of her lifetime. The memory almost made her chuckle—worked at loosening the tears scratching about the borders of her eyes. How ludicrous, her thirty-six-hour-old idea of adventure. Moving to New York City, spending the summer working in a world-famous museum. Learning filing procedures, memorizing bits of information about exhibits and the building's architecture so she might lead tours, making certain the free brochure holders were filled—

Adventure . . .

The repealing of the law of gravity, though, Bridget thought, finally turning away from the mirror, closing her eyes, *you've got to admit, now that's something that happens in an adventure.*

Feeling her knees going soft, the muscles and ligaments of them twitching, failing her, Bridget folded her legs under herself and sat on the floor—consciously doing so before she simply collapsed instead. As she leaned against the bed next to her, her mind overflowed with images from her past day and a half. Her parents at the diner, making jokes, inserting little reminders about safety and watchfulness when in the big city, more warnings at the airport, last moments of opportunity slipping from their hands, realization finally dawning on them that their little girl was all grown up—

She remembered the confidence she had felt, boarding the plane. There was no sense of escape, no desperate hurrah over the throwing off of some imagined chains. Bridget liked her home, her family, her life, felt in no way put-upon or held down. It was a good, comfortable life.

But it was not enough for her.

Life in Montana was simply too easy, and she was ready for more—had known as she waved good-bye to her parents that she was going to be all right. That nothing was going to stop her from "making it on her own." And why not? After all, things had always come easily for the long-legged beauty.

"Yeah," she said aloud, daring to peek at the mirror once more. From her position on the floor, she could only see the top half of her head, nose up and no more. Staring into her eyes, knowing herself well enough to realize what she was seeing there, she finished;

"And see, look how easy it's going to be to make it all the way to crazy."

And then, finally, Bridget Elkins broke down and gave in to the tears she had been desperately holding back since she had watched four men get blown apart, been interrogated by the police, run from a burning building, and basically discovered that she could rely on absolutely nothing she had ever believed throughout her entire life.

"MY HEAVENS, GENTLEMEN, WHAT A GATHERING. TO WHAT DO I OWE the honor?"

Knight had gotten off at the sixth floor of the museum to find his office staked out by a cluster of men whose look signaled nothing but trouble to the professor. Dix had been correct—"cops and like worse" were indeed in evidence, and in far greater numbers than Knight had actually expected. Dollins' assessment that "the feds" would be stopping by had also been correct.

In fact, if Knight was reading those gathered correctly, he had both Brooklyn and Manhattan detectives, members of the state police, FBI agents, and, he was fairly certain, CIA spooks in attendance with the rest.

"Don't be shy. Somebody speak up."

Despite his encouragement, none of the men or women in the hallway said anything to him. Making his way as pleasantly as possible through the throng of obvious underlings, the professor headed directly for his office. Finally, when he reached what he was reasonably certain had to be an FBI man, one who had parked himself directly in front of the door to Knight's chambers, he was told;

"They're waiting for you in the big conference room."

"Oh, are they now? How exciting." The professor felt like saying a bit more, had several sarcastic bon mots lined up, but held off on delivering any of them. As much as his first inclination was to do so, instead he simply smiled at the messenger before his door and turned for the room the agent had designated. Rummaging through his pockets for a vial he had brought from home, he thought as he palmed the thing;

"No sense in making enemies—especially of grunt-level functionaries. Besides, throwing wit to the likes of these, what did

Thurber say? 'As futile as a clock in an empty house.' Let's save the A-list material for their superiors, shall we?"

Throwing open the doors to Conference Room A, Knight walked in with his head down, his hands fumbling within his bag, looking as if he thought he were there to teach a class, not to be interrogated. Paying no attention to those gathered, he walked to a table against the wall that held four pitchers of ice water and a herd of glasses. Passing his hand over the pitchers as if unable to decide which one he liked the best, the professor finally picked one and poured himself a glass of water.

Then, glass in hand, forcing himself to present a calm exterior, the curator walked directly to the seat obviously left for him. Still rummaging around within his black leather shoulder bag, he finally withdrew a pad and pen, placed them on the table before him, then sat down quietly.

"Professor Knight—"

"Oh yes—I'm sorry, may I help you?"

"May—" The speaker cut himself off abruptly, not allowing whatever he was about to ask to escape his lips. The fellow appeared to be in his late thirties, early forties, tallish, sandy hair—thinning somewhat, brown eyes—just drab enough to be anyone. His suit was just expensive enough to make him either a dishonest cop or a run-of-the-mill government agent. From the somber cut of his clothes, Knight was willing to bet FBI.

Whoever this chap might be, Knight thought, *it's apparent he's used to giving orders and being both feared and obeyed. Well, let's see how that's working for you this morning.* Deciding that small bit of information gave him all he needed to know, the professor continued to stare innocently at the speaker, waiting for the inevitable to begin in earnest.

"Yes," the man started again, his tone unchanged, his attitude showing he planned on following his normal approach to such matters. "I believe you can help us, Professor. I certainly know that you had better help us."

"Really?" Knight filled his voice with a sort of bemused guilelessness, creating a persona for those in the room that bespoke a kindly, somewhat confused mouse of a man, one who not only spent most of his time working in quiet, dusty rooms by himself but who also preferred it that way. "Tell me, why would that be?"

"Why would—?" Again the speaker cut himself off before repeating Knight's complete response in amazement. The man began to speak again, but this time he was interrupted by a woman sitting several seats down from him. Dressed in a proper dark blue business suit, thick dark brown hair just beginning to be shattered by streaks of gray, she was Abigail Brinkley, the main director of the Brooklyn Museum. This was one of the only people whom Knight knew in the conference room, and certainly the only one who knew him well enough to understand exactly what he was up to at the moment.

"Professor," she said, her tone implying that she did not have time to watch him have sport with the officials gathered there that morning, "these men represent various local and federal agencies. Mr. Klein here," she said, indicating the man with whom Knight had been toying, "is with the FBI."

"Oh my," the professor answered, moving a hand toward his lips as if surprised by the information. "The FBI—really? And, and why are they here?"

"They're here, Professor," Brinkley growled ever so slightly, hinting at her displeasure with Knight's usual shenanigans, "for the same reasons our lawyers Mr. Feldon and Ms. Grillstein are here—because of what happened downstairs last night. You do remember being here, downstairs, after hours last night, don't you?"

"Oh yes, my—how dreadful, how simply terribly dreadful. Oh, Abigail, have they told you, all—"

"Look," snapped Klein, the normal cool demeanor he had been trained to display slipping more every moment he spent in the professor's presence, "let's knock off this game, all right? You knew you were going to be seeing the police again today. And, unless you're willing to admit that you're some kind of simpleton, you had to have known the federal government would be wanting to talk to you as well."

"Of course I expected the lot of you," answered Knight with a sudden surprising candor. "But I also expected to be interviewed as a witness, to be asked for cooperation, not threatened by a drab, unimaginative, buttoned-down bully whose idea of tactful interaction with the public is to dispense vague hints of being run through some legal grinder."

"Professor Knight, we have no intention—"

"Oh, please—don't compound the arrogance of that sloppy, boilerplate opening salvo you fired at me by lying about it. Hallway lined with silent, brooding enforcer types, scowling faces in dark suits all around the table, my seat, positioned with my back to the wall, centered so that all eyes can glare at me, why not just spread a towel out covered with thumbscrews and sharp, pointy things and be done with it—"

"Professor Knight!" Brinkley snapped her words furiously, but the professor raced past them, telling Klein;

"The legendary FBI—pfah. You and yours are so used to cracking nuts with a hammer, it never dawns on you to try any other approach."

"Now see here, Knight, your director, Brinkley, has promised us your full cooperation, and I—"

"Cooperate with you I certainly will, and without hesitation," interrupted the professor. "But be intimidated by your gestapo tactics? No, I think not. Five places to your left you will find Detective

Sergeant Denny LaRaja. Ask him how long I cooperated with the NYPD last night."

"Professor Knight was a model witness," the detective answered, enjoying the chance to tweak the FBI's collective nose. "He worked with us for hours until a fire broke out in the station house, forcing us to postpone any further interviews until this morning."

Knight glared at Klein, his eyes daring the FBI man to escalate the situation any further. For a moment, it seemed as if the government agent was willing to do just that, but then something within Klein caught hold of his emotions, shoving them back down into the recess where he usually was able to keep them stored without any problem. Nodding to the professor, the FBI man acknowledged;

"All right, perhaps we've all grown a bit too defensive of late. But if you will grant that we have a reason to be concerned when someone sets off explosives in a public place these days without any further admonishments over our tactics, I'll admit we should be seeking your cooperation rather than demanding it."

"Well," answered Knight, allowing one side of his mouth to curl into a smile, "any man who can use a word such as 'admonishment,' in a sentence and make it sound unforced certainly deserves a second chance in my book. Shall we proceed?"

Agent Martin Klein pursed his lips for a moment. He had just been played like a rookie by an expert. After eighteen years with the bureau, a twice-decorated senior agent with a corner office, it was not something he appreciated. Indeed, so annoyed was the FBI man that he found a part of himself wanting to start probing the professor for weaknesses, to have him investigated on the off-chance there was something in his background that could possibly be used to embarrass him, or even land him in court. Another part of Klein's mind, however, whispered that perhaps he actually was allowing the routine of his job to turn him into somewhat of a paint-by-the-numbers type rather than the investigator he had trained to be.

Besides, he thought, grinning within his mind, *he complimented us on our vocabulary. How bad can he be?*

Deciding getting some answers and trying to assemble an accurate picture of what had happened the night before was far more important than rubbing salve on his ego, Klein nodded in the professor's direction, saying;

"All right, let's give it another run. After all, we can always throw you in irons for impeding an investigation later—right?"

"There you go," answered Knight with a laugh. Slapping a single palm against the tabletop before him, he added, "That's the spirit." And with that, everyone present began revealing what they knew to one another.

CHAPTER SEVENTEEN

Although Bridget had her cab take her to the Brooklyn Museum, she did not enter immediately. Instead she crossed the street to wander for a while within the Brooklyn Botanic Garden situated on the hillside leading up to the summit upon which the museum rested. As she stared down through the trees and well-tended gardens, she thought on the view of the city she had received the day before.

From atop the Empire State Building, Manhattan had appeared as it did in movies and on television shows—endlessly flat. But Brooklyn seemed built of hills and valleys, far greener than the rest of the city, more tranquil and inviting—

"More like home," she told herself.

She allowed herself a few more minutes of self-delusion, just enough time to steel herself to enter the museum and to get on with pretending that her knowledge of the basic rules of physics had not changed. Going back across the street, she entered the front door of the museum roughly an hour and a half after the professor had done so. The museum had been closed to the public for the day because of the police investigation filling the main lobby, but even her temporary ID had been sufficient to allow her entry. Knight had left word that she be admitted when she arrived. What neither of them knew was that Detective LaRaja had done so as well.

Staring at the various forensic teams puzzling over the scant evidence to be found, the dozens of yards of yellow police tape festooned everywhere, and the general confusion to be found in every corner of the lobby, the redhead suddenly realized she had no real idea as to what she should do.

She had no way of knowing, of course, that Knight was still in Conference Room A, or that he would be there for quite some time. Although neither of them had realized it when they had spoken at breakfast, the professor had given her no actual instructions for her first day. No meeting place or time—no assignments. Nor had he given her the name of anyone else to whom she might report.

Indeed, it was not until she entered the main lobby that she realized she had no idea where Knight's office was located, or even if that was where she would find him. Staring once more at all the official activity taking place, however, she decided that whatever she was going to do, she should probably find some other place to do it. Trying to make her way around the various taped-off areas, she suddenly found an extremely thin black man of medium height headed in her direction. The fact that he was wearing a museum guard's uniform did not completely dismiss her apprehension, something that made her realize she was far more nervous about the current situation than she had realized.

"Ms. Elkins . . . ?"

In seconds, however, the man had introduced himself as Dix Mitchell, a friend of Knight's whom the professor had asked to watch out for her. Hearing that her new boss had thought to have someone watching out for her greatly improved the young woman's attitude, much of her fear dissipating as the back of her mind accepted the idea that she might not be completely alone and on her own in "the big city" after all. When she asked where Knight was at the moment, the guard explained not only where the professor was but also what he would be going through as well.

"He thought maybe you might want to avoid that mess if possible, so he told me to send you in to Human Resources. You gonna have to get it smooth with them anyway, so you might as well go on to it and do it now. Skip bein' browbeat by these—" Dix nodded in the direction of the various official types in the lobby, pausing as he obviously sanitized the phrase he was about to use, changing it to a weaker, but more socially acceptable, "ah . . . officers—"

When Bridget covered her mouth, a touch of a chuckle escaping her lips nonetheless, the guard narrowed his eyes, making a face that let the young woman know that if his skin were not such a dark shade she would be seeing him blush right then. Touching his arm softly, she said;

"Please, don't be offended. I think it's sweet."

"Not supposed to cuss on duty, anyway," he offered, letting a bit of his trademark grin show through despite Knight's admonishment to not turn his charms in Bridget's direction. As he raised his eyebrows toward her playfully as well, to both ease the tension and let the redhead know there were no hard feelings, she leaned in conspiratorially close, telling him;

"Maybe some night after work we can go somewhere when you're off duty and you can teach me how to cuss New York City style."

Dix smiled, insisting that such would be his pleasure. After that, he pointed out the way to Human Resources, assuring Bridget that if she could find a "short, round, nasty black woman that answers to Judith" she would be in good hands. The redhead thanked the guard for his help, then turned in the direction that had been pointed out for her. Heading for the museum's human resources department, she hoped she would not have to search through too many "short, round, nasty black women" before she found one named Judith.

"HELLO, EXCUSE ME . . . WHERE COULD I FIND JUDITH?"

"Oh, don't tell me . . . you're Elkins—Knight's new intern—aren't you?" the speaker had called out from her office door. She was indeed a short woman, one far rounder than she was slender. Nothing about her labeled her as "nasty," but then Dix had impressed Bridget as one of those men who viewed women as fitting into a very limited number of possible categories. As Bridget nodded in agreement, the woman in the doorway depressed a button on the clock on her desk and then had started to cross the open area in the middle of the human resources department when another woman called out from a cubicle;

"Of course she's Knight's new intern. Look at her. It just proves God hates all of us."

"Excuse me . . . ," answered Bridget with a bit of hesitation, not quite certain how to take the second woman's comment. Feeling somewhat foolish for not saying anything, she was about to answer when Judith cut her off.

"Don't pay attention to that gasbag. She's all full of the idea she's someone who's goin' to fly while the rest of us walk. Trust me," the round woman snapped over her shoulder at the other, "it ain't goin' to happen, girl."

By this point, several of the women in the human resources department had left their desks and joined Judith and Bridget. It was clear that part of their reason for doing so was the simple any-excuse-to-stop-working mentality of all offices where people are sequestered in cubicles. Denied the sun, fresh air, and any real reason to remain motivated outside of collecting a paycheck, most workers in such situations were usually ready to take a break at the slightest diversion.

Bridget was used to such behavior—indeed, had held several jobs where, temporary as they were, she fell into the same pattern without much coaxing. But this gathering, the young woman thought, was something different. There was a genuine curiosity in their approach, as if she were a movie star or, perhaps more accurately, a sideshow freak. Bridget might have been younger than all the women suddenly circling her, but she was old enough to know when she was being examined. Of that much she was certain. The only thing she could not fathom was why.

Bridget felt, however, that the inspection process went along painlessly enough. The others all introduced themselves, asked the name of her hometown, what state it was in, if she had any siblings, parents still alive, still together, where she went to school, if she had a boyfriend waiting back home, et cetera. As the women gathered around her, Bridget did grow a touch uncomfortable due to the way she had dressed. For her first day she had chosen a dark gray pencil skirt with a discreet pinstripe, matching jacket over a tucked in, button-down white blouse. Feeling playful when she had first assembled the outfit, she had decided to make a cute wink to the fifties and add a string of pearls and even heels, despite her height.

Now, towering over the others, most of whom were dressed in far less fashionable attire, all of whom were wearing either sneakers or loafers, she found herself becoming more and more self-conscious as she noticed various glances being stolen specifically at her wardrobe. After a few minutes of everyone pointedly looking but no one commenting, she almost wished someone would say something one way or the other.

However, Bridget did find herself enjoying the attention.

While still in Montana the young woman had worried that New Yorkers might live up to their, in many ways deserved, international reputation of being hard and distant—that she might never make any friends in the city. Judith and the others, however, made Bridget feel more than a little welcome, something for which she had not quite been prepared. As the barrage of questions began to slow, the redhead told the others;

"You know, I just want to say thank you all so much for . . . I don't know, being so friendly, I guess. You hear a lot about New York and New Yorkers, and well, I guess I really just needed something like this after last night—"

"What happened last night?"

"Ah, you know," Bridget answered, not certain if she was being teased, "out in the lobby, those men who . . . you know . . . the thieves—"

"What're you sayin'?" Judith eyed Bridget with a mixture of suspicion and sympathy. "You saw that? You were here? You were with the professor—"

"He was the only one inside. I, I was outside—"

And suddenly the furor began once more. Now the other women's questions came in earnest. It was not an unreasonable development. Like most places of daily commerce, the Brooklyn Museum was not usually the scene of gunfire, explosions, or the resulting massive police investigations. As far as Judith and the others were concerned, this was a chance to get the inside scoop on the most exciting thing that had happened in their workplace in years.

Bridget answered their questions slowly, trying not to make any mistakes—to not reveal that which she knew about the professor that she was assuming no one else did. She had been circumspect in her responses to the police the night before, but she had been able to hide behind a mask of shock then. Also, she knew the pair of older men were going easier on her because they had Knight to pummel with their queries. Her fellow workers, however, only had her as a source of information and were determined to drag every morsel they could find from the younger woman.

Eventually, though, what little Bridget had to offer was obtained, and the human resources staff broke down into the typical ritual often referred to as "comparing scars." Each in turn told her most harrowing story of life in the city. Bridget was fascinated by all of their shared experiences, but none more so than the one related by Judith.

"I lived my whole young life in the Bronx. Daddy didn't like the city, didn't want us mixin' with all the white trash—you-all know what I mean. Anyway, until I was fifteen, I never once got to set foot outside the Bronx. So one day, my cousin Rhonda, she wants us to hop the A train and head on down to Manhattan. I'm all full of myself, so I go. We get on the train, and I swear, the minute we go past One Hundred and Tenth Street, this homeless piece of shit gets on the train, and I mean, he stinks. He reeks. Half the people in the car get out at the next stop and jam into other cars. Rhonda and I, we stay. But then, he starts takin' off all his clothes."

"In the train?" asked a somewhat shocked Bridget.

"Yes, sittin' there stretched out on a bench, peelin' out of his coat and shirt and shoes, and T-shirt, *and* pants, and we're watchin', and we can't believe it. And then, yes, this wrinkled old, dirty, scarred-up white man slides out of his drawers, piles them up with everything else, and sits back to start . . . inspectin' himself. Like there's no one else there, like he's in his livin' room or somethin'."

"Oh my God, girl," asked one of the other women, "what did you do?"

"What do you think we did," answered Judith, her scowl barely concealing the grin forcing its way across her face. "We got out at the next stop, walked across the platform, and we went straight back to the Bronx, which I found no reason to leave again until I was twenty-three."

All the women, Bridget and Judith included, laughed over the story's ending. The response also served as a silent signal to the group to return to their desks. All office workers need to break up the monotony of their workdays with such diversions, but they also had to realize when enough fun had been interjected into their day and that it was time to get back to their desks and actually earn their paychecks.

Since Judith's job was to introduce newcomers such as Bridget to the paperwork side of their first day on the job, the older woman took the redhead in hand and led her back to her office. As they took up seats on separate sides of Judith's desk, the round woman said;

"All right, here it comes. Time to fill out all the forms for the museum, the city, the state, the feds, for the insurance company, oh, I'm telling you, girl, you are about to have just ever-so-much fun." When Bridget merely grinned in response, Judith said;

"You know, we've been puttin' you through the wringer. Before I hit you with form city, you have any questions you want to ask? Just tryin' to be fair and all."

"Actually, there is one thing I'd like to know." When the department head nodded, Bridget asked shyly;

"I was just curious . . . do you know how old Professor Knight is?"

And with that, Judith slapped her hands together and threw her head back to laugh. Then, as quickly as she could, the department head stabbed the button on her clock once more, crying out as she did so;

"We have a winner!"

CHAPTER EIGHTEEN

"All right, Professor," said Klein, looking more than a touch frustrated. "Much as I hate to admit it, I guess that's probably about all there is we can drag out of you over this thing."

"I should certainly hope so," answered Knight, exhaling an honestly tired sigh as he did so. Packing his pad and pen back into his shoulder bag, he added, "We did seem to cover the same ground fairly endlessly, but in all fairness I do suppose you're only doing your jobs."

"Yes, that's true," agreed Klein, "and though I hate to say it, we're not actually done yet."

"Not done?"

The professor's tone was one of both puzzlement and unconcealed exasperation. So far he had tried to be as co-operative as he could possibly allow himself to be. He obviously could not tell the authorities anything like the complete truth, could not admit to flying about the museum, or that he had positively recognized the intruders as magic users. And he knew he certainly could not talk of the ring he had used to cause the thieves' bullets to ricochet off his person, or that he had used it to shield himself and Dollins from the heat and smoke in the station house basement.

Having so much to hide, Knight had purposely provoked the FBI man in the beginning so that when it came time to cooperate his manner might not arouse suspicions. At this point he was fairly certain his story as finally presented had been accepted. But, he had gone over the confrontations in the museum and outside the police property room from what he felt had to be every conceivable angle. What, he wondered, could there possibly be left to discuss? When he voiced his question, Klein told him;

"Professor, you can't really be this naive—can you?"

"Oh," injected Brinkley, a look of pity forming on her face, "you don't know our little Piers Knight like we do."

The museum director had sat through every minute of the three-hours-plus interrogation because it was her job. Unlike the jobs of curators such as the professor, who rarely, if ever, had to interact with the outside world, Brinkley's job was to be the public face of the Brooklyn Museum. She met with the corporations looking to make donations to help their public image, as well as the ones she was hoping to convince they should be doing more for their public image. She also had to have an open door for any city officials who might need to be cajoled for this reason or that, for the various neighborhood organizations or businesses that wanted to interact with the museum and any other type of outside interest that needed a human face with which to deal.

That meant she had to be present for every possible moment of Knight's questioning. She would have the board to report to soon over the incident of the night previous, and she would need solid answers for them. After all, controversy was not something that could be tolerated. The board knew donations had a tendency to evaporate when proper public institutions suddenly became sensation enough to generate headlines in the jaded New York City media. Brinkley's assistant had been monitoring not only the local radio and television stations throughout the day to see what their news reports had to report about the night previous, but also dozens of the more popular message boards.

Had AOL gotten their hands on the story yet—plastered it on the screens of a hundred million computers? Were the chat rooms buzzing from one end of the Internet to the other? Were the conspiracy nuts drawing lines from their pet insanities to her museum? Brinkley knew it was bound to happen. It was not a matter of "if," she felt, but only "when."

"Really, Agent Klein," said Knight, more than a slight trace of irritation sneaking into his voice, "possibly I am as naive as you think. But, sir, after all we've covered, what more can there be?"

The director was somewhat afraid to hear the answer to that question—had been asking it of herself for the past three and two-fifths hours. What would the media make of the mysterious deaths, or of the curator entering his museum with a young woman—an intern, no less—after hours, in the dark? Brinkley had not met Bridget yet, but her assistant had been certain to get a look at the girl as soon as she arrived. The image of the young redhead the director received on her cell phone did nothing to quiet her already-jangled nerves.

Oh God, she had thought, looking at Bridget's stunning face, perfect cheekbones, languid eyes, long lashes, perky smile. *Oh my dear God. . . .*

It was enough to make her slip a hand discreetly into her bag for her antacid tablets. This girl had the kind of looks that editors would invent stories about simply to be able to justify the use of her image. Brinkley knew Knight, of course—absolutely knew he was not the kind of man to take advantage of a young woman. Indeed, it was that strict ethical code of his that made him think it was all right to do all of the foolishly improper-looking things he was forever doing.

"Professor," said Klein, his voice hinting that he was about to enjoy himself, "hasn't it occurred to you to wonder why the FBI has involved itself in this matter? Let alone"—the agent moved his head slightly to the right, indicating the pair of operatives everyone else at the table had simply assumed were CIA—"some of the other interested parties assembled here today?"

"Well, I simply assumed it was because there was an explosion here in the city. One that didn't involve a faulty gas main or the such for once."

"That's absolutely right, Professor," answered Klein.

As he revealed a bit of a smile, suddenly both Knight and Brinkley felt twin stabs of apprehension. Both realized clearly that the FBI man must have been holding something back, something he had been waiting to unleash at the proper moment. In his mind, the professor cursed the agent, thinking;

Goddamn it all, I should have known. Push us for hours, pound away on every little, insignificant detail from every angle, over and over, and when we finally sigh and relax that it's all over, then the bastards reveal that it was all to frazzle us—that they haven't even started yet.

"And," asked Klein, "when the government gets involved with explosions, what's usually the reason?"

"Well, 'usually,' in this modern age of wonders of ours, it's because of terrorism. Yes?"

"Very good, Professor. And so, you being so quick with the smart answers, riddle me this: What motivation would we have to be looking at this as a possibly terrorist-related incident?"

Knight paused for a moment, throwing every facet of his mind into answering the question. Perhaps there was something going on he had not considered. And then an idea so absurd it made him begin to chuckle came to the professor, one so idiotic he was certain it had to be correct. Unable to stop one side of his mouth from curling into a smile, Knight suggested;

"The Dream Stone, the piece being stolen by the thieves in question, I had come back to thc museum, as I have reported more than once today, to prepare for the arrival of Dr. Ungari. Are you saying that this is all because Ungari is Egyptian?"

Sitting back in his chair, Klein enjoyed his moment. Turning his neck from side to side so that the cartilage within his spine made audible clicking noises, the agent answered;

"That was the red flag that got us digging. Remember, there's more than one type of terrorism in this world. A lot of countries out there are still extremely resentful over the pilfering of their national treasures by the industrialized nations in the past. And what nation is the Dream Stone from, Professor?" With a sigh, Knight answered;

"Syria."

"Yes, one of the world's leading exporters of terrorism, no matter what our State Department says 'officially.' But I'll stop wasting all our time here. We wouldn't have bothered you over this because of Ungari. An Egyptian who moves back and forth between Syria and the United States? Please, he's been on our radar for years. He's squeaky clean."

"Then what's the problem?"

"The problem, as you put it, Professor, is one Hamid Bakur. Know him?" Knight thought for a moment, then shrugged, admitting he did not recognize the name. Smiling widely now, Klein said;

"We didn't recognize the name, either. At first. He's Ungari's assistant—has been for the past five years, ever since the doctor started digging up this lost Syrian city of his. Bakur was assigned to him by the Syrian Directorate General of Antiquities and Museums. No big deal—right? Except that his name is not Bakur." As all those seated around the room stared, waiting for the FBI man to get to the point, everyone feeling some level of apprehension as to what exactly that point would turn out to be, Klein sat forward, crossing his hands on the table before him as he announced;

"His real name is Hamid Ras Morand. He has connections to some twelve different red-flag organizations, including the Golden Jihad, Bits of String, Flaming Vengeance, among others. He has fronted for all of them, has law degrees from both Iran and Great Britain. And yet he's been digging in the sand for half a decade as if he knew something about archaeology, placed there especially by a government we wouldn't trust to spit on us if we were on fire."

Knight felt his mind going empty. Caught completely off-guard, he could think of nothing to say. If Klein's information was correct, and Knight had little reason to think it was not, then things had just gone from very bad to much, much worse.

"So, Professor, care to tell us what you know about our boy Hamid . . . and why you invited him to come to New York?"

CHAPTER NINETEEN

"Oh, come now, see here, Klein," snapped Knight, his eyes narrowing as his indignation flared. "I would think you would know I did not invite this Hamid person anywhere. I didn't even know he existed until you told me about him."

"And I believe you, Professor," answered the FBI man in a tone Knight accepted as one not masking any hidden purpose. As the professor calmed slightly, Klein continued, adding, "But you did invite Ungari, who is on his way here to inspect a carved rock he could just as easily have gotten the information he needed from through the phone lines. Agreed?"

Knight nodded his head, answering quietly;

"Agreed."

"Splendid. And so, now that we're all in agreement, what shall we do about it?"

The professor sat back down slowly, his eyes seeing nothing, his entire manner that of one lost in thought. Klein had not spent as many years as he had in the bureau without learning something about reading people's body language. It was obvious to him that Knight was wrestling with a decision. Rather than interrupt the professor's thought processes, the agent decided to wait and see at exactly what decision the academic arrived. It was only a handful of seconds afterward when Knight finally looked up, focusing his attention on the FBI man as he said;

"Last night, when I was being interrogated at the police station, this same idea about the Dream Stone was put forth. I have to admit, even after thinking upon it for quite some time now, I still have no idea how to answer it. When I first spoke yesterday to Ungari about the damn thing, it didn't dawn on me to question his coming to America."

"It didn't seem odd to you," asked Brinkley, her tone more curious than challenging, "at all?"

"No, ma'am," snapped the professor, somewhat annoyed at being attacked by a member of his own team. "Not really." Turning away from the director to the others around the table, the curator softened his tone, explaining;

"In the way of giving some background, understand, everyone, that I haven't seen Ashur in quite some time. I believe the answer is simply that I was merely excited over the prospect. Old friends, reunited in triumph. Something to celebrate. At that moment, I was only seeing the affair as a grand coup for the museum. First relics released from the world's oldest city, one of our artifacts helping solve the puzzle, providing a translation for the written language of mankind's first great civilization. Beyond that, the sudden validation for the Dream Stone also meant the same for my great-great-grandfather, the man who discovered it. The family name, restored, made whole . . ."

Knight's voice trailed off into a regretful whisper. Sitting stock-still for only a moment, the professor sighed, then turned his attention back to the FBI man.

"You must forgive the academic mind-set, Agent Klein, but no, I'm forced to admit I wasn't thinking much of terrorism when I asked an old colleague to come here. I was thinking only of my predecessor, and of the prestige an exhibit of Memak'torian artifacts would generate for the museum. If anything—"

Despite the level of overwhelming boredom that had set in around the long table in Conference Room A, all eyes turned to stare at Knight as he suddenly went silent. The professor had thrown himself off into some random thought, abandoning those in the room in mid-sentence to follow whatever notion had flashed within his mind through to its conclusion. After several seconds, he blinked hard, then told the others;

"Forgive me, but something important just dawned on me. . . ."

"Yes . . . ?" asked Klein and Brinkley at the same moment.

"Stereo," joked Knight, pausing only to give the pair a moment to register sour looks, then said, "It may be nothing, but it's just come back to me that I did not actually invite Dr. Ungari to come here."

"No?" Klein leaned forward. "Then who did?"

"I remember it quite clearly. He invited himself. Said he deserved a vacation, and that I deserved a chance to bask in his 'all-encompassing radiance.' That's why I brushed it aside, didn't think of it. He was joking; we discussed hitting the town—it was like we were planning a party. I just—"

"Forget it, Professor," responded the FBI man sympathetically. "This is the way of things. It's not your job to be suspecting every little thing. And besides, not only did you not know about Bakur; it's quite possible Ungari doesn't know anything about the man's background as well."

"Really?" The surprise in Brinkley's voice prompted a response from one of the other FBI agents present.

"Bakur was assigned to Ungari by the Syrians, ma'am," the woman said. "Back in the day, the Soviets would assign a KGB agent to every American scientist, politician, or even entertainer that found themselves traveling within any of their territories. The agents served in the roles of translators, travel coordinators, drivers, whatever, but they always had their eyes and ears in place. Bakur most likely is simply keeping tabs on a non-Syrian for the government."

"And, as it's a non-Syrian with an acceptable excuse to be traveling in and out of the U.S.," added Klein, "as well as one for shipping large crates here, Ungari is certainly someone they would have covered."

"Which leaves us still with the question," said Knight, "of why Ungari would want to personally inspect the Dream Stone."

"That is, as they say, the question, Professor," agreed Klein. "What do you think—got any answers?"

"NO, DAMN IT—I MISSED IT BY THIRTY SECONDS . . . ?"

"Less, looks like."

"It's just not fair."

The speaker was a Ms. Danielle Green, one of the secretaries working under Judith in the museum's human resources department. She had picked the time slot designated "15 to 20 minutes" in the department's current pool. Bridget quickly came to the realization that the betting had something to do with her, or more specifically, something to do with her and the question she had asked about the professor. She was having more than a little trouble, however, determining how people could be betting on something as trivial as that.

"Confused?" When Bridget agreed with Judith's assessment,

the department head smiled, then explained. "Our pool was on how many minutes it would take you to ask someone how old Professor Knight is. And to save you makin' another inquiry, I've been in this department longer than anyone here—okay? And that's how I knew we could bet on such a thing because there hasn't been a female who's worked for this place in all the time I've been here that hasn't wanted to know the same thing."

"Don't feel embarrassed," offered Danielle. Placing her index finger to her chin, the woman scrunched her shoulders coyly, saying, "You're not the first pretty face to fall for the professor's smooth satchel of charm."

"I, I didn't . . . I mean . . ."

As Bridget flushed, the other women's responses ranged from small grins to full-bodied laughter. Putting a sympathetic hand to the redhead's shoulder, Judith told her;

"Don't take it the wrong way. That man, damn, he's simply got the Devil's charm about him, leakin' out of every pore. Don't you think, ladies?"

The five other women gathered in the central area of the human resources department all made noises of approval running from nasty smirks to deeply suggestive groans accompanied by some rather explicit hand gestures. As the giggling among the group began to get out of hand, meaning loud enough for people outside the office to overhear, Judith clapped her hands together and brought an end to the disturbance. Claiming they as a group had wasted enough time, the department head declared that she needed to get Bridget to fill out all her necessary paperwork and that everyone else needed to get back to their jobs. Once she had Bridget safely in her office and behind a closed door, Judith said;

"Forty-three."

"Excuse me . . . ?"

"Professor Knight, that's how old he is. At least, that's what the records we have on file here say. If you can believe that." As the department head walked around her desk to her chair, Bridget took a centrally located one on the other side. Then, as she settled her ample self into her swivel chair, Judith added;

"I mean, you've seen him . . . you tell me—you think that man could possibly be forty-three?"

"I have to admit, he . . . but then, he doesn't look any older."

"Is that what I asked you?"

The younger woman took a deep breath in through her nose. Her mouth was a thin straight line, clamped tight, her eyes hooded. She was avoiding looking at the woman on the other side of the desk, remaining silent not because she wished to avoid the conversation but because she was trying to really be a part of it—to offer some contribution that would make her sound not quite as silly as a few of the other women in the office. Finally, she looked up and answered;

"I'm a country girl, all right? I did just finish my undergraduate work at the University of Chicago, so I know a little bit about cities and the people that live in them, but I'm probably not as sophisticated as the rest of you."

"Hedgin' your bets here?"

"No," Bridget said slowly, "just trying to be honest. I'm admitting that I can't even pretend to know everything. So, if the records say he's forty-three, then, all right, I guess he must be. But he just seems so . . . oh, I don't know what the word would be, I mean, mature, wise, but he's funny, and playful, do you know what I mean?"

"All too well," agreed Judith with a sigh. The younger woman could not tell if the department head was referring to all the other women whom the professor had apparently enthralled or maybe to her own feelings. Curious, Bridget asked, "What do you think of him?"

"Child, I don't know how any man that young got that smart and that sexy, but if he came in a darker shade I'd be on him like lies on a politician's résumé. And," she added with a chuckle, "if my husband would conveniently disappear for a while. I mean, even after all this time I can't tell you what it is that man has, but I certainly would like the chance to lick some of it off him."

When Bridget's eyes went somewhat wide with surprise, Judith scoffed, adding in a low whisper;

"Oh, like your brain hasn't been flirtin' with the idea of givin' him a wink and sayin', 'Come hither.' "

Blushing, the redhead admitted;

"The thought had crossed my mind, if I remember correctly."

"I'll bet it did," answered Judith, laughing softly as she did so. Reaching for the forms she did need the professor's new intern to fill out, Judith added, "And let me just wish you good luck tryin'. I'll tell you this much, the man ain't gay, but he ain't escorted no one from here home as of yet. And believe me, more than a few have tried."

"It's a shame," said Bridget, not thinking about what she was saying. "He really does have a charming home."

Judith's eyes went wide to the point of comic exaggeration. Her one hand clutching the now-forgotten forms, she held her other out to point at the younger woman on the opposite side of her desk. Her eyes suddenly narrowing to coldly suspicious slits, she asked;

"You've been in this city one day, and you've seen the inside of Professor Piers Never-Does-Anything-But-Eat-Sleep-and-Work Knight's home? Exactly which rooms did you see?"

"Nothing happened," answered Bridget, her tone revealing she was slightly shocked that someone would think so.

Not ready to leave things at just the registering of the younger woman's indignation, Judith demanded the whole story. Her insistence on getting all the details of the evening before was born more out of disbelief than anything else. By the time Bridget had explained the set of circumstances that had led to her sleeping on the professor's couch, the department head had been placated. Oddly enough, Bridget thought the older woman might actually have been relieved to hear the entire story.

As she finally settled into filling out the half-dozen various forms required to be on file in the museum's human resources department, Bridget's mind reviewed the past twenty-four hours of her life. Since her arrival in New York City, she had seen one of the greatest cities in the world from its highest point. After that she had enjoyed one of the finest meals she could have ever imagined in one of the most wonderful restaurants she had ever known.

She had also seen a man levitate, watched men get shot and then destroyed by an explosion, seen a walking wraith, been interrogated by the police, escaped the clutches of a being made of fire, learned that magic very possibly might be real, and slept in the home of a man many of her new coworkers apparently fantasized about on a daily basis.

Hmmph, she thought. *Not bad. Now, I wonder what the second day's going to turn out like?*

CHAPTER TWENTY

After Bridget finished filling out the small booklet's worth of forms the museum bureaucracy required, then came a tour conducted by Danielle. It was an exhaustive introduction, one that took the young woman from one end of the museum complex's expansive basement to the other and then the width and breadth of floors one through six.

The tour had been designed to show newcomers as much of the Brooklyn Museum and its inner workings as possible. In Bridget's case, her guide had taken into account the necessity of showing her charge the museum, especially as it might relate to her duties under Professor Knight. Although she might well be "borrowed" on occasion to help guide tours through the museum or do other general tasks, mainly she would be concerned with keeping her boss focused.

"The Big K," as Danielle referred to Knight, "is a special case. He'll keep you busy."

"Taskmaster?" Bridget responded, obviously curious.

"No, not really." The shorter woman paused for a moment, then added, "It's more as if he has no real sense of time. I mean, he'll ask you to work through the night on something, not because he's one of those evil bosses . . . he just . . . gets caught up."

After that, as Danielle continued the tour, marching Bridget first through the various exhibit levels, the special displays in the mezzanine, through the Beaux-Arts Court and the various upper galleries, she also led the newcomer to all the various offices and departments hidden behind the scenes. The round little woman knew Bridget's day-to-day would be much more concerned with places like the study center, the on-site storage vaults, and the library.

Of course, Danielle also went out of her way to introduce the redhead to as many other staff members as could be found. By the time the finish of the workday arrived for the Human Resources staffer, Danielle said in a joking tone, "There you have it, all of our big, fat, marvelous workplace laid out before you. Now, come tomorrow you're going to remember all of it and the names of everyone you met—right?"

"Oh, certainly," answered Bridget with a slightly sour humor. The redhead wished she could forgo propriety and reach down and rub her aching feet. Instead, she silently cursed her choice to wear heels that day, responding with a weak joke. "You're Fred, aren't you—or was that Bill?" Danielle laughed in response. Smiling wide, the older woman said;

"Don't worry; it's easier to get the hang of it than it looks. Besides, once the professor starts working you, you probably won't see anyone else, or the light of day, for that matter, for years to come."

"That's certainly comforting." Danielle chuckled, after which she gave Bridget a friendly hug, saying;

"Don't worry; you're going to be fine."

The redhead hugged Danielle back, letting her know she thought she might just be fine at that, thanks to the thoroughness of her tour. After that, the older woman left Bridget in the central lobby to return to Human Resources so she could gather her coat and purse and such and head for New Jersey and home.

Still having no home of her own other than her suitcase, however, which itself had not left the professor's spare bedroom, Bridget went off in search of her new boss. Deciding to try the obvious first, she was greatly relieved to discover Knight working in his office. Dropping herself into a chair, she kicked off her shoes, groaning in relief as she exclaimed;

"What a day!"

"I imagine your comment signifies that you have met the sturdy and wonderfully efficient Judith Johnson, as well as the rest of our delightful human resources flock. Most likely one of them was then charged with dragging you up and across the various lengths of our fine museum, from the fascinating art of the feminists' era backward down through the ages to the artifacts of ancient Egypt. At the same time, I imagine, you were introduced to several score people, had your head thrust into a few hundred rooms, galleries, and chambers for up to ten, maybe even twenty seconds apiece." The professor paused for a moment, then added drily;

"All of which you're expected to remember on the morrow. Yes?"

Bridget's only response was to nod and smile quietly. Fussing with papers on his desk, the professor told his assistant;

"Some good news—"

"I'll take it."

"I managed to keep the dogs of war busy enough so that they didn't feel the need to summon you for further questioning, so that's something anyway."

"Something I appreciate," answered Bridget honestly. Stifling a yawn, she asked how he had managed to do so as she tried to figure out how to rub her feet with any kind of propriety while wearing a pencil skirt. Continuing to thumb through the papers, folders, envelopes, and such piled over a foot high in his in-box, Knight responded absently;

"Well, it didn't hurt that LaRaja and his people shared their transcripts of what you had to say last night with everyone involved." When Bridget questioned the word "everyone," the professor told her of the FBI and CIA coming on board with the case, as well as why. He then outlined the hours of questioning he had endured throughout all of the morning and half the afternoon, giving her the boiled-down essence of the entire affair.

"First off," he said, "it seems the bozos—that will be my label for any and all of the knuckle-dragging cretins I had the pleasure to dance around endlessly with today—the bozos have decided to graciously believe what I have told them. You were an innocent bystander and I must be telling the truth because what else could make sense."

"That's good—yes?"

"Well, yes, I suppose—as far as it goes." As Bridget simply stared, waiting for an explanation, Knight added, "What I mean is I'm fairly certain they have no further interest in you. The bill of goods you sold Detective LaRaja last night was enough for them all. For which, by the way, let me finally say, 'Thank you, very much.'"

"Oh, please, Professor—it was no big deal."

"Yes," Knight responded. Looking up from his unending piles of paper, the professor's normally reserved and calculating eyes went soft for a moment as he told her, "It was. You lied to the authorities, or at least forgot to tell them everything to which you were witness. Which in their humorless eyes is part and parcel of the same thing. Either way, I greatly appreciate that, as I would hope you must know."

"What else could I have done?"

"Not to put ideas in your head, but you could have done any manner of other things. For one, you might have acted like some brainless ninny and started caterwauling to the police that you thought you saw me levitating, that you suspected I somehow caused the deaths of the intruders. You could have made mention that you saw a fifth figure with the others that appeared to be a ghost or a hologram, that whatever it was, it was this thing that caused the explosions, after which it disappeared without a trace."

"Yeah, and have them cart me off to the loony bin."

"Here in the big city, it's not politically correct to use such terms," Knight told his assistant only half-jokingly. "You have to say 'escort me to a restful and therapeutic mental health facility.'"

"Oh, okay—I'll make a note of that. And if they just decide to cart me off to a federal detention facility?"

"I'll send you a postcard."

Bridget pushed against the back of her chair, needing to feel her spine solidly against something. Stretching her arms up and over her head then, she let out a noisy yawn, one that went on for longer than the professor would have thought possible. When she caught him staring at her, she asked;

"What?"

"Nothing. Just impressed with your lung capacity." Several quips came to Bridget's mind, but she pushed them aside, asking instead;

"So anyway, what else did they say, or ask, or whatever?"

Knight gave up trying to sort through the monstrously large pile of things in his in-box. Giving over his full attention to Bridget instead, he ran through the entire list of points brought up by the "bozos." He did not have much in the way of new things to tell her. The only piece of information previously unknown by either the professor or Bridget had been the existence of Hamid Bakur, as well as his ties to the variety of terrorist organizations the FBI agent had listed. Knight also told Bridget of the quandary over why Ungari would travel all the way to the United States when there seemed to be no need for him to do so.

"Did you come up with any ideas on that one?"

"No," answered the professor honestly, his tone somewhat depressed. "And I must admit the whole thing has me fairly stumped. We went around in circles on that one for almost two hours, and in the end all our great minds found they had generated no worthwhile ideas whatsoever."

"So they gave up on it," asked Bridget hopefully. Shaking his head, Knight told her;

"Not hardly. Apparently one or the other of our bozos was able to get a bead on Ungari. He should be arriving at JFK sometime in the morning."

"Are they going to arrest him?"

"That was my first thought as well, but it seems they're going to meet his plane, and then have him shadowed to see what he does. If I heard it all correctly, they plan to slip some kind of device into his cell phone when he comes through customs so they can listen in on his calls."

"Hmmph, our fascist government at work."

"Oh?" Knight opened both his eyes wider than normal, taking on a slightly comical doe-eyed-innocent look. When his assistant snorted in response, immediately questioning his patently phony visage, the professor told her, "Well, my dear, I'm just hoping you don't disapprove of our government's tactics in this case."

"And exactly why not, good sir?"

"Because it's pretty much what I did to them."

CHAPTER TWENTY-ONE

Less than half an hour later, Bridget and Professor Knight found themselves at another of his favorite restaurants. This time it was New Corner of Brooklyn, an out-of-the-way Italian place nestled in the shadow of the Verrazano-Narrows Bridge, one specializing in a quiet atmosphere and family-style dining. And although the menu featured a cuisine almost diametrically opposed to the one the night before, their meal was not all that different an affair from the one they had shared the previous evening. The chefs were just as talented, the waiters equally experienced. The decor proved to Bridget to be charmingly inviting, and their wait for both a table and service was so brief as to be practically unnoticed.

New Corner was an extremely low-key restaurant, one often used by many of its clientele as a decompression chamber. The place was nicely isolated in an extremely quiet residential neighborhood on the borderlands of Bay Ridge and Bensonhurst. The surroundings seemed to soak up much of the daily chaos of the city, relieving its patrons of their stress. Thus, the fact that the pair in the corner booth were not enjoying themselves as they had the evening previous was in no way the fault of the establishment.

Rather, too much had changed in both their lives in an extremely brief span of time for even the Corner to heal their wounded spirits in the span of a single meal. Delightful to the palate as their meals turned out to be, neither was in a mood to celebrate, to ask revealing questions or chatter about much of anything. They were worn-out—too tired to eat and too upset to talk about it. Finally, however, in an attempt to play the grown-up in their relationship, Knight asked, "How's your scampi?"

"It's all right," answered the redhead absently. Understanding her mood perfectly, the professor made a motion with his eyes toward her hand, commenting;

"You realize, no matter how much longer you slide that piece of shrimp around, I fear it's not going to be able to absorb any more butter."

"You don't think so, eh?"

"My goodness," exclaimed Knight in an exaggerated tone. "Bless all the tiny monkeys, is that the hint of a smile I see there, creeping over my ever-so-blue dinner companion's thin but wildly attractive lips?"

"You, good sir, are a barrel of trouble."

"Yes," responded Knight, twirling a half-dozen strands of linguine around his fork. "That has been, for quite some time now, the popular opinion. But enough of this depression." Popping the forkful of pasta into his mouth, only a few drops of white clam sauce dripping onto his chin, the professor announced as he chewed;

"Let's get down to business."

"Which business is that?"

"Well." Smacking his lips in appreciation, realizing he had just begun actually tasting his food for the first time that night, Knight set his fork down and began buttering a piece of bread as he said, "To start, we acknowledge we both had days best described as . . . now, what would the best, the most fitting, word in the world possibly be . . ."

"Crappy?"

"Why, yes—that's an excellent choice. Yes—a marvelous word. A pair of crappy days we have just experienced, and now we need to put them behind us. And I do believe I know one way we could try to do so."

"Thrill me, boss man."

"Well, if I remember correctly, I owe you all sorts of explanations. To tell the truth, I'm frankly surprised we didn't start chattering like mad folk in the car over them."

"Didn't feel like it," admitted Bridget. "Danielle really did wring me out with the museum tour. And, before that, your harem left me a little speechless."

"My 'harem'?"

Bridget stared into the professor's eyes, a trifled startled to discover that the curator seemed to have no idea to what she was referring. When the redhead hesitantly explained her comment, giving him hints of how the women in Human Resources had discussed him, she found herself growing both slightly amused at and embarrassed for Knight.

He genuinely did not appear to be aware of their feelings toward him.

Touching his chest with one hand, holding the other out before him in an imploring manner, he asked sincerely;

"Really? Moi?"

"Indeed. But, oh come on now. Are you telling me you had no idea of the effect you have on some women?"

"Well," the professor answered, ducking his head slightly, "I've never had a terrible amount of trouble finding a companion for the theater, or museum events, or whatever. But, you make them sound as if they were . . . I don't know, fanning themselves as they spoke about me."

"It was a spectacle," answered Bridget with a giggle.

"Very well," said Knight, unconsciously sitting a bit straighter. "I suppose from now on I'll have to send anything needed from me by Human Resources via the mail room."

"It might be for the best," teased the redhead.

"Yes, well, anyway, on to explanations. I mentioned to you earlier that I had bugged our bozo friends—correct?" When his assistant agreed, the professor added;

"I shall explain. There is a powder employed by the fakirs of India when they want to share mystical journeys or visions. All that is done is they mix it in water, everyone to be involved in the experience drinks a portion, and for the next eighteen to thirty hours they basically all share one mind." As Bridget merely stared at Knight, her own mind struggling to process yet another bit of the fantastic that had been presented to her as being nothing out of the ordinary, the professor added;

"Really."

"And you can hear everything each of them is saying, or thinking—"

"Both."

"And they can hear you?"

"No." When Bridget returned to simply staring, waiting for an explanation, Knight obliged, telling her;

"I can hear them, because I know how to hear them. It comes from a number of things, really. I know the water was spiked; I know how to manipulate magical, or more precisely elemental, energies. What they will dismiss as 'background noise,' or a headache, daydream, whathaveyou, I will, shall we say, turn up the volume on and listen in to whatever they are saying, or hearing. Or what they are thinking."

"And you're doing this now?"

The professor nodded in response, finally taking a bite of his heavily buttered piece of hearty, sesame seed–encrusted bread. "It's like background music. As long as they're not saying or thinking anything important, my mind ignores all of it. If, however, something I would need to know comes up, then my conscious mind will start to pay attention. Sort of a transcendental-meditation version of that TiVo thing."

"Okay," responded Bridget, her head shaking and nodding at the same time. "And you can do this because, as you said, you 'know how to manipulate elemental energies.' That's what you said—correct?" When the professor agreed with her quote, she added;

"That's something I was wondering about. Ever since you let me hold the Disc of the Winds, what you said about it has bothered the back of my mind."

"And what was that?"

"You said that all you had to do was expose it to the air and up you went. Yet, I was holding it, out exposed to the air, and I didn't go floating out of my seat. Why's that?"

Dipping another piece of bread into his white clam sauce, scooping up several large slices of clam with it, the professor took a dripping bite, then returned the bread to his plate so it could soak up more sauce while he said; "Well now, here we go. That is, as they used to say, the sixty-four-thousand-dollar question. You've basically just asked me to explain how it is so-called magic works in our universe."

"I have?"

“Oh yes indeed,” responded Knight. His hand up, signaling for a waiter, he said, “And you know what? As soon as we can get our dinners wrapped up for some imaginary dog, I think I’m just going to go ahead and show you.”

CHAPTER TWENTY-TWO

In less than twenty minutes, Professor Piers Knight and his new assistant were riding along through a lush and sprawling cemetery. They had been stopped at the large red sandstone main gatehouse, and by the attitude of the guard Bridget had been certain they would not be allowed entrance. After the man on duty went in to check his "Allowed Visitors" roster, he returned and waved Knight through without any further delay.

As the professor drove along one of the winding roads leading farther inside, he told his companion;

"Here's a hopefully interesting fact. Green-Wood was among the first 'rural' cemeteries to be created within the city. By that I mean it was a business—a thing not attached to any particular church. The place covers nearly five hundred acres. Astounding to find something like this in the middle of a major city."

"And we're here because you need a cemetery to perform magic?" Bridget's tone betrayed the slightest bit of trepidation on the redhead's part. "What? We're going to be collecting graveyard dirt, or robbing tombs?"

"Oh, for heaven's sake," responded Knight. He did not look at his assistant as he spoke, for the roads within the cemetery were twisting affairs and, with the sun rapidly setting, it was best for any drivers there to keep their eyes focused on where they were going. Still, he told her;

"No, truthfully we could have gone to any of a hundred different places. I chose here because it's private and quiet. For what we're about to do we don't need any spectators. Security—as I mentioned before."

Finding the spot he wanted, the professor stopped his car, then hopped out quickly to move around to the other side and open Bridget's door. He extended his hand to help the redhead from the car because he had been forced to park on an uphill grade and the angle would be a trifle tricky for one exiting from the passenger side of any vehicle. As they made their way carefully across the well-kept lawn covering most of the area, Knight said;

"This has been, as you might have guessed from the size and grandeur of some of the mausoleums, the place to be put to rest in Brooklyn for quite some time—almost one hundred and fifty years now, I believe. Many a famous sort under the sod here—the engravers Currier and Ives are here somewhere, Boss Tweed, Horace Greeley, oh, C. L. Tiffany, and his son, Louis. Oh, and the fantasy illustrator Roy Krenkel, the fellow whose paperback cover paintings were responsible for the big Edgar Rice Burroughs revival back in the fifties, he's here. And then there's—"

The professor broke off his lecture suddenly, however, as he came to a somewhat boxy tombstone, one carved as if to resemble a child's idea of a house. In a circle carved into what would be the roof's peak were three words: "Jane, My Wife." Below, the bas-relief carved into the front of the headstone showed a man leaving his home, presumably on his way to work, leaning on his gate. His gaze appeared to be directed toward a woman standing at the front door to the home, a small dog sitting on the steps to her left. After Bridget and Knight had stood silently before the headstone for a long moment, the redhead broke the silence.

"All right, this is what you wanted me to see, I'm guessing. Am I supposed to also guess why?"

"No," answered Knight quietly. "Jane and Charles Griffith are buried here. The sculpture represents the last time Charles saw his wife alive. When he returned home that evening after work, he discovered his bride had died of heart disease. He had this monument erected, and then proceeded to visit her every week for the next quarter of a century until his own death, in the early 1880s, I believe, at which point he was interred here next to her."

"Touching, but the importance of all this is . . . ?"

Knight involuntarily dropped his head several inches, taking a deep breath at the same time. Although he had honestly meant to go through with revealing the secret behind his abilities to the young woman, a part of him reached out, flogging him with hesitation, throwing up all the familiar warning beacons it had at hand. It reminded him of the disasters he had created for himself in the past on those occasions when he had done with others as he was about to do with Bridget.

Calming his paranoid streak, reminding himself that there had been tremendous successes as well when he had done such over the years, he reached out and touched the tombstone, beginning his explanation as he did so.

"The first thing anyone must realize is that there is a vast difference between 'knowing' that magic is real—actually understanding it—and 'believing' it is real. My easiest example would be yourself. You now 'know' magic, what most people would label as magic, actually does exist. You've seen it in operation. But, even though you know magic is possible, deep inside you there is a part of you that still keeps you from really believing it."

Continuing to touch the tombstone, Knight closed his eyes. Although it was obvious he was attempting to keep his voice steady, his tone clear and unemotional, it was equally obvious that something was happening to him. As his assistant watched him, the professor seemed to grow straighter, taller, stronger. His entire body appeared to be vibrating, not the jerking, uncontrolled spasms of someone attempting to stay awake all night from ingesting too many energy drinks, but instead the steady, humming vibration of a well-oiled machine.

"As I said earlier, we can both handle the same objects, speak the same words, perform the identical rituals, whatever, and I will be able to produce a result whereas you will not. Even though we do everything exactly the same, even though you know that magic works because you've seen it with your own eyes, you will not be able to make anything work."

Releasing the tombstone, taking a backward step at the same time, Knight opened his eyes once more. His face was split apart in a full and infectious smile, one that appeared to have planted itself upon him of its own volition. Brimming with a sudden vitality, he announced;

"This is what has protected those we have labeled as magicians throughout history. We know a secret the rest of you do not. This is the reason the grand majority of people can read spell books, play with Ouija boards and the such, and nothing happens. It takes energy to perform magic, just as it does to do anything else."

"But not the kind generated by steam power, or electricity, I'm guessing."

"Correct." Taking Bridget's hand, Knight pulled her down to the ground as he himself suddenly sat down, his back coming to rest against the Griffiths' headstone. As Bridget settled herself against it as well, the professor continued, telling her;

"No. It takes human energy, emotional energy—elemental energy. The Empire State Building, to give us a familiar point of reference for instance, fills up with the stuff all the time. Can't help it. Millions of people every day, they look at it, they think, 'Tallest building in the city.' As they do, their awe, their respect, their fear of heights, admiration for accomplishment, love of art deco design—all of it—it pours into the building, waiting for some magician or another to come along and drain it out."

"I guess you did so yesterday?"

"Well, one always checks, but that's the problem with big, splashy landmarks. All the wannabes, the amateurs, the slop artists, they're constantly hovering over such sites, gorging themselves, fighting over the crumbs. The World Trade Center memorial site, or the Verrazano-Narrows Bridge, Times Square, the vultures haunt these places. But something like this," he said, patting the gravestone gently, "these are the places that get overlooked. The story of the Griffiths is well-known, appears in plenty of the guidebooks. Green-Wood is itself a tourist attraction, but not the kind that attracts the sorts of erstwhile magicians who can only think of unlimited power."

Then, pulling the Disc of the Winds from a pocket on the inside of his sport coat, the professor held it out between himself and Bridget, telling her softly, "It's the kind I prefer, softer, quieter—pure. Undiluted. And, when gathered properly, it's, well . . ."

Reaching out with his other hand, Knight gently took Bridget's hand and closed her fingers over the disc.

"It's magic."

And so saying, the pair began to levitate upward into the darkness that had begun to fill the cemetery. The professor did not allow them to travel more than a few feet upward. First, he could not take the chance they might be spotted by someone else despite both the growing gloom and the fact that the graveyard was closed to the general public at that time. Second, he did not want to take a chance of Bridget losing her grip and suddenly falling to the ground. There seemed little chance of the latter happening, however. Clutching on to the disc with an almost desperate grip, the redhead exclaimed;

"Professor, we're flying!"

"Well, we're floating at any rate, but essentially, yes, at the very least we are giving that appearance. Now, do you think you understand?"

As the couple settled back to the ground, Knight replaced the disc within his jacket while Bridget attempted to regain her composure. Not able to do so sitting, she rose in a single, bounding motion. The pain in her aching feet forgotten, she began pacing back and forth before the professor, her hands in constant, somewhat comical animation. Waving them both frantically to emphasize her points, she said;

"My God, oh my God, it was unbelievable; it was like in a dream. I was floating, levitating, whatever you want to call it—it was *magic*! Just like you said . . . and we were off the ground . . . we were—"

And, just as suddenly as the young woman had risen and become practically a blur of random activity, she then stopped, frozen, her attention completely removed to a point outside herself. Studying her quickly, Knight could tell that something new had entered the picture, something so riveting that it had immediately commanded all of his assistant's focus. The professor got no sense of uncontrollable fear or terror from Bridget, but still, the extremely heightened sense of agitation he was getting filled him with concern.

TWENTY-THREE

"Is, is," the redhead stammered slightly, her frightened amazement stumbling her tongue, "is that a *ghost*?"

"I don't think," answered the professor, "there is a much better word for that which, considering your question, I assume you are seeing as well." As Knight studied the shape in the distance before them, eyes fastened to the undulating contours of the thing, examining the structure of the gliding wraith as best he could, Bridget asked;

"This, this *is* a cemetery. Are there . . . ghosts, um, like always running around in these places normally?"

"Well, more so than on your average street corner, I would suppose," answered the professor absently, his concentration fixed primarily on the glowing shape still approaching their position. "I mean, reasonably, if you decide you want grapes, and you go to a fruit stand, you have a much better chance of finding some there than, say, at an auto dealership. But—"

"I get the idea," answered Bridget curtly.

Perhaps, he told h
what it is that's stole

Rising from the gro
able to scan the cemetery

When he did so, he was a
tral apparition floating across th
she had. Sighing, unable to fathom
serve such a never-ending series of
muttered;

"I've got to start praying to a better

CHAP

By this point the young woman had moved completely behind Knight. Eyes wide, unblinking, pulse running rapidly, she stared with a horrified fascination as the silent form continued drifting slowly onward toward them. Part of Bridget's mind was working desperately to calm her increasingly jangled nerves. It whispered to her that she should not have anything to worry about, reminding the young woman that if the specter actually posed any sort of real danger the professor would have at least said something to her by then, if not removed her from the area.

At least, Bridget told herself, she hoped he would. Swallowing hard, the young woman made a fist of her left hand, squeezing until her fingernails were digging sharply into her palm. Biting at her lower lip, she concentrated on the pain in her hand as a distraction from her fear. Then, when finally she felt she could speak without stammering, she asked;

"So, okay—now what? What does this damn thing want from us? I mean, is it after us? Is it coming to us, or is it just flying around? Since you're staying so calm, I'm thinking that you've seen ghosts before—yes? Were they like this one? Can you tell I'm rambling because I'm scared out of my mind?"

"You do an admirable job of covering it, my dear," answered Knight in a vague, distracted voice.

The professor realized that Bridget certainly must be frightened to a great extent—not that he held such against her. Unless she had encountered some kind or another of spectral phenomena previously, which apparently she had not, it was only natural for her to be unnerved by the sudden arrival of such a figure now.

The only question I have for you, my spectral friend, the professor asked himself, *is are you something out of the blue, unrelated to everything else we've been forced to survive lately, which would only prove that God is a bastard who* does *play dice with the universe, or are you yet another piece to the ever-widening puzzle we're being encouraged by Fate to solve?*

It took a moment for the pair of observers to realize the glowing form had slowed its approach drastically, to the point where it barely seemed to be moving at all. Knight felt he might know the reason why. Ghosts, at least those specters that represented the life force of some departed human being, were for the most part nothing like they were portrayed in legend or by the various entertainment mediums.

Thinking he might have uncovered a clue as to why the shape had slowed its advance, Knight turned to his assistant. Taking her by the shoulders, he stole her attention by staring directly into her eyes, forcing her to look away from the wraith and at him instead. Feeling the tremors racing throughout her body vibrating within his palms, the professor told her;

"Listen to me: I don't believe there is any reason for alarm in this. But I do believe your, ah, 'apprehension' might be the reason it's stopped moving. Your fear might actually be acute enough to keep it at bay."

"Is, is," Bridget stammered, her teeth chattering as she spoke. Stopping, she dug her nails into her palm once more, forcing herself to focus, then said smoothly, "Is that a good thing, or am I messing things up?"

"Sadly, there's no way for me to know without making contact," Knight told her honestly. "So, that's what I'm going to do. But, I want you to stay here. I'm going to go out to it, try to, anyway, just to see what happens." As the young woman's eyes went slightly wide, despite her best efforts to control her reactions, the professor added;

"Don't worry, I'm really quite certain there's no danger to either of us in my doing so. What I'm afraid of is that this might have something to do with everything else that's been crashing down all around us." Moving one of his hands to her chin, he touched it lightly, saying;

"I simply can't take the chance of losing a clue that might tell us what the devil's going on around us."

Bridget nodded, smiling briefly at Knight's touch. As he removed his hand from her chin, beginning to turn away, the redhead touched him on the arm, halting him for a moment. As his head swung back, she told him;

"Just so you know, despite everything that's been happening, I'm not sorry I left Montana."

Giving her a comically leering smile, one meant to amuse her, he shifted his tone to one that was a fair approximation of Groucho Marx's voice and said;

"And, just so you know, I'm not at all sorry you left Montana, either."

After that, Knight turned back toward the still-hovering specter, focusing all his attention on the freestanding apparition. The thing had taken up a position some sixty to seventy feet away from the pair. Moving slowly, the professor took a step in the wraith's direction, holding his palms out toward the entity. He understood that human energy was released through the eyes and palms. If the thing waiting across the manicured cemetery lawn still possessed any level of consciousness, Knight wanted it to be able to read his intentions, to understand that he neither feared it nor meant it any harm.

"Whatever it is you want," he whispered to the wind, hoping the words could somehow reach the thing glimmering before him, "I want you to have it. So please, stay there now—wait for me. I'm here to help you."

As Bridget watched she unconsciously began moving forward, returning to the Griffiths' tomb. Grabbing hold of it, she bent low, unaware she was hugging the solid block as a shield. From the imagined safety of her position she then scanned the scene before her with fearful fascination as Knight continued onward, taking one smoothly measured step after another. The redhead was no Scully to his Muldar, at least not yet—but she was ready to make the effort.

Continuing her observations, Bridget noted that Knight moved carefully, never rushing, making certain to keep all his movements uniform. Shifting her gaze from the professor to the apparition, Bridget began studying the thing as well, trying to get some sense of exactly what it might be—or what it might want.

She had heard the term "ectoplasm" over the years when various sources had spoken of parapsychology and ghosts, but she had little idea of what it might physically consist. Besides, if she remembered correctly, ectoplasm was something that was created when the spirit world came in contact with a human host, such as a medium in contact with some beyond force or another. But this thing hanging in the air before them, it was not even connected to the ground, let alone in contact with anything living. Forcing herself to blink, Bridget ran her tongue over her teeth, working to generate some spittle in her fear-dried mouth. As she did, she asked herself;

So, is this what you had in mind when you told everyone you were looking forward to all the new experiences New York City had to offer?

The comment made the redhead chuckle, a diversion she greatly needed. Even bitter humor, she told herself, was better than none. Using the moment to rein in her terror, to get her fear at least under some minimal amount of control, she took several deep breaths, telling herself that if Knight thought everything was all right, then it must be so. Then, working to bring her curiosity to the fore, placing her faith in her new boss instead of in the self-preservation fears urging her to run for her life, the young woman mumbled;

"Besides, anyone who thinks I'm going to start running across a graveyard, in the dark, in three-inch spikes no less, has got another thing coming."

As she continued to observe, Knight's journey finally came to an end. As he drew within arm's reach of the wraith, the thing began moving once more, advancing in a forward motion. Bridget's one hand shot out involuntarily in surprise, the other hanging on to the gravestone tenaciously as the specter moved in to envelop the professor's entire body. Covering him like a great transparent cocoon, the specter began to swirl, changing shape and form, sliding across Knight's body in a motion that seemed half dance, half some manner of communication.

The ghostly form writhed and swirled, beginning to move faster and faster over the professor, under his arms, between his legs, across his chest, racing in between his fingers, under his clothing, rippling his hair as it breezed about each individual follicle. Finally, as Bridget continued to watch, Knight finally made some reaction to his intercourse with the spectral presence. His body began to jerk, to spasm, not uncontrollably, but in a fashion unnatural enough to bring forth a rush of concern within the young woman.

The professor had assured her that such meetings were rarely violent or dangerous, but had not guaranteed it. As she reviewed his words in her head, she realized he had said a number of things meant to calm and reassure her, but he had never firmly stated that nothing could go wrong.

It's doing something to him, thought Bridget. Clinging to the tombstone, her brain tore itself apart trying to think of what she might be able to do to help, but she could not think of anything. She knew nothing of ghosts, not about communicating with them, combating them, dismissing or summoning or feeding them—nothing! Tears gathering in her eyes, her mind throbbed with shame, but there was no way available to her to assist Knight. If the professor had been wrong to go out to meet the thing, what could she do? He was the magician. He was the one explaining everything to her.

Is that who you are, Bridget Elkins?

The voice sounding in her mind startled the young woman. For a moment she froze, not able to grasp her conscience's meaning.

Crippled by fear—useless?

Then she realized the man struggling a handful of yards in front of her had done nothing since their first meeting other than befriend and protect her. If he was now in danger from having once more put her safety before his own, what was she doing still kneeling in the dirt?

Filled with a sudden resolve, Bridget threw herself to her feet and, with no plan in mind other than trying to help another human being, she launched herself at Knight and the specter.

"Here comes Scully," she muttered, managing to cover slightly under half the ground between them before the sky was shattered by a monstrous peal of thunder, followed by a darkly colored shaft of lightning that struck the professor, dissipating the specter and sending both Knight and his assistant hurtling through the air.

CHAPTER TWENTY-FOUR

"Professor, for God's sake—speak to me!"

Bridget had recovered first. Such made sense, of course, since she had received only the barest edges of the explosive blast that had knocked Knight end over end. His body had come to rest badly against a sizable gravestone, one that halted his trajectory both violently and instantaneously.

Considering the force with which he had struck the quite solid granite, his assistant was certain he would need medical attention.

Pushing herself back up onto her feet, she had raced to his side, working as gently as she could to untangle his limbs and then gently rearrange him into a more comfortable position.

"Come on, boss—say something. Anything. This is no time for one of your pranks."

Bridget fought the ever-tightening strands of terror working to fasten themselves to her mind. She remembered enough of her high school health classes to know it was dangerous to move any accident victim. But Knight had landed in such an awkward heap, his face buried against the ground under his own weight, that if she did not at least straighten him out it was possible he might suffocate before anything else could happen to him. The young woman did so slowly, taking care not to unduly jostle his neck or spine. She took great care also while checking his arms and legs for possible breaks, watching his face as she gently ran her hands over each limb as well as his rib cage.

The professor's expression did not change as she did so, showing no indication that he was in any localized pain that might indicate a break or even a fracture. His assistant considered that a fortunate turn of events but struggled with what she might do next. The young woman had felt Knight's chest, put her ear to his nostrils. She knew he was breathing regularly. Raising his eyelids, she said a silent prayer of thanks as she noted that his eyes had not rolled upward into his head.

He's alive, she told herself, making a checklist both to keep herself calm and to see if by doing so she might think of anything else useful to which she could be attending. *He's breathing. He's not broken, or at least, if he is he's not broken severely. His pulse is steady. And his clothing and skin don't seem to be burned very badly, either.* Staring for a moment, she then asked aloud;

"Are you in shock?"

Taking one of Knight's hands, she rubbed it vigorously, doing her best to warm it, to try to force the unconscious man's mind to react to stimulation. After she began to feel his flesh heating, she took his other hand, then did the same with it.

"Come on, Professor," she whispered, talking as she rubbed, words spilling out of her, hoping to both reach some part of Knight's mind as well as bolster her own failing nerves. "It's dark and it's cold and for all I know that thunder and lightning are going to be followed by rain. Rain and more ghosts and then what? The walking dead? Mummies? Vampires?" Having said the last bit in jest, Bridget suddenly blinked hard, exclaiming loudly;

"Jesus, coffins everywhere. You maniac, did you really *have* to bring me to a cemetery for this?"

"Well . . . ," Knight suddenly responded, the single word almost lost in a hacking cough, his voice weak and distant, "it did . . . seem like a good idea . . . at the time."

Bridget let out a cry of sheer delight, squeezing the professor's fingers so sharply his eyes opened as he yelped in pain. Letting the hand she had been rubbing drop to his chest, she grabbed him in an awkward rush and hugged him to herself, shouting as she did;

"You're alive—you're all right!"

"Listen to me. . . ." Knight's voice came to her as if through a tunnel, the tone of it hollow and distant. "I believe myself to be essentially unharmed—"

"Oh, thank God—"

The professor waved one hand feebly, cutting Bridget off. His voice reduced to a hiss, he told her;

"I appreciate the concern . . . but I'm not certain how long I may be able to remain conscious. I think . . . at the very least, it is probably best we get ourselves back, back into my car."

Gasping down a lungful of air, Knight whispered the answer to which pocket held his keys, then threw all the effort he could muster into forcing himself up and off the ground. Even with Bridget's help he did not have an easy time regaining his footing. Leaning on his assistant, he struggled to stay upright as the two of them made their way back to his car. As they neared his vehicle, the professor whispered;

"You can drive—yes?"

"Everyone outside New York City can drive," Bridget assured him. Propping him against the passenger side of the car, she held

Knight upright with one hand while getting the front door open with the other. After that she helped the professor slide into the front seat, managed to get him safely strapped into place, then closed his door, ran around to the other side, and did the same for herself. Once behind the wheel, she quickly familiarized herself with his controls, finding the lights, locking the doors, getting the heater turned on, and so forth.

"Good," Knight mumbled absently. "Good. Oh, and . . . one more thing . . ."

Bridget waited for Knight to complete his thought. When he did not, she glanced over to find him gently snoring. Knowing he could not be allowed to sleep in his condition, the redhead tugged at his arm, first gently, then with force. When he swam back to consciousness for a moment, she snapped;

"Professor, you can't go to sleep. You know that. You have to stay awake—right?" When Knight agreed with her assessment, his assistant asked him;

"All right, then. Now, think back. Just before you passed out, you said there was one more thing you wanted to say—do you remember what that was?"

"Yes, I do. Thank you for reminding me." The professor swallowed hard, coughing once more as he did so. Finding his voice with a minimum of effort, he fixed Bridget with as focused a stare as he could manage, then told her sharply;

"No hospital . . . no doctors."

The redhead immediately questioned him on the point, but Knight put her off, promising to explain once he had recovered. So pitifully weak were his responses, the young woman had no choice but to stop arguing the point—at least for the moment.

Deciding the most important thing would be to get the professor to his home and make him comfortable, the young woman finally put the car into drive and began moving forward. As she did so, however, it finally dawned on the redhead that she had been ignoring the big picture to focus on the details. Yes, of course, she admitted to herself, making certain the professor was alive, that he could be moved, et cetera, was certainly important. But, she had so focused on his condition she had momentarily forgotten what exactly it had been that had forced that condition upon him.

Yes, she told herself, *there's the little matter of your shining playmate, and then thunder and lightning out of a clear sky. Oh, yes sir, Professor Knight—*

Unfortunately, most of her mind had to continue to pay attention to the immediate. She needed to keep Knight conscious, not only because keeping his brain active would greatly increase his chances of making a full recovery but also because she did not even know how to drive back to the sprawling cemetery's main gatehouse without directions from him, let alone all the way back to wherever in the "greatest city in the world" his home was located.

I'm going to get you home in one piece, she thought, *yes indeed. We're going to make it, all the way, safe and sound. And then, if you think you've done some explaining already, mister, you ain't 'splained nuthin' yet.*

Questioning Knight as to which way to turn at an intersection, Bridget threw all her focus into not only keeping her boss awake and functioning but also driving without running off the ill-lit road or hitting anything. And, as she did, on the now-forgotten hilltop behind them, strands of shattered energy began to pull themselves together once more.

CHAPTER TWENTY-FIVE

Professor Piers Knight proved to be a great deal heavier than his assistant would have thought possible. The drive from Green-Wood to his home had not proved terribly difficult for the young woman. Somehow the professor had managed to both keep himself conscious and give Bridget understandable directions. On top of that, the traffic had been unexplainably light for so early in the evening. Having heard horror stories of the highway nightmares that routinely snarled the streets of New York City, remembering all too well the soul-draining purgatory that was the Chicago City Loop, the redhead had been greatly relieved to only have to find her way through a strange city, in the dark, forcing her passenger to stay awake long enough to give her directions.

Once they arrived at her passenger's brownstone, however, all the energy seemed to simply drain out of the man. To her credit, this did not cause Bridget to panic. She believed she understood what had happened. Knight had marshaled his strength, forced his body to keep going by telling himself all he had to do was stay awake long enough to make it to his home. He had given himself a task, then thrown every ounce of will he had behind the singular idea of getting it done. Once he had accomplished this one stated task, however, his body had then shut down.

Bridget likened his feat to pulling an all-nighter. She had seen it happen plenty of times—students promising themselves they could sleep only after they studied for twenty or thirty straight hours and then took the exam for which they had been studying. She remembered classmates doing such on a regular basis, hurling all their effort into making it through to the point where they completed their test. Some even garnered high marks doing such, but they also often ended up falling asleep in their classroom at the end of the exam.

"All right, Professor," Bridget said, staring down at him through the passenger-side window of his car once she had it safely stored within his garage, "I guess we have to do this the hard way."

Intelligently, Bridget first went through Knight's home from the garage to the living room, opening all the doors and turning on all the lights. Returning to the garage, she managed without a great deal of difficulty to open his door without letting him slide out and onto the floor. Getting an arm under his shoulder, she then hoisted him out of the car and began the exhausting procedure of half-dragging, half-carrying him to his living room.

Bridget Elkins was a tall, strong young woman. She exercised, ate a proper diet, and worked hard to stay fit. When she first began tugging on Knight to remove him from the front seat, the redhead had not anticipated getting him inside to be that great a production. As she attempted to lift the professor out of the car, however, she found him almost impossibly heavy.

"Jesus, Knight," she cursed, struggling to get the man upright, "you got rocks in your pockets?"

Up the trio of steps out of the garage, into the kitchen, down the hallway, with each step the professor seemed to grow heavier. By the time she reached the doorway to his living room, Bridget was more dragging him along than carrying him, his feet catching the hallway's long throw rug as they moved. Bunching around his feet, the rug began slowing them down even further. Worse, it threatened to overturn the hallway's small, three-legged half-circle area table. Bridget caught the disaster in the making just in time, seconds before the stand's display of carved stone pieces was sent hurtling to the floor.

"You know," growled Bridget, perspiration dripping down her forehead by this point, "maybe you've got too much 'dust-collecting junk' in this house, after all."

Kicking the professor's feet free from their entanglement, Bridget threw all her remaining strength into lifting her burden up and over the bunched rug and then hurriedly dragging him into the living room. Unable to lower Knight to the couch, she instead simply fell with him, pushing the professor's unconscious body onto the piece of furniture while she came to rest on the floor next to it. Seeing that she had managed to drop him on his back rather than his face, Bridget considered her struggles a job well done and simply collapsed next to the couch, not interested in anything else at that moment other than catching her breath.

After only a few minutes she got herself up onto her knees so she might check on Knight's condition. The redhead did not know exactly what she could do for the professor, but she did decide not to try to second-guess him. He was completely unconscious at that point, and Bridget could see no amount of slapping or shouting was going to awaken him once more. Yes, she knew to allow him to remain unconscious was dangerous, but he was the one who had insisted she not take him to a hospital, not call any doctors.

All right, fine, she thought. As she stared down at her patient, her brow wrinkled with concern as she asked herself, *Hell, maybe you're right. Nothing else about you makes sense—why not this? Even so, where exactly does that leave me?*

Placing her hand to Knight's forehead, she checked to see if he felt warm. As best she could tell, he had no fever. As she bent low to listen to his breathing, that seemed regular to the young woman as well. Looking his face and hands over in the light, she saw that what burns he had sustained were superficial. His clothing seemed to have suffered the effects of the oddly singular lightning bolt far more than he had himself.

Lightning, she wondered, *as if everything else we've been through wasn't enough. Worse yet, I don't know if that bolt was just a coincidence, or another attack on him, or . . . maybe it was his way of getting rid of the ghost.*

Knowing she had no way of solving such questions on her own, Bridget decided all she could do at that point was attempt to make the professor more comfortable. Setting about to do what she could in that department, she first got a pillow under his head, then removed his shoes. Thinking it could not hurt, she then removed his socks as well. Next she loosened his tie, then decided she might as well take it off completely and unfasten the top couple of buttons of his shirt as well. As she did, something caught her eye that caused her to undo a third button, and then a fourth. And a fifth.

"Oh my God . . ."

Pulling Knight's shirt free from his pants, she stared in a sort of fascinated horror at his chest. It was decorated with several quite terrible scars, ones so ragged and vicious the young woman could not imagine what might have caused them. The one she first noticed, the worst of them by far, was a monstrous gash that ran from his right shoulder diagonally down across his chest to finally disappear behind the left-hand side of his waistband. It was accompanied by two others—ones running parallel down either side of the first. Both of these were minor in comparison, but taken together with the central one they created a picture of an injury so devastating it was a wonder Knight could have possibly survived it.

Shutting her eyes against the sight, feeling herself beginning to tremble once more, Bridget pulled the edges of the professor's shirt-front together and rebuttoned several of the buttons, no longer capable of confronting the hideous image. Afterward, realizing there was nothing else she could do for Knight at that moment, she decided to see what she might possibly be able to do for herself.

Returning to the upstairs room where her suitcase still remained open on the bed, Bridget moved to the large mirror attached to the dresser to make an assessment of her own condition. The young woman was more than a little stunned by what her reflection had waiting for her. Her hair was in complete disarray, her carefully piled do from the morning now a hanging mass of pins and wild strands. Her makeup was badly smeared.

Worse was the condition of her outfit.

Struggling to carry Knight had left her jacket and blouse horribly wrinkled. Her constricting pencil skirt looked as if it might be completely ruined. The streaks of mud along her thighs were one thing, possibly not so bad. But, the darkly ground-in grass stains at her knees looked as if they might be permanent. Her panty hose had somehow been practically shredded.

Then suddenly Bridget realized she was not wearing her shoes. How long had she been without them, she wondered. Where had they been lost? Were they somewhere in the grass of the cemetery? Resting on the floor of Knight's car? Kicked off somewhere within his house? It troubled the young woman that she could not remember taking them off or losing them—that she might have driven the professor's car barefoot without even realizing it.

Oh well, she told herself, slipping out of her jacket. *I'm not going to worry about any of this now. It's just not worth it. What I am going to do is take a nice hot shower and just maybe even, once the water gets good and hot, let myself have a nice long cry.*

The tears starting flowing down Bridget's face before she had managed to finish undressing. They did not stop throughout her shower, or even after she turned out the lights and slid under the covers of Knight's guest room bed.

CHAPTER TWENTY-SIX

Professor Piers Knight woke in the morning with more than a touch of reluctance. His entire body was a throbbing mass of pain. His eyes hurt too severely for him to actually dare to go ahead and open them. His teeth ached. And for some reason he could not comprehend in the least, his tongue itched. As his conscious mind shrugged, laboring to pull itself together, however, the questions it began enumerating forced him to begin searching his slightly damaged memory for answers.

Where are we? it wanted to know first and foremost. *Feels like home—smells right. But how did we get here? And from where? Where was I? Oh, damn all the fools who plague me so, what's gone and happened to me now?* And then, less self-centeredly, his brain inquired;

And where's Bridget? Is she all right?

And with that last thought the professor's eyes came open sharply despite his reservations over allowing them to do so. Their opening proved to be every bit as painful as Knight had expected.

The touch of light that entered seemed to burn them, forcing him to both cry out and close them once more immediately. As he gasped in shock, he found his hands reaching out in opposite directions, desperately searching for handholds as a stabbing dizziness sent his head crashing back toward his couch. Through the throbbing agony, however, still his mind questioned him: Where was his assistant? What had happened to them both? Could he have possibly allowed her to come to harm?

Oh, what have you done now, you great, bloody idiot?

As his hands came in contact with his couch, Knight concentrated all his energy into one burst, pushing with all the strength he could muster so as to force his body into an upright position. Once up, he braced himself with both arms, hanging on by digging his fingers into the fabric of his sofa to keep from backsliding. The effort from the ascent as well as the effort spent in staying vertical left the professor gasping in pain. Blinking, trying to both reopen his eyes as well as fight through the various gnawing pangs still stabbing at him, he shook his head slightly, demanding answers from himself.

Oh yes . . .

As information began pouring into a section of his brain where he could actually make use of it, the professor realized where he was, began remembering what had happened to himself and Bridget. Assuming that if he was on his couch, in his own living room, things must be at least secure for the moment, he paused to take stock of his situation. Pulling down a deep breath, Knight made himself stand up, to see if he could do so, if nothing else. Upon making it to an upright position without having to hold on to anything, he commented;

"Well, that's something, anyway."

Slowly, making certain to attempt no sudden moves, the professor began bending his various joints a few at a time—knuckles, elbows, wrists, knees—checking them for further small agonies as well as flexibility. Twisting his neck, rolling his shoulders, swiveling his hips, he found all the movements more or less painful, but he also noted that his suffering was receding with each new set of motions. After only several minutes, he sat back down on his couch, reasonably confident that he had sustained no breaks, fractures, or sprains the evening before.

Taking a deep breath, he held it down for a long moment, then exhaled it harshly. Repeating the procedure several times, feeling himself stabilizing further with each breath, the professor believed himself strong enough to risk a small shout.

"Bridget?"

When no response was forthcoming, Knight scratched at his head. He was positive his mind had gathered all the facts of the evening previous for him. The specter had merged with him, they were struck by lightning, Bridget had helped him to the car, got them both home—

But then he realized that much—and no more—was all he actually remembered. Her pulling the car into the garage, shutting the door. That was it. How he had gotten inside his home after that, onto the couch, shoes and tie removed, shirt open but jacket still on—had his assistant managed all that? And if she did, where was she? Still asleep, perhaps?

The professor's head turned to check the time. The daylight streaming through the windows had already alerted him to the fact that he had slept at least the night away. Focusing on his longcase clock standing in the corner, he saw that the time was nearly ten thirty. Staring at the five metal human figures mounted on the timepiece's crown, he asked them;

"Fine, it's still morning—but *which* morning?"

"It's only Thursday, Professor." Turning suddenly, Knight found his assistant standing in the doorway leading to the kitchen. Scratching his head once more, he asked;

"Oh, hello, didn't you hear me call you?"

"I did. Didn't you hear me answer?" The professor thought for a moment, then said;

"No, I guess I didn't. Appears I'm not as recovered as I thought I was. What about you, though? Are you all right?"

"I'm fine," the redhead said in a voice warm with assurance. "But then, why shouldn't I be? After all, you're the one that was struck by lightning."

"Yes, I hate when that happens. Don't you?"

"Haven't had the experience yet," answered Bridget, wondering if Knight was teasing her or not. "I'll let you know, though. Until then, why don't you tell me how *you're* doing?"

"All in all, I believe I'm fit enough. Although I don't remember anything after your managing to get us to the garage."

Sitting down in an overstuffed chair across from the couch, Bridget filled in the remaining blanks in Knight's memory. Once she had covered her struggles in getting the professor onto his couch, she told him;

"After that, it was a shower and beddie-bye for me. And I slept very well, too, thank you very much. After that, I got up, came down to the kitchen, rummaged around for a few odds and ends, and put a pot of soup on. You had a half a chicken and enough vegetables to make something that should, at the very least, not do you any harm. My mother made soups like this for everything from colds and scraped elbows to broken hearts."

"And did they help?"

"Every single time," she told him, wearing a grin that dared him to contradict her. Knowing women at least well enough to see the foolishness in such an action, Knight made a show of sniffing at his underarm, then offered;

"Well, why don't I drag my aching carcass upstairs, take a much-needed, very hot shower, dress in something less wrinkled than my current ensemble, and then come back down to try your version of your mother's soup?"

"That sounds good," answered Bridget. "Then, while you're warming your throat and making yourself feel wonderful all over, you can tell me how one makes it thunder and lightning out of a clear sky."

"All right. . . ."

"And how one does so without getting any rain, or any more thunder or lightning for that matter."

"Good idea. . . ."

"And—"

"Yes," snapped Knight, wishing he had some right to be annoyed. Knowing he had none whatsoever, however, he surrendered to the inevitable, saying, "And we'll have a little impromptu seminar on ghosts and the spirit world as well."

"Enjoy your shower, Professor."

Knight grumbled to himself about the unfairness of life throughout his entire trip upstairs and even through most of his shower.

CHAPTER TWENTY-SEVEN

"You know," said Knight, staring at his soupspoon, his tone that of one imparting the wisdom of the ages, "this concoction of yours isn't half-bad."

"Oh my," answered his assistant with mock humility. "It's ever so kind of you to say so, good sir." Bridget, elbows on the kitchen table, threaded her fingers, then rested her chin upon them. Batting her eyes at the professor for comic effect, she then switched to an outrageous southern accent as she added;

"How you do go on. Why, I do declare, you'll turn my head, Piers Knight."

"That's 'Professor' Knight to you."

"Yeah, whatever," answered his assistant in her regular voice. As the professor went back to his soup, Bridget continued, telling him, "Okay now, spill it. Just what the hell was that we went through last night? As opposed to all the other hells we've been through since I got to this crazy town."

"Not enjoying the marvelous diversity which is New York City, are we?"

"Let's just say it's not shaping up the way it was described in the guidebooks. Oh, and for the record, what I saw last night seemed a lot closer to *The X-Files* than to any Homeland Security project." Assuming a more comfortable pose, Bridget took a spoonful from her own soup bowl, then said;

"Listen, I'm trying to keep it together here—do you understand me? What I'm saying? I am just ten inches from losing it. Big-time. This morning, I have to ask myself, gee-whiz, what bit of information from the common-knowledge lexicon are we going to throw out today? I've already lost Sir Isaac Newton and the Amazing Randi as experts-one-can-trust—who gets thrown on the dustheap of history next? Mendeleev? Adam Smith? I am, literally, afraid to ask."

Knight raised a hand, conceding defeat. Giving his assistant what he hoped was a sincere look, he asked;

"Have I denied you any information so far?"

"No, but that's not my point. Don't you get it? My world is shattering here. Half the time I think you're telling me the truth, which is all that's keeping me sane. But then, you start feeding me qualifiers, 'was I flying or floating,' talking about national security, like you're misleading me, maybe covering your tracks, trying to protect yourself—"

"Bridget, I . . ."

"I need to trust you, and if, how can I, if you don't trust me, I mean . . . I just, I have—"

As Bridget's breathing began to come in more rapid bursts and her words started to slur as she jumbled them one against the other, the professor raised his hand once more, begging her to halt before she did herself injury.

"Ha-ha, very funny."

"Not terribly amusing, I admit," he told her, "but perhaps necessary to capture your attention. Now please, calm yourself. Trust me, you *are* handling things, and very well I might add. I've seen others, over the years, who would have been screaming in the night by this point."

"Try me around bedtime," she told him sourly.

"Touché," Knight responded, half-smiling as he did so. Sitting back in his chair for a moment, he admitted, "Listen to me: You are a much stronger person than you realize. You have come through everything that has happened to us both so far with admirable fortitude. In all honesty, I don't know anyone else who could have done as well."

"Please," snapped Bridget, feeling she was being patronized, "you have to know plenty of others who do what you do. You must all have some secret club where you confer, converse, and otherwise hobnob with your brother wizards—"

"Did you just quote *The Wizard of Oz* at me?"

Bridget blushed, then started to giggle. Giving his assistant an exasperated look, Knight forced himself to swallow another spoonful of soup. Appreciating its healing warmth, he commented on how much better it was making his throat feel, then got back to the more serious matter at hand.

"As I was saying, you, Ms. Bridget Elkins of Wolfbend, Montana, you are indeed handling things well. I'm not trying to tell you that you haven't gone through a great deal, or that it hasn't taken its toll. What I'm telling you is that—"

The redhead's eyes stared intently as Knight suddenly stopped talking. He did not appear to her as if he were having any sort of medical problem, a flash of pain, beginnings of a stroke, headache, et cetera. No, to the young woman he looked like a man considering something. As his gaze met hers, as they both probed each other, searching each other's eyes for answers, Bridget could tell the professor was on the verge of making some monumental decision. When he blinked she knew whatever problem he had been looking to resolve, he had found his answer. Taking one more spoonful of soup, he said;

"Sorry for the delay. I . . . I wonder, do you have any idea how much I trust you?"

"Ah, I assume, like a great deal, and me without a security clearance or anything. I mean, I hadn't really thought about it—"

"I'm sure you didn't. It's the kind of thing truly honest people don't concern themselves with." Letting his spoon slide into his bowl, Knight moved his left hand across the table to take Bridget's right. Holding it gently, wanting there to be contact between them as he spoke, needing their auras to mingle at least slightly so the back of her mind would be positive he was telling her the truth, he explained to her gently;

"I trust you a great deal, probably far more than you realize. You're thinking I'm merely talking on such matters like the flying, the ring I told you about, the Disc of the Winds, magic use in general. But trust me, dear Bridget, it goes far beyond that." As the redhead nodded unconsciously, Knight continued, telling her;

"I didn't worry about letting you sleep here. In this suspicious and litigious age, that's something—especially after your little 'boundary-setting' speech. You think me telling you about my use of magic is a big deal, my dear, let me remind you, young lady, I let you drive my car. You think about that for a moment."

Bridget lowered her head in response, her wide mouth breaking into a smile she was desperate to keep from erupting into uncontrollable giggles. As the professor looked at her inquiringly, she told him;

"I'm sorry, but every time you start to seem the least bit sexy, you say something that sounds like my dad."

"Oh, you are a cheeky monkey, aren't you?"

The two made slight conversation for a moment, both of them putting some effort toward downing a bit more of their soup while it was still at least somewhat warm. After a half-dozen rapid spoonfuls, Knight wiped his mouth with the napkin his assistant had set out for him. Replacing it on the table, he then told her;

"As for last night's unusual weather, I don't have any kind of explanation for that outside of, yes, as I'm certain you've been suspecting, its creation was most certainly magical in nature. It not only came on too swiftly, but I could feel the residue of dark bindings running all through the bolt when it struck me."

"But," asked Bridget, "what was it all about? If you're saying it was sent, then who sent it? Why were you struck?"

"Good questions all, and I will be looking into them," the professor assured her. "I can tell you this much: I felt something of the same directional threads leading off from this attack as I did those in the basement of the police station and the museum lobby."

When the young woman asked if that meant all the attacks were coming from the same source, Knight explained that the sources of the attacks were different, but the guiding force behind them was the same. Then he told her;

"What you may not understand, however, is that last night, the lightning bolt wasn't meant for me."

"They were after me?" Bridget gasped as she spoke, unable to imagine why anyone would do such a thing. Before her fear response could run away with her imagination, however, the professor raised his hand, telling her;

"No, the bolt wasn't meant for you, either. There was another presence there last night, if you remember." The redhead's eyes went wide as she whispered;

"The spirit? Someone wanted to zap the ghost? Why?"

"Because he was trying to tell me something."

" 'He'?" Bridget questioned the single word, her eyes narrowing. "Why are you suddenly calling what we saw last night a he?"

"Because, my dear, what you saw last night was the essence of the recently departed Detective Sergeant Dollins. And if I am correct, he has something very important to tell us."

CHAPTER TWENTY-EIGHT

Much to Bridget's intense frustration, the professor could make no speculations as to what the specter of Detective Dollins might have been trying to tell him the night before. Nor did he have any concrete ideas at that moment on how to find out, either. As he explained to her, no longer attempting to guide Bridget down any misleading pathways such as Homeland Security issues;

"I might know various bits about magic and the supernatural and the lot, but apparitions and their motives have always stayed a bit beyond me."

Electricity, however, the professor knew quite well. As they finished their soup, Knight explained to his assistant what an extremely effective tool it was for reducing ectoplasmic energy to nothing more than a flurry of noncohesive atoms. Even if Dollins' spirit somehow survived the blast, the professor assured Bridget, it would still take the thing quite some time to reassemble itself.

Not that either of them could worry about such matters

right then. It was Thursday, which meant it was a workday, which meant both of them were expected at the museum—were already late, in fact. Swallowing the last of the broth in his bowl, Knight replaced the faded piece of china on the table as he said;

"Well, of course, if you'd like to play a bit of hookey, I am the boss, well . . . as far as you're concerned, anyway. I think you would certainly be justified in lounging about for a day. Or if you wanted to take the time to finally connect with your sorority sister, get settled in out there in Queens—"

The professor looked to Bridget for an answer and was surprised to find her smiling. Wondering what she might have to grin over, outside of the fact that like any chef she could simply be pleased to see he had finished his soup, he asked the reason for her good cheer. Her eyes filled with a sudden mischief, she told him;

"I'm not so certain Queens is the best place for me this summer. Someone once told me it was 'lumpy.' "

"Did they now?"

"Oh yes," she continued, adding, "how did they describe it now?. . . . Oh, I remember, they said it was 'only good for taking up the overflow.' "

"Not very kind of them. Perhaps even a bit condescending, if you think about it."

Knight's voice had gone soft as he replied to the young woman. He understood what was happening between them, knew what his assistant wanted—realized why she was having the difficulty she was in asking for it. As the silence in the kitchen began to shift slightly from the type that is restful to that which is uneasy, he swept aside the growing awkwardness, saying;

"You know, this was rather a good pot of soup."

"Why, thank you."

"Well, and you're welcome, certainly. But, I was actually going somewhere with that. You see, it's just that, being a stuffy old bachelor, I've kind of grown out of the habit of having anyone else around. This was rather a delightful change of pace, and so . . . I was just wondering. . . ."

"Yes . . . ?"

"I've been reflecting, as it were, I mean . . ." Making his voice as light as possible, Knight spread a bit more than his usual half smile across his face, then continued, saying, "With you privy to so many of my secrets now, that perhaps I should be keeping a closer eye on you."

"Sir . . . ?"

"You'll forgive me," the professor said, hoping he was making his true intentions clear. "I feel a little awkward asking this, and I certainly wouldn't want to appear forward, or in any way improper—" Unable to contain herself, Bridget cut Knight off, blurting;

"Please let me stay!"

The professor sat quietly on his side of the kitchen table, elbows planted firmly, hands held before his face, suddenly not quite knowing what to say next. Knight felt a certain embarrassment, for he had been building up to asking the young woman if she would like to stay. He thought that was what she had been leading toward, thought he knew why she wanted to do so, and had been trying to make such easier for her. Bridget's unexpected outburst, however, not only caught him completely off-guard but left him a trifle flustered as well. Before he could regain his composure, the redhead added;

"I'm sorry, but I'm just so scared. All I can think is that I don't know what's happening to me—to us. And that you don't know what's happening to us. And if you don't know . . ."

"Well, it's not like—"

"Professor, please—if any of these crazy things come after me,

I'm finished. I don't want to be gunned down or burned to death or blown up or struck by lightning. And going to Queens isn't going to make me safe. Running back home to Montana isn't going to make me safe."

"The way things have been going," the professor reminded his assistant, "I'm not so certain you're all that safe around me, either. And please, I don't say that to dissuade you, but to remind you that, as you said, I really don't have any idea as to what it is that's been happening around us."

"I know all of that," answered Bridget softly, her tone trembling. Looking at her, staring into the clearly frightened green eyes staring into his own, Knight felt his heart crumbling. He could not turn the young woman away, for no other reason than she was most likely completely correct in her assessment of the situation.

"And . . . I don't care."

Rapidly the professor turned the recent rash of events over in his mind. There was no question that he did not know what was going on. Or, for that matter, why it was happening, either. For all he knew, the very second young Bridget Elkins got too far away from him, some other doorway from beyond would open and launch forth some new entity to ensnare his helpless assistant, simply because whatever was going on behind that door, the progenitors of it felt destroying her could help their cause. A part of his brain asked him, and not very subtly, if he was willing to take her in simply because he liked her full figure and long legs. Growling at himself, he made the cynical side of his nature aware that he intended to offer her what sanctuary he could in *spite* of her many pleasing attributes.

"I know it's an imposition. But I just know I'm not going to feel safe anywhere else." As she spoke more rapidly with each word, tears began to roll down Bridget's face while she sobbed, "It's like I'm losing my mind. When I look in the mirror, I'm not certain who it is I'm seeing there. Every shadow, in corners, passing the window, I, I—"

"It's all right, my dear. . . ."

"And I promise, I won't ask another embarrassing question. I don't care why you didn't want a doctor to see you, or why you have giant scars running across your chest, or—"

And then, the professor put a finger of one hand to his lips while he took one of hers in his other, squeezing it gently.

"As for my aversion to doctors, the bodies of those who store magical energies tend to throw off the readings of medical instruments. Everything from MRIs to simple blood-pressure machines, none of them seem normal, and questions begin to mount up which can't be answered. I knew my body would repair itself, but I, well, I was too frazzled at the moment to explain that to you. The lightning and all." Sensing that his assistant was almost calm, he began again;

"And, as for the scars—"

Before he could even really begin his second explanation, Bridget suddenly began crying in earnest, sobbing harder the more Knight tried to comfort her. They both then began apologizing to each other, her for breaking down so completely, him for knowing nothing about how to treat women. Talking over each other, they blurted;

"I think you know something about women, but me—"

"I wish I could somehow reverse all this. I'm so sorry that—"

"You don't have anything to apologize for—"

And then suddenly the professor and his assistant stopped talking and stared at each other for an instant. Hearing what each other had been saying, the pair started chuckling over how foolish they sounded. Handing the redhead a paper napkin from the dispenser on the table, Knight commented;

"Modern life really has screwed up just about everything,

hasn't it?" Bridget merely nodded, doing what she could to dry her face. As she did, the professor said;

"Very well, as far as your friend in Queens, or your family, for that matter, is concerned, my housekeeper left me two months ago to get married. My home is a mess; my pantry is bare. I've been living on canned beans and spaghetti and will soon forget to bathe without supervision. For taking care of me you get free room and board close to the museum, as well as a ride to and from work every day. Is that enough of a story to placate all parties?"

"I would think so," answered Bridget, smiling brightly as she gathered up their bowls, spoons, and used napkins. Running the hot water in the sink, she tossed the refuse in a nearby container Knight kept there for that purpose, then started cleaning their dishes. She was about to thank the professor further, not only for his generosity but also for understanding her feelings, when she noted that he suddenly appeared to be transfixed, as if listening for some faraway sound. As she finished the dishes, Knight announced;

"Well, if you're thinking you want to be where I am, then you'd better get ready to head into the museum."

"What is it," she asked. Drying her hands on the oversized T-shirt in which she had slept, she added, "You seemed so far away for a moment there."

"I was," answered Knight. "I finally heard something in the minds of one of the bozos worth hearing." When his assistant inquired as to what that might be, the professor told her;

"I overheard a phone conversation Mr. Klein was having with one of his underlings. Dr. Ungari's plane has just landed at JFK Airport. Ungari and Bakur are in New York City."

"Okay," answered Bridget, her tone suddenly bright, "guess I better get cleaned up. After all, I'd hate to have less than perfect makeup for my third day in the greatest city in the world. I mean, God only knows what's going to happen today."

Watching Bridget leave the kitchen, Knight nodded his head unconsciously, telling her, "Indeed, God only knows."

And, he thought, frowning as he did so, *as usual, the bastard is keeping the information to himself.*

CHAPTER TWENTY-NINE

Knight had been inside the museum for no more than twenty minutes when Martin Klein walked into his office unannounced. Of course, since the professor could still hear the agent's thoughts, he was in no way surprised by the FBI man's arrival. Indeed, it pleased Knight to act as if Klein's sudden appearance there were the most natural thing in the world, as if he were merely a delivery boy from the corner deli, bringing the professor a coffee the way he did every morning. Looking to get some sort of reaction out of Knight, the agent said;

"Ungari is on his way here."

"But we knew that," the professor answered, not actually looking up from his paperwork, "didn't we?"

"I don't mean he's still heading to America, Knight. I mean he's here, in New York, and headed for the museum."

"Oh well," responded the professor matter-of-factly, "that seems logical." Setting aside the report in which he had been pretending to have a deep interest, Knight finally looked up at the FBI man, telling him;

"His entire reason for leaving Syria in the first place was to come to the museum, to examine the Dream Stone—correct? Well, and to visit with his old friend, of course, namely myself. So, I don't understand the fuss. I mean, why in heavens wouldn't he head straight here?"

"Fine." Klein spat the single word. Taking pity on the FBI man, the curator told him;

"Listen, I do understand that you are, trite as the cliché might sound, simply doing your job. And given the circumstances and all the, well, all the crazy shit, for lack of a better phrase, that has been going on around here, it's probably for the best that we have you here to do your job."

Klein stared at the professor for a long moment, not certain what to make of his last little speech. The agent's surface instinct was to feel a measured amount of relief, his ability to hope flooding him with the suggestion that he might finally be able to relax a bit around this impossible character cruel Fate had introduced into his life. Knight, or at least the man's antics, had been twisting the FBI agent's guts in continual knots. His stomach's acid content had escalated dramatically since the museum assignment had started, and his stress levels along with it. He had not been sleeping well, either.

"Professor," he said after a cautious moment's pause, "I would so greatly love to believe that's how you really feel."

"Oh, you can," answered Knight, allowing his tone to flood with sincerity. With his being in such close proximity with the agent after melding their minds, Klein's every thought came to the curator with echoing clarity. Until the mixture the professor had slipped into the water at the meeting the day before wore off, it would be impossible for the man to hide the slightest idea or feeling from Knight.

Thus it was that he now knew for certain the FBI man was seriously attempting to do a job he believed in, without any real animosity or suspicion aimed at Knight himself—excepting, of course, for that which he deserved for having acted as he had toward the man.

There you go, he thought, *getting yourself in trouble once again because you think you're so clever.* Feeling a marked level of genuine sympathy for Klein at that moment, the professor told him quietly;

"I suppose I should actually render unto you an apology. I've displayed some of the classic arrogance of the ivory-towered academic toward you, I'm afraid. And for no good reason. You really do believe this Morand person might be a threat, and I have no proof to the otherwise."

Klein simply continued to stare at the curator. The agent greatly wanted to believe what he was hearing. He possessed a sharp set of instincts for sizing people up, for knowing when they were telling the truth or simply some portion of it with which they wished to distract. Knight had proved to be such a troublesome enigma so far, however, even with his usually reliable judgment telling him the professor was finally dealing with him squarely, still the agent found a segment of his mind urging him to caution simply because Knight had proved to be so adept at jerking him around. Giving in to his hopes, he answered;

"I don't necessarily believe Bakur, and I use the name he wishes people to believe is his because I don't want to encourage any slipup—"

"Of course."

"I don't believe Bakur is plotting against the museum, or that he's up to anything specific at the moment. It's simply my job to watch such characters. And when they're connected to cases like this one, explosions in public forums, mysterious fires in government facilities . . ." The agent spread his hands wide in a plaintive gesture, hoping to encourage more cooperative remarks from the professor. Knight obliged him, answering;

"No, I completely understand. I do. And I understand that I haven't been much help, either. All I can say in my defense is that I'm very protective of my museum, and . . . well, no man likes to admit such, but—"

"But," filled in Klein, suddenly feeling a certain sympathy toward the curator, "it's kind of rattling to be around dead bodies and people shooting at each other, and explosions, and being forced to run from burning buildings—all in a very short period of time? If that's where you were going, don't worry about it. I've been trained for such eventualities, and I think I'd be a bit off my feed if I'd gone through everything you have in the past couple of days, myself."

Damn, thought Knight, the side of his mouth curling into a smile, *I think I'm going to have to like this fellow. Well, there goes my standing with all the liberals on the board.* The professor felt his smile spreading across his entire face as a voice from the back of his mind added;

Which means, of course, there goes your standing with the entire *board.* Extending his hand across his desk, Knight looked the FBI man squarely in the eye, then asked;

"Do you think we might start back at the beginning, with you being pretty much the same person you have been since you arrived, and me attempting to be . . . well, shall we say, more of a grown-up?" Taking Knight's hand, Klein answered;

"At this moment, nothing would please me better, sir."

The two men shook hands, both relaxing as contact with each other told them all their senses could comfortably absorb. Both were possessed of strong defensive shields and impressive skills when it came to analyzing the motives of others. Both of them were men hard put-upon when it came to trusting new people. They had reached that instance with one another where a decision had to be made one way or the other, though, and both were relieved to finally have found a point where they could be comfortable in the other's presence.

As they released each other's hand, the phone on Knight's desk rang. Excusing himself, the professor answered his call. He did so quickly, giving instructions to have someone escorted to his office. Replacing his handheld phone in its charger, he looked up at Klein, then said;

"As I'm certain you've deduced, it seems I have visitors. Care to guess who?"

"Ungari and Bakur have arrived, I take it?"

"And will be here in a matter of minutes." The FBI man nodded to Knight, then, finally cracking a smile of his own, said;

"Okay then—I guess it's showtime."

CHAPTER THIRTY

"Dr. Ashur Ungari," said Knight in his most formal voice, "may I introduce Mr. Martin Klein. Marty is the museum's newly appointed liaison to the outside world in all matters governmental."

"Pleased, I am most certain," said the doctor, taking the FBI man's hand. "And while we are making with introductions, might I introduce my own governmental attaché, Hamid Bakur." While the thinner, shorter man who had arrived with Ungari moved forward to shake hands with both Knight and Klein, the doctor expounded further, adding;

"Hamid is working with me as my assistant, and also as my official contact with the Syrian government—given to me by the Syrian government."

A natural actor, the FBI man betrayed no reaction when Ungari so casually announced Bakur's true nature. The agent's mind raced over what such might possibly mean. It obviously indicated that the doctor understood his assistant's true assignment, to keep his eyes on Ungari and report all that happened at the Memak'tori dig site back to the Syrian government. But, wondered Klein, did the doctor know Bakur's other connections? Was Ungari trying to tell Knight or himself something?

Probably not, the agent thought. *After all, even if he had all the facts on Bakur's terrorist connections and was trying to warn us about something, there'd be no need to do so in public, in front of him.*

The FBI man, on the one hand, found himself trusting Ungari more in that moment. Yes, the suspicious parts of the agent's brain were feeding him a score of devious reasons as to why the doctor had made his introduction the way he did, but Klein chose to ignore them. Standing in the man's presence, shaking his hand, Klein felt no sinister vibrations. Following his gut instinct, he found himself willing to relax his guard slightly as far as Ungari was concerned—at least for the moment.

Knight, on the other hand, was not quite the thespian Klein was. The professor had come up with the idea of introducing the FBI man as a museum employee. He did have a quick and agile mind; of that there was no doubt. But, in many ways Knight was not an overly duplicitous man. Upon hearing his old friend introduce his assistant as a functionary of the Syrians, he could not help raising one eyebrow. Catching the motion, in a tone heavy with challenge, Bakur asked;

"Something distresses you, Professor?"

"Oh heavens, I think 'distress' might be too strong a word," answered Knight politely. "Let us say instead that I was simply surprised."

"And at what would your surprise be aimed? At the fact that the Syrian government takes an interest in what happens to its national treasures? That after more than a hundred years of open theft on the part of the West, that finally we would say 'no more' to those who would rob us of all they could carry away?"

The shorter man spoke in clipped, polite sentences, his tone that of a polished academic. There was nothing of the accusatory to be found within his voice, just, of course, his words themselves.

Speaking in just such a hypothetical tone, the professor answered him, asking;

"Heavens, are you saying the Syrian government feels the Brooklyn Museum is out to plunder the Memak'tori site?"

"Why would it not?" Bakur's eyes flashed ever so slightly as he said, "It is not a person, after all. People can be judged for their qualities, for integrity, for honor—a corporation cannot. And, is a museum anything more than that? For all the marble columns and solemn sense of history, is all of this with which you surround yourself, Professor Knight, anything more than just another business?"

"Since you have history on your side, Mr. Bakur," replied Knight, working to draw the man out further, "let's not go down any foolish paths. All men have trouble in their past. No one's ancestors come off particularly clean. Countries other than yours come to mind, where what are now considered as treasures were then thought of as merely lumps of rock to be removed. Amazing, the ignorance of one's own culture some peoples can maintain."

"Especially when such ignorance is encouraged by those who would victimize such innocence."

"Well said," admitted Knight. "But then, sir, that's why we have laws about such things these days. Or are you of the type who doesn't know how to forgive or forget?"

"Gentlemen," broke in Ungari, his tone revealing he was somewhat concerned where the tempers of his assistant and his friend might lead them, "surely we—"

"Doctor," said Bakur, cutting into Ungari's interruption, his tone still silkenly calm, "the professor has asked a question—he wonders if the memory of the Syrian people can be mollified with ephemeral trinkets. I think he might possibly be an honest man, one who believes the West can truly police itself, despite the ever-building mountain of crushing evidence to the contrary."

"I believe my question concerned the Syrian people's disposition toward the Brooklyn Museum." Allowing a bit of his actual feelings to color his voice, Knight continued, saying, "To be perfectly frank, I could care less what the rest of the world does or thinks. My only concern is the reputation of my little slice of the world—this particular set of walls and the history of all mankind which they contain. And, I tell you, sir, that I shall defend it as dearly as you or anyone else will defend what is theirs."

"Very impassioned, Professor," responded Bakur smoothly. "I am quite certain your ancestor, the man for whom I assume you were named, the Piers Knight who helped create your precious Brooklyn Museum—your great-great-grandfather, yes?—he, too, must have felt quite certain this 'noble' establishment of yours was correct in all its dealings." Adjusting his thick, horn-rimmed glasses, more for the reason to make a dramatic pause than anything else, Ungari's assistant then added;

"Tell me, how many of the acquisitions he made for the Brooklyn Museum were justly compensated? Pieces like the so-called Dream Stone, which, of course, the viewing of such is why we are here in the first place?"

"Professor," came Klein's voice, a certain shakiness foreshadowing his following words, "perhaps this would be a good time to tell the gentlemen what has happened—yes?"

"Something has happened?" Ungari's voice was shot through with concern. Unlike the pleasant tones of his assistant, the doctor's words conveyed a dread he seemed incapable of concealing. As he turned his head back and forth from Knight to the FBI man posing as his assistant, the professor finally answered his old friend, saying quietly;

"The Dream Stone has been destroyed."

The doctor's reaction to the news was one of utter shock, followed by an unbelieving fury. Cursing in Egyptian, he managed to rein in his anger after a moment, at which time Klein related the story of the attempted theft. The professor allowed the agent to do so, both of them assuming that "the museum's liaison to the outside world in all matters governmental" would be the one to pass along such information. Of course, knowing far more of the details of the incidents, Knight felt far safer letting Klein do the talking, since he only had the official version of the story and thus could not possibly let any secrets slip.

While the FBI man explained all that had happened, the professor wondered about Bakur's reaction to the news. He was the one, after all, who seemed so concerned over the stolen treasures of Syria, and yet here was one, possibly one of the most important ever discovered, one with the potential to unlock some of history's greatest secrets, now lost to all time.

Yes, Knight realized, certainly the museum would have copies of the text. The secrets themselves would not be lost. But the stone itself, losing it would be like allowing the Mona Lisa to be consumed in a fire. Despite the millions of copies of the painting, exact matches down to the brushstrokes and filigree cracks, the loss of the original would be a devastating blow to the world of art—an irreparable hole in the fabric of history.

And yet, thought Knight, not certain what to make of his observation, *this man so concerned with his nation's antiquities does not seem very upset over this news.*

The professor was willing to grant that Bakur was an extremely in-control personality type, the kind of man capable of not blinking in the face of the most devastating news. Still, why would he choose to control himself at that moment when anger over Western carelessness would only strengthen his position?

Unless, thought Knight, *he's not showing any reaction because he already knows.*

And then, before anything more could happen, a slight tapping came at the door to the professor's office. Knight's simple response to "enter" brought a quite excited Bridget into their midst. After the professor made introductions all around, starting with Klein's new identity as a museum employee, Knight's assistant bent close to his head and whispered into his ear. Allowing himself a moment to grin wickedly, he announced;

"Everyone, I believe my assistant has some information that will be appreciated by everyone here." Giving the young woman a nod, indicating she should share her news, Knight then sat back and studied the faces of the others as Bridget said;

"Gentlemen, I do believe the Dream Stone may not have been destroyed."

CHAPTER THIRTY-ONE

Bridget's news, of course, threw all those assembled within the professor's office into quite a tidy frenzy. As soon as he had grasped her words, Knight immediately threw his complete attention toward Bakur. Focusing all his well-honed powers of observation upon the Syrian, he was not surprised to find that his old friend's assistant was suddenly capable of showing quite an extensive array of emotions. Quite a number more, in fact, than the professor could account for reasonably.

That man is something a bit more than elated, Knight reasoned. Narrowing his field of vision, he continued to stare—unblinking—thinking, *His surprise here is most genuine. Overwhelmingly so. And yet he evidenced no such level of emotion when told the treasure he had come seeking was no longer in existence.*

Somehow, the professor was completely convinced, the man calling himself Hamid Bakur had known of the theft and ruin of the Dream Stone before he had ever entered the Brooklyn Museum—probably before he reached the country. But what appeared even odder than that to Knight was the fact that where the assistant almost certainly knew of these incidents, the doctor employing him almost certainly did not. Filing away these newly learned bits of information, the professor commandeered his own assistant's attention, silencing the others so they might all learn what she could possibly mean by her announcement.

"Has news come from the police department," he asked, going to the only feasible possibility of which he could think. "Did they somehow find the Dream Stone intact in the rubble? I admit, such seems so utterly impossible, but—"

"No, no, nothing like that," the young woman insisted. Smiling as she spoke, obviously enjoying her center stage moment, she told the others, "The piece removed from the museum was destroyed; there doesn't look to be any question about that. However . . . as I'm certain you remember, you did give me an assignment when we arrived here this morning—yes?"

"Well," mused Knight, still not certain where he was being led but willing to be led, "I asked you to go down to the old files, Section F, to try and find any of the original drawings and etchings that were made of the piece, anything from the old days, back when it was first brought to the museum . . . but—"

When the professor simply shrugged at the redhead, she smiled, then continued, saying;

"I did as you asked, of course, and when I did, one of the things I found was a complete diagram for reproducing a replica of the Dream Stone. It was earmarked for a world's fair–like symposium held somewhere in California in 1935. Now, remember what you said, Professor, that the men carrying the Dream Stone seemed awfully strong, because they were carrying it so easily? What if—"

"Oh my God," Knight blurted, actually slapping his forehead at the same time. Wincing from the force of his blow, he whispered, "I don't believe it." After allowing himself a moment to let Bridget's news soak in, he asked her, "Did you check it out? What did you find in—"

Bridget cut her employer off, reminding him;

"I don't have clearance to enter the storage units on my own. That's why I came back here." Before anyone else could speak, Dr. Ungari broke in, his voice overwhelmed with hope as he asked;

"Is it possible, Piers?"

"I wouldn't want to make any promises I couldn't keep, Ashur, old friend," answered the professor, an uncontrollable smile stretching itself across his face, "but I think this calls for an immediate reconvening of this little meeting. Gentlemen, and, of course, you as well, my dear, most wonderful of creatures ever to walk this earth, what do you say, all? Shall we adjourn to Section F?"

AFTER A BRIEF INSPECTION OF ALL THE VARIOUS BITS OF PAPERwork that had sent a quite excited Bridget to Knight's office, the small party made its way into the sub-basement from where the team of intruders had removed what until that moment all had believed had been the actual Dream Stone. The area was still festooned with yards of yellow police tape, but none of the assembled gave it the slightest notice. Ripping it aside without regard, the party made its way forward into the narrowly set shelves until they reached the aisle in question.

"Well," said Knight, pausing to allow himself a nervous swallow, "this is the place. If the Dream Stone is still intact, it's either here or it isn't."

So saying, the professor climbed several steps up a small, wheeled ladder, flashlight in hand. Shining his light along the shelf in question, he ran his hands over something out of the line of sight of the others. In a voice barely able to crack a whisper, Ungari asked;

"Piers, is it there? Is it the Dream Stone?" Turning, his face breaking into the widest of smiles, Knight answered in a tone trembling with relief;

"I can't be certain just from touch, but if it isn't, it will certainly do until something else comes along." Then, trying to move the large piece of stonework with one hand, the professor grunted, then added;

"Oh yes, I do believe we have the correct piece this time."

As a small burst of cheers went up in the confined area, the doctor pushed another of the small, mobile ladder units over to the opposite side of the aisle. Rapidly climbing to a height equal with Knight's, Ungari pulled on the end of the stone closest to him while the professor manipulated the other. As the two men worked the ancient piece closer to the edge, both Bakur and Klein moved forward, each eyeing the ancient treasure.

"Dr. Ungari," his assistant cried out, "perhaps we should offer some assistance. We would not want the stone to fall. If even the slightest marking were to be chipped—"

"Just get yourself in position, fellah. . . ."

Bakur went silent, staring coldly at Klein. After a moment, however, he realized what he was doing and forced himself to blink, then finally did as the FBI man suggested. With their supposed coworkers ready to back them up, Knight and Ungari finally pulled the Dream Stone to the edge of the shelf, then held it aloft as best they could as the other, younger men got their hands beneath it. The situation proved tensely awkward for only a moment, though. Working together, in seconds the men had the large stone slab out of the aisle and on an inspection table in the light. As they simply stared, Bridget asked;

"Is it the Dream Stone? Was I right?"

"Yes, you were correct, my dear," answered the professor, chuckling as he did so. "The thieves must have gotten their information by going through the storage records that predated the Californian exposition. When the copy was made, the real piece was removed to deep storage while the lighter copy was returned to its old place after the show."

"But if it was lighter," asked Bakur, "how were these thieves so easily fooled?"

"They didn't have the same kinds of materials to work with in the thirties we do today. Then they would have simply had a copy made out of soapstone. Fake or not, they wanted the copy to look real, and the easiest way to make certain something looks like it's made out of stone is to, well . . . make it out of stone."

As everyone continued to allow their spirits to climb, Ungari's assistant patted the Dream Stone sharply, then announced to the assembly;

"Given the strange events surrounding the recent need for this quite valuable piece, I think that no more time should be wasted. I am sure you would agree with me, Doctor, that we should begin immediate proceedings for shipping the Dream Stone back to Syria without delay."

"Begin what?" Knight stared at the younger man with a curious fascination. Moving closer, the professor asked, "Please, illuminate me, my dear fellow. What exactly is it that makes you think this piece is going anywhere?"

"This treasure was stolen from my people by Western freebooters posing as scientists," snapped Bakur loudly. His voice echoing in the narrow aisle, he added, "But now it shall be returned. And such will be done immediately."

"For starters," interrupted Klein, moving forward to stand next to Knight, "you might want to use your inside voice. As a follow-up, I do believe you're in no position to be making demands."

"The Dream Stone must be returned!" Bakur's hand slammed against the ancient slab once more, a blow so violent, the fact it did not force even a wince from Bakur surprised everyone else present. Then, to make matters worse, the professor suddenly realized the younger man was considering a rash act.

"Do you hear me?"

So agitated was Bakur becoming, Knight could see his left hand moving toward the inside of his sport coat. The professor, as well as Klein, both came to the realization that the man was armed and beginning to go for what had to be a weapon concealed beneath his jacket. As each of their minds raced, wondering what exactly to do, Bakur shouted once more.

"I said, do you hear me?!"

"They heard you," came a new voice from behind the crowd. "Now hear me, mister. That stone's going somewhere all right, but not with you."

CHAPTER THIRTY-TWO

"Ah, there you are, Detective LaRaja," said Bridget, her voice as calm as if announcing nothing more startling than the return of a waiter to take orders all around. Keeping her tone pleasant, she added, "I see you were able to make it, after all."

"Oh my heavens," answered the gray-haired detective quietly, "why, I wouldn't have missed this party for anything—goodness no, Ms. Elkins."

When Bakur began to make resentful noises, demanding an explanation of LaRaja's earlier statement, Knight was quick to make introductions all around, making certain that Ungari and his assistant knew the detective was the local authority in charge of the museum-break-in investigation. The professor was also careful to "reintroduce" Klein to LaRaja as the museum's newly installed liaison to governmental agencies. LaRaja allowed one eyebrow to elevate to show he would like an explanation for the subterfuge but that he was also clever enough to make no mention of such desires in front of the newcomers. Growing more irritated with each passing second, Bakur demanded;

"Fine. Excellent—now we are all well acquainted. Very well then, explain yourself, policeman. What did you mean when you said that the Dream Stone would not be returned to Syria? Who are you to interject yourself so? This is an outrage. It is beyond outrage. This is an affront to the international community, you humorless little man. I would have you know that civilized nations have laws concerning—"

Dropping all pretenses to any form of civility, LaRaja fixed Bakur with a stare so brutally cold it shocked the younger man into an abrupt silence. So uncharacteristically grim was the detective that even Knight felt himself somewhat taken aback. Never having seen LaRaja so intense, the professor joined the others in playing mute as the detective answered the Syrian, telling him;

"Let me tell you something about outrage, sonny. Seeing your best friend shoveled up and stuffed into bags because he died—burned alive—trying to defend your damn stupid, useless piece of rock, now that, that's a goddamned outrage. Listening to some punk pontificate about the rights of an outlaw nation, one that floods the world with cowardly murderers, that's another goddamned outrage."

"Who do you think you are speaking to, old man? Do you know who I am?"

Both Knight and Klein wondered what Bakur might be attempting. He appeared to no longer possess any regard for concealing his role as an extension of the Syrian government—a pose neither man could understand. Moreover, Bakur almost seemed to be on the verge of reverting to his terrorist roots. The FBI agent, like the professor, had spotted the telltale bulge beneath the ranting man's jacket. Both assumed he must have picked the weapon up somewhere along the way, most likely at the Syrian embassy, since there was no way he would have been able to bring one aboard a plane. Even diplomatic courier pouches received no such privilege anymore. Before either could comment, however, LaRaja raised his voice to answer the questions posed to him.

"Yes, as a matter of fact, I do believe I have some idea of just exactly what it is that I'm addressing. I'm talking to a punk. And just in case you missed my meaning there, that's you." As the shorter man stewed, his expression showing clearly that he was not used to be treated in such a manner, LaRaja continued to tear at him, saying;

"You're a punk—period. I don't care on whose authority you think you're acting, or how high up some jerkwater political ladder you can climb when you need to, you're still nothing more than a punk. And a fairly cheap one, at that."

Bakur began to shake as an inexplicable rage built within him. It seemed obvious to everyone else there, including even Ungari, that the detective was purposely goading the Syrian. Understanding that he was an agent of his government, most likely trained to resist such situations, none in the room could fathom how Bakur could so easily be pushed to the brink of foolishness. And yet with each word the detective jolted the younger man ever closer to that particular edge.

"Whatever else it might be, this miserable Dream Stone of yours is the key to all the insanity going on around here," LaRaja told Bakur. "And so, like I said, it's going somewhere, all right. It's going with me."

"You have not the right—"

"I have all the right in the world, sonny boy," snarled LaRaja. Thumping Bakur in the chest with a solid index finger, the detective physically moved the Syrian backward as he poked him repeatedly, telling him, "That miserable piece of crap is evidence in a police investigation, and that means if I want to lock it up and keep it from the sight of man for the next hundred years, I can do just that, and there's nothing you can do to stop me."

The color drained from the younger man's face, his swarthy complexion going an odd, sickly pale. The change was so rapid the others could practically follow it even in the feeble lighting there in the museum's sub-basement. Coupled with the ways his limbs were trembling, the way his very skin seemed to be vibrating, it appeared it would not be long before Hamid Bakur would snap. Trying to make his actions appear normal, Knight shifted his position, placing himself in between the younger man and Bridget. As he did so, Bakur responded to LaRaja's threat, spittle flying from his mouth as he shouted;

"You cannot do this to me. I will not allow it. I—"

"Oh, give it a rest, little boy," growled the detective. "You're not going to do anything, and here's why. You have no legs to stand on in this matter. The best you can do is get your miserable terrorist government to lodge a protest. And if you were thinking of finally sliding your hand all the way inside your jacket, perhaps you should take a look behind you."

As Bakur's head jerked awkwardly, everyone else followed his lead. So absorbed had the group become in the small drama playing out between the two, they had failed to notice LaRaja was not the only new arrival in Section F. Standing several steps back in the gloom were four uniformed police officers, all of them standing with their hands on, or at least near, their holsters.

"Give us the excuse, 'Mr.' Bakur."

Wide-eyed, blinking rapidly, the terrorist agent gave every impression of getting ready to do exactly as the detective suggested. Then abruptly Bakur's manner changed, his mood turning from crazed to calm in less than a heartbeat. Pushing his hair back on his head, pressing hard as he did so as to contain the inordinate amount of sweat greasing his scalp, Bakur straightened his suit jacket, offering;

"You are quite the quaint provincial, Detective. You must be a welcome addition to meals held out-of-doors, and perhaps children's parties. I shall take your advice, sir, and see about, as you said, lodging a protest. Although I think I might take my petition to a higher authority than the 'terrorist government' you have suggested."

And, so saying, the eerily calm man turned and headed for the exit. With a hand signal from LaRaja, two of the uniformed police officers turned and followed Bakur, ready to escort him all the way to the front door. Making rapid apologies for his assistant, Dr. Ungari begged off, explaining that it would be best for all if he was to accompany the younger man and try to contain whatever actions he was contemplating. The others expressed their understanding and concern, allowing the Egyptian to save face and depart. Ungari practically had to break into a trot to be able to reach the elevator before its doors closed.

"Well," said Knight, once the museum's visitors had removed themselves from earshot, "that was certainly an interesting little display."

"Yes, it was," agreed Klein, "but quite an effective one."

"Thank you, gentlemen," answered LaRaja. His "bad-cop" persona neatly tucked away, he continued, saying, "It's always nice when one's work is appreciated."

"So," asked the professor, his tone suggesting honest curiosity, "what were you thinking was our next move, Detective?"

"You mean now that the little grease stain has been removed from the picture?"

"Something like that," answered Knight with a chuckle.

"I'd say now we decide exactly what we're going to do with that damned hunk of rock of yours, that is, before Mr. Charm figures out what he's going to try and do with it."

CHAPTER THIRTY-THREE

"Did I mention, by the way, my dear," asked Knight, "exactly how impressed I am with your first day's work on the job?"

"No, come to think of it," answered Bridget, pretending to be quite severely wounded over the fact. "You have not. Typical, though, of a male-dominated society. Oh, the indignities. Oh, the humanity. To think—"

"All right, Tallulah—"

"Who?"

Knight looked from his assistant to Klein to LaRaja and then back to Bridget. The detective's eyes revealed that he had understood the professor's reference to the onetime star of the international stage, so well-known for making hugely overdramatic much of the tiniest of moments. Klein's gaze, however, was as devoid of any idea over the meaning of the name as Bridget's.

Taking pity on them both, Knight said merely;

"Ah, youth is so truly wasted on the young. Still, age

brags of its common knowledge and does nothing more than send youth to resentfully bragging of its own—"

"Who said that?" asked LaRaja.

"Someone dead longer than Tallulah, I'm afraid," the professor answered. "So perhaps we should get down to business. And the first business I would like to take care of is to say, well done, my dear." Blushing slightly, Bridget made an overly affected curtsey in Knight's direction, telling him;

"It was nothing, really. I just stumbled across the diagram while I was looking through the other papers, and I realized the possibility—"

"No, no," interrupted Knight. Waving his hands in the air, he cut his assistant off, adding, "I mean, yes, of course, I'm impressed enough with you realizing what you might possibly have uncovered as quickly as you did. I'm talking about your other bits of resourcefulness."

"Can I ask you to shower me with compliments for a moment, just so I'll know what it was you considered so resourceful?"

"Women," growled the professor playfully. "The price we pay to be allowed the privilege of their company." Bridget smirked in response, giving Knight the opportunity to roll his eyes back in her direction. While Klein and LaRaja both chuckled, the professor's features softened as he added;

"You're apprenticing here, young lady, so yes, I will give you a catalog of what you did correctly so you can continue to do such things throughout your career." Counting on his fingers, Knight announced;

"You used your brain. You thought. That single characteristic of yours outweighs any other. You made the connection that the Dream Stone might still be intact. You remembered what you had been told of Bakur and realized what that particular news might mean to him. You then brought the detective here on your own, along with enough firepower to keep our visitor from causing a scene."

"You know, Knight," said the FBI man in a tone too sincere to be anything but honest, "I do believe my opinion of you has been elevated somewhat simply because this young woman is willing to keep company with you."

"I know mine has," added LaRaja softly. Klein laughed at the detective's comment. The professor was tempted to chuckle himself, but he realized that despite the fact that Bridget had jokingly asked for compliments, she was becoming more than a little embarrassed by the overwhelming amount of them. Attempting to come to her rescue, he said to the lawmen;

"Fine, gentlemen, your begrudging admission of my greatness is faint praise, indeed, and yet it thunders in my ears. However, with Ms. Elkins' fine example before us, perhaps we should cease wasting time and get back to business."

"What do you have in mind, Professor?"

"Well, Mr. Klein, I do believe the good detective here was correct. The Dream Stone must be removed from the museum. Let me ask you gentlemen, are you as convinced as I am that our Mr. 'Bakur' had something to do with the attack on the museum?"

The conversation became quite animated at that point, Knight's question sparking instant agreement. Everyone had been aware of the fact that the terrorist had to have been armed. Those present in the professor's office had also noted Bakur's lack of surprise at the news the Stone had been destroyed, as well as his overwhelming show of emotion when it was announced it might not have been.

"Fine, we're all in agreement then. Bakur is almost certain to have had something to do with the first theft. Most likely the attack on the police station as well. To me, that means he most likely will make another attempt." Turning to the detective, Knight said quietly;

"I know how personally you must be taking this entire affair. Jimmy Dollins was a good man, and I suspect an excellent friend. But I think it best for all if Agent Klein here is allowed to remove the Dream Stone."

"You want me to take it to FBI headquarters?"

"No, sir," answered the professor. His manner suddenly terse, he said, "You've nothing there that the police didn't have at their disposal. No—I'm thinking you need to relocate the Dream Stone to a military facility. And not a National Guard station such as Brooklyn's Fort Hamilton. Close it might be, but it's most likely not manned by what we may need."

"What are you thinking, Professor?"

Knight lowered his head for a moment, taking a deep breath, one he held for quite a long moment. Finally releasing it, he looked from the FBI man to the detective, then back again, before finally answering Klein's question.

"Understand, gentlemen," he started, "that I know my place in the world's affairs. I offer my advice merely as, shall we say, a consultant. But that being said, I think our Mr. Bakur is quite mad. He threw killers armed with guns and explosives at a museum. No one seems to know what he threw at the police station, but a sizable portion of it was burned to the ground as a result."

"If," inserted the FBI man, "he is our man."

"Are you thinking there is some other possibility," asked Knight quietly. When the federal agent admitted he had no other ideas on the subject, the professor continued, saying;

"I believe Bakur is quite agitated now. He most likely believes his next attempt to secure the Dream Stone will be his last. Thus, I cannot believe he will resist throwing all his readily available resources at it."

None of the others thought anything different. The assembly continued to speak for a few more minutes, but with little debate.

Klein assured the others it would not take much to find a general interested in protecting something terrorists wished to place their hands upon. Leaning in close, Bridget asked the professor in a whisper;

"Why not have your friends at Homeland Security handle things?"

Knight had to pause for a moment, uncertain as to whether his assistant was serious or she had finally realized how he had been attempting to sidetrack her with such talk over the previous few days. Feigning deference to Agent Klein, he asked the FBI man to continue. His tone filled with assurance, Klein said;

"Let me get on it. I'm fairly certain that within a half-dozen phone calls we can have the Dream Stone on its way to upstate New York, where it'll be ringed with more than enough tanks and commandos to keep it safe."

"Safe, yes—maybe," started LaRaja, then asking, "but safe from what—exactly?"

"When it is explained how your station house was destroyed," responded Knight, "then we shall both know. Tell me, Detective, have your forensics people, or your arson experts, has anyone put forth a theory as to what happened in that basement that makes any sense whatsoever?" When LaRaja admitted that so far no one had been able to even determine the conflagration's point of origin, let alone what might have caused it, the professor offered;

"Gentlemen, I tell you now, as I am certain you both believe yourselves, there is something going on here that we do not understand. Whether they're using some form of extreme science with which we are not familiar, or some ancient, impossible magic—for lack of a better term—someone out there, somewhere, is willing to do whatever they must to procure the Dream Stone for themselves. I do not have the slightest idea what they feel they might use it for, but I fear that even without knowing what they are up to, it is of monumental importance they be stopped."

After a long, silent moment, Klein finally shattered the quiet. Nodding his head in short, barely perceptible motions, he told Knight;

"I'd make some kind of wisecrack about your flair for dramatic overstatement, if I didn't think everything you said was right on the money. I'll be letting people know this thing should be moved A, S, A, and P, and surrounded by as much firepower as possible when it arrives."

"If you don't mind, Agent Klein," LaRaja started, his tone firm and cold. Resting his hand on the Dream Stone, he finished, saying, "I'd like to tag along to wherever this thing ends up. Be there whenever the fun starts." The FBI man was about to answer the detective when Knight interrupted, saying;

"I understand your feelings, Denny, but if you wouldn't mind, I believe I have something more important for you to attend to right here in Brooklyn."

CHAPTER THIRTY-FOUR

It was later that night when Detective Denny LaRaja met the professor and his assistant on the front steps of the Brooklyn Museum. The police officer informed the pair that he had heard from Klein. The Dream Stone, for the moment at least, appeared safe. The uniformed patrolmen who had accompanied LaRaja to the museum earlier in the day had escorted the FBI man when he had removed the antiquity from the premises. Now the artifact was hundreds of miles to the north, headed for the U.S. Army installation maintained at Fort Drum. The detective related Klein's assurance that the military was prepared to take extreme measures to protect the Dream Stone.

Knight thanked LaRaja for the information with honest sincerity. The potion the professor had spiked the meeting-room water with had almost completely worn off, at least as far as Klein was concerned. He had not heard anything of the agent's thoughts since the episode with Bakur. The back of Knight's mind was, however, still filled with the thoughts of Abigail Brinkley. The museum's director had downed three glasses of water during the meeting, taking one back to her office with her when their meeting finally broke up.

I swear, Knight mused to himself, *if she doesn't solve the overwhelming problem of whether to go strapless or not to the Weinstein formal, I may have to drive a pencil into my ear simply for the relief.* Attempting to distract himself from such thoughts, the professor asked the detective about the facility in question.

"The whole place is one big wilderness," LaRaja told him. "I used to do National Guard training there."

"Really," quipped Knight, trying to hide a smile. "I didn't know the Guard dated back to the Civil War." Ignoring the professor, the detective turned to Bridget instead, saying;

"And this is how he treats those trying to help him. Do take note."

"I've known him less than half a week, and believe me, I've already filled half a notebook." Although he knew she was teasing, the detective did not smile back at her. Instead, he shot her a knowing, sour look, pointing his thumb over his shoulder at Knight as he advised the redhead to;

"Refer to it often. It'll come in handy if you're going to continue to hang around with the likes of him." Then, finally turning back to the professor, LaRaja added; "Anyway, wise guy, just to let you know, the whole get-the-damn-thing-out-of-the-city-and-away-from-people idea has been covered. Also, the place is the home of the 10th Mountain Division and the 42nd; that was my Guard division."

"And that means?"

"And that means, young lady, that there's never less than ten thousand military personnel on hand at any one time. Considering that both units store all their weapons there, and that includes a large number of Bradleys and Abrams—" Bridget's eyes filled with such immediate confusion that the detective stopped to explain;

"The latest in armored personnel carriers and tanks. Anyway, my point is if that thing can't be protected there, I don't know where else it would be any safer."

"Oh, I agree," said Knight honestly. "I'm just happy it's out of the city."

"Klein also said the people he has tailing both Bakur and Ungari report that neither one of them has done much of anything suspicious since they left the museum." As the three got into LaRaja's vehicle, Knight pulled at his chin as he mused;

"Nothing that would look suspicious to the untrained eye, anyway."

"Now there," said the detective, "is one of those statements that just beg to be questioned." His hand falling away from his keys, he listened to them squeak as they rocked back and forth hanging from the car's unengaged ignition. Turning across to the professor, who had chosen the front seat, leaving the back for Bridget, LaRaja asked;

"So tell me, Piers, just exactly what kind of training is it you think you have that the FBI is lacking?"

Knight sighed softly, wondering what exactly to say in response. He had already divulged far more to his assistant than he would usually ever admit to most people.

"For once something is simply too big for you to hide away from it. There is something terribly wrong with all this business, and if you do nothing, good people will suffer. Don't make me quote Edmund Burke. I will, you know." Facing LaRaja, the professor told him;

"I promise you, all will be answered once we get to where we're going this evening. I'm hoping to be able to simply show you what I'm talking about, but if when we arrive at our destination, if there is nothing to show you, then I will endeavor to explain myself. Although, frankly, that way will be far more unsatisfactory, and most likely leave you unconvinced."

"One picture," added Bridget suddenly, "is worth a thousand words, Officer."

LaRaja pursed his lips, staring at the young woman in his backseat. In his mind, the detective knew he had to play that evening Knight's way. By breaking protocol, by agreeing to work outside the department's knowledge, he had placed himself in the professor's hands. It was the kind of thing he would never do without a staggeringly important reason. Discovering what really had happened in the property room, to his best friend, in the lobby of the Brooklyn Museum—all of that was important enough, LaRaja decided, to give Knight at least one more day's breathing room. Nodding to Bridget, acknowledging the truth of her statement, the detective turned back to the professor with one last question.

"Okay, we can let that one pass for now. But tell me, Piers," he asked, "answer this one puzzler. The Dream Stone might be safely upstate now. But how is our boy supposed to know the thing isn't here in the city anymore? What's to keep him from launching another attack on the museum anyway?"

"Detective," started Knight slowly, his tone suggesting he might be a tad uncertain as to how he should proceed, "the answer to that question also has a great deal to do with why I wanted to see you tonight." As the awkward silence between the two men suddenly grew a touch uncomfortable once more, Bridget leaned forward, offering;

"Officer LaRaja, I know the professor is asking a lot of you. You wanted to be wherever the Dream Stone is because you want to pay back whoever it was that killed your partner. You gave up that chance to help us, without any explanations. Now, you would like a few. Am I right?"

"Do you blame me?"

"No, sir," answered Bridget. "But I know what the professor is hoping we can do tonight. All I want to say is, something happened to us that . . . how to say it? If . . . if I'd been told what was going to happen, I don't think I would have handled it very well. I would have doubted it actually happened, because I would have suspected that I wanted to witness such a thing so badly that I made it happen in my mind."

"What my assistant is trying to say," said Knight, "is that I'm hoping the same thing that happened to us will happen to you tonight. My first reason is that if you see what we saw, that further confirms that we actually did see it." The professor paused for a moment, then added;

"My second reason for wanting you there is, if I'm correct in the assumptions I've made about our experience, then you might be the one man on earth best suited to deal with it."

"And that's all you're going to tell me, isn't it?" Looking across the front seat at the detective, Knight nodded, answering;

"If it's enough to get us there without any further questions, then yes."

LaRaja considered the professor for a long moment, then finally moved his hand back to his vehicle's steering column. Turning his key in the ignition, he gave his gas pedal a couple of gentle taps to start his engine warming up, then said;

"Okay—give me a direction to point this beast in, and let's get going."

CHAPTER THIRTY-FIVE

"You know," said Detective LaRaja, his voice low and respectful, "if I'd been forced to guess where we were going to go tonight, I'd have to admit that this place would have been way down on my list."

The detective had parked his vehicle less than twenty-five feet from where Knight had parked the evening he had brought his assistant to the Green-Wood Cemetery. Standing in the middle of the sprawling graveyard in the oppressive darkness, LaRaja and the professor faced each other in the gloom while Bridget remained in the car. If there was to be a repeat of what had happened the night before, he wanted his assistant safely away from them, if for no other reason than she may be needed to rescue himself and the detective in the same manner she had saved Knight the other evening.

"I would have been surprised if you'd been able to predict our destination, myself."

"So, man of mystery, you were pretty tight-lipped

about where we were going. Now that we're here, you think you might want to give me some idea as to exactly *why* we're here?"

"I want you to see something, to experience it," answered the professor. His head in constant motion, looking first one way and then another, he strained his eyes against the black all about them—searching. Without facing LaRaja, Knight added absently, "Please understand, it took a while for things to begin the last time we were here—'we,' Bridget and I. Let's give the moment a bit of time to see if anything's going to percolate this time as well, if you don't mind?"

"So, you mean, this could all be for nothing? You don't even know if anything—"

The professor cut the detective off with a hand motion, whispering to him, "No—I cannot guarantee you that anything will happen. But I can assure you that nothing whatsoever will happen if we fill the air with negativity." His eyes filled with an earnestness the detective could not ignore, Knight added;

"I hate to sound all turbans and tarot, but please, Denny, just a few minutes." Then, focusing his attention directly on LaRaja, locking eyes with the officer, the professor's voice filled with a pleading note as he asked;

"You've trusted me as best you could so far in all of this. Trust me just this one last time—all right?"

Crossing his arms over his chest, the detective nodded as he sighed deeply, throwing his mind to wondering about exactly what he might have gotten himself into this time. There had never been any doubt in his mind that Knight was holding back a great deal of information about whatever was going on all about them—he and his late partner had both felt so. But then, LaRaja reminded himself, they had both suspected as much every time the three of them had come in contact for any reason, and so far the professor had proved himself in each instance.

Of course, thought the detective with a touch of a chuckle, *then again, maybe it just comes down to the fact that Piers Knight is simply an odd duck who somehow always seems to end up in the middle of weirdness.*

LaRaja had no problem with such a notion. New York City, after all, was filled with plenty of characters who made it their business to immerse themselves in all manner of lunacy. Some were thrill seekers; others craved attention, or mere publicity. They were the easiest ones to handle. Worse by far were the self-appointed saviors, the noble protectors, and, of course, the never-ending parade of voyeurs who were underfoot at every official investigation. Those were the souls whose interference caused policemen to go gray before they were thirty.

"Worse than the damn media," mused the detective. "How they find us . . ."

LaRaja stopped there. His problem had never been the fact that the crazies were capable of sniffing out crime scenes. It was the fact that they wanted to—that they actually wished to be there—that had always puzzled him. There was no cop he had ever known who enjoyed surveying a murder site. Comforting rape victims, searching rooms for the limbs of dismembered children, trying to determine if the blunt-trauma markings on a corpse's face came from a chair leg or a knife sharpener, one became inured to such casual horrors—it was simply an occupational survival mechanism—but to actively seek such things out, to view them as some sort of . . . what would the word be . . . entertainment?

"You seem distracted, Denny."

"Yeah, I suppose you could call it that."

The professor stared at LaRaja for a quick moment, preparing to do what he had to do next. Knight had known since asking the detective to meet him that night that he was going to have to reveal at least a few things about himself he would have preferred to keep private. He needed LaRaja whole and functioning if he was going to accomplish what he was hoping to that evening. And to do that, he had to ensure the detective believed what he experienced.

Completely and utterly.

You know what needs doing, Piers, a voice from the back of the professor's mind whispered to him. *So for once in your life stop stalling and just get it done.*

"Something happened here the other evening," Knight said sharply, hurling the words out from his head. Damning the part of his mind that tried to force him to keep every aspect of his life a secret, knowing that what he did then he did for the greater good, he continued on, saying, "Here, in this graveyard, Bridget and I encountered a ghost."

"What?" asked LaRaja, his expression showing traces of amusement. Pointing to a particular nearby gravesite, he joked, "Crazy Joe Gallo raising hell again?"

"If only things were that simple."

The detective simply stared at Knight, his mind incapable of giving him a clue as to where the professor might be attempting to lead him. Unconsciously the hardened mask of skepticism he had learned through all his years on the force settled across his face. Until he chose to have it otherwise, nothing about him would reveal the slightest trace as to his inner feelings. Whatever Knight wanted to tell him, the man would have to do so without the benefit of any clues as to what reception his words were receiving. Understanding that, Knight continued.

"It was not a random specter, either, but one come to visit me on purpose." The professor paused for a moment, expecting LaRaja to possibly ask a question or make a comment. When nothing was forthcoming, he continued.

"I don't believe it's any secret that Jimmy maintained certain suspicions about myself and my activities over the years. I'm quite certain you have them yourself. And why shouldn't you? It's not like . . . well, I mean . . . it's—"

Flustered, years of hard-learned self-preservation tactics screaming at him to stop, Knight suddenly found himself tongue-tied. Embarrassed. Frightened. Anger at his cowardice rushing through his entire being, he dismissed his fears, shutting them away as he finally continued, saying;

"I apologize for that—all of it. But please understand, I'm trying to do something now that is very hard for me. I am going to tell you . . . exactly what you want to know."

LaRaja's eyes grew slightly wide. It was an involuntary reaction. Despite his decades of on-the-job conditioning, the detective could not stop that one slight slip from occurring. As he stood there in the darkened cemetery, suddenly LaRaja's focus narrowed to a tightly controlled sliver in reaction to what he had just been told. Gone was the feel of soil and short-clipped grass from beneath his feet. Gone was the sensation of the evening's slight breeze weaving through his thinning hair, the sight of the sky full of stars above his head, or the sounds of crickets and faraway cars mixed within his ears. The detective was standing too close to Knight not to feel his sincerity. LaRaja understood what he was being told—as well as why.

"This must be pretty important."

"I think it is, yes. You need to understand what is happening, what might yet happen. For you to do so, you will need to know that I believe everything I am telling you."

"Of course," offered the detective, carefully watching for Knight's reaction, "you could just be crazy. I do deal with the tinfoil-hat brigade on a regular basis, you know. They believe what they're telling me pretty passionately, too."

"I understand," answered the professor, "and if you wish to

think of me as merely another harmless crackpot, that's fine. That's not the kind of reaction that worries me."

LaRaja nodded. Saying nothing more but wearing an expression that announced that he planned to be as open as possible, he waited for whatever it was the professor was offering to him. Knowing he could ask for little more from the detective, Knight swallowed, then said;

"I told you we saw a ghost here earlier. I'm telling you now that I've seen them before. I've seen worse. There are in this world, Denny, all manner of things. Most, thank Heaven, are locked away, barred from reaching mankind. The Bible stories of Solomon, sealing Hell things away for eternity—more than just flights of fancy. He was not the first, nor was he the last."

LaRaja felt the moisture in his mouth begin to evaporate. He had heard such talk before—far too often. But this was different. Knight was a man with everything to lose, and little to gain, by revealing what he claimed to believe to the detective. Of course, those others over the years who had spoken to him of like things were in the same position as the professor. The only difference was, Knight understood the possible consequences. The others—the crazies—they spoke with an unshakable belief, the tone of which indicated they fully expected anyone hearing them to instantly accept anything they said as proven fact.

But the professor's voice was different. There was no doubt in LaRaja's mind that Knight was afraid to speak as he was, that he understood completely what kind of a leap of faith he was asking the detective to make and how damaging it could be to him if that leap was not attempted.

"The world is filled with dark forces, and sinister men willing to use them. But they're never . . . what you would think. Novels, Hollywood, the entertainers of this world . . . they never get these things right—not even close. There are no men in opera capes living forever on the blood of young women who confuse the erotic with murder. But there are vampires. Twisted, unnatural parasites that exist beyond the understanding of men. There are witches and demons and wizards, an entire underground race of nightmare and wonder of which most mortal beings have not the slightest clue."

"But . . ." LaRaja choked slightly, so dry had his mouth and throat become that he found he could not form words. Taking a moment, he forced himself to produce a small ball of saliva, then swallowed it, adding, "But you do. Correct?"

Still sitting in the car, listening, Bridget held her breath, waiting to hear the professor's response. Knight nodded, staring directly into the detective's eyes as he gave it. It was a hesitant motion, a delay conveying not his lack of faith in what he had to say but his fear that his faith would not be shared. Then, before either man could say more. Bridget interrupted their conversation by calling out;

"Professor, I think you were right."

As both men turned toward the detective's car, they saw Bridget pointing off to her left with both hands. Following the directional cue, Knight viewed what he had fervently hoped he would find that evening. LaRaja beheld something practically beyond the scope of his comprehension. Moving slowly across the cemetery, curling around some gravestones, passing through others, came the same type of wraith that had approached Knight and his assistant in the same spot so recently.

"This . . ." The detective cursed himself mentally, damning the fear that was freezing his blood, overloading the circuits of his mind. Knight had told him what to expect. Was he less of a man, he snarled at himself, than some cocky academic? Responding to the insult, his policeman's soul denying all fear, LaRaja forced himself to finish his sentence.

"This is what you were hoping to show me?"

"I believe it must be—yes."

The glowing, mostly transparent shape continued forward, heading straight for the two men as best it could. The apparition did not seem hampered by the growing wind as much as it did by some form of apprehension. Studying the figure, Knight wondered at what the difference might be between the two manifestations. The ghostly form did seem somewhat changed from the previous evening. Larger, he thought. Brighter, perhaps. Heartier.

Next to the professor, however, his companion's mind was filled with different issues. All the time he was working to face down the approaching horror, a dozen different voices sounded within LaRaja's head, urging him to flee. They reminded him of how close his car was, that the key was waiting in the ignition, waiting for him to throw his vehicle into motion. He could still make it, they whispered. Pleaded.

Others were more sinister.

They questioned Knight's motives, suggested that perhaps the professor meant to destroy him, to feed his soul to the approaching nightmare.

"Why not," asked one. "If you can believe this much of what he told you, why not all of it? Is this one of those dark forces he claimed the world is filled with, and if it is, is he one of those sinister men he says are so willing to use them?"

The detective found himself beginning to shake. He understood Knight's warnings now, realized the academic had been trying to prepare him for just this kind of doubt. Then, as terror clawed its way into his soul, a small voice from the furthest recesses of his brain reminded him;

You believed the girl when she said she was here before. She saw this thing, and she came back. What exactly are you afraid of, Dennis, that doesn't scare a young woman still wet behind the ears?

And then, the glowing shape came within inches of the two men. Without hesitation, Knight stepped forward, plunging both his arms into the undulating specter. As he did so, he turned his head slightly toward the officer, shouting;

"Do the same as me—join me!"

Trembling, but closing his eyes all the same, with a prayer on his lips, Detective Denny LaRaja did as instructed. The professor put a hand on the smaller man's shoulder then, holding it tightly, forcing his senses to remember that he was not alone, that human contact was right there next to him.

LaRaja needed the guiding hand, for fear was invading his senses from every angle. Even knowing Knight was there at his side was not comfort enough to keep the desire to bolt from flooding his every thought. And then a sudden realization hit the detective—one so astounding as to be almost beyond his capability to accept it.

Part of him realizing that he must be right, that the professor could have brought him out there for no other reason, LaRaja was just beginning to speak when the skies barked and another terrible bolt crashed down from the Heavens, striking them all.

CHAPTER THIRTY-SIX

"All right now, son, let me see if I've got this whole thing straight." The major general speaking to Agent Klein did not appear to be a particularly confused man. He also did not appear to be an extremely happy one, either.

"You've come here to have us protect a rock?"

The speaker was Major General Mark Harris, a ramrod of a fifty-year-old, slightly gray, with metal-flake eyes and a jaw that appeared capable of withstanding a blow from a two-by-four. As he stared upward from his seat behind his desk, unblinking, the agent before him answered simply;

"Yes, sir."

The FBI man knew enough about military protocol to both not address the officer by either his rank or name, and also to not respond to anything more than he had been asked. He had answered the question put to him. To do more would be to offer offense. It would be a silent admission that he thought the major general did not know his own mind. In most of the outside world, such protocol seemed a particular type of arrogance, one that outraged liberal thinkers used to breaking into spontaneous debate over the slightest, most insignificant of things, often for no more reason than the mental exercise.

To the military mind, however, order and discipline were not simply niceties. They were ways of conduct that, if not followed at the right time, could lead to the deaths of thousands, to the destruction of cities or the fall of nations. Klein had been well trained in dealing with the various patterns of thought among leadership personalities. He would handle a CEO in a much different manner from a military commander, from a police officer, from a politician.

And, he thought, forcing himself not to smile, *from an academic, as well.*

"Okay, Mr. Klein, now that you've gotten yourself all the way up here, tell me, why do I want to do this?"

The agent understood the major general's question. The officer was not asking to be convinced to follow his orders. He was looking for whatever information Klein might possess outside those orders. Immediately the FBI man launched into a complete recitation of the history of Hamid Ras Morand. He kept his report brief and concise, detailing all he knew of the terrorist's various criminal activities as both a soldier of the line and a director behind the scenes. When Klein got to Morand's most recent assignment, the watching over of Dr. Ungari and the uncovering of Memak'tori, he asked;

"If I might be allowed to offer a speculation, General?" Receiving a nod from the commanding officer of Fort Drum, the FBI man continued, saying;

"I've dealt with Morand in person recently. The encounter was brief, but long enough to lead me to form the opinion that he wants to—needs to, really—take possession of this Dream Stone very badly. Symbol of a cause, national pride, a totem meant for good luck, I have no idea exactly where his internal justification lies. But whatever his reasons, it's my opinion that the man is clearly obsessed with getting his hands on the thing."

Klein paused in his explanation not only to swallow a deep breath before continuing but also to give Harris a moment to absorb all he had been told. The agent had done his homework on the major general in what limited time he had possessed. The officer had done several tours in the Middle East, working his way up the chain of command during every war, occupation, and skirmish available. The man knew more than a little about the mind-set of the Muslim fanatic. Harris had also nearly died in more than one surprise attack. Starting again, the FBI man lowered his tone to the conspiratorial as he said;

"We brought the piece here, sir, because we believe Morand has access to some sort of sophisticated, possibly experimental weaponry. When the piece was being stolen initially from the Brooklyn Museum, the thieves suddenly murdered one another, and then were blown to bits. Speculation by our best experts hasn't given us anything tangible to work with. Worse, when what they thought was the stone was moved to a police station, the building was somehow burned down from the inside. Stone and steel rooms obliterated. Metal doors melted from within. And, sir, the tiny bits of explanation the pros have handed us to work with make sci fi look tame."

The general considered what he had been told for a moment, then questioned what Klein had meant when he said "what they thought was the stone was moved to a police station." The agent explained the mistake the thieves had made in as brief a fashion as he had everything else. Harris gave him a slight stare, then lowered his eyes so that the FBI man would have no access to his thoughts while he contemplated all he had been told.

The first thing the officer reminded himself of was that there was no use in debating the protection of this hunk of rock. Klein and the others he was working with in New York City had used the chain of command quickly and efficiently. Before the agent had arrived, the major general's office had already received orders to comply with the FBI's requests in this matter, adding the somewhat disturbing tagline "no matter how outlandish." With that much a given, the officer's main duty was to figure out just how to keep this thing out of terrorist hands with as little risk to his men and equipment as possible.

Harris had risen through the ranks quickly, half of his brilliant rise due to plain dumb luck, the other to always being organized, on top of each situation as outlined, but also by being as prepared as possible for the unexpected. He saw before him in Klein and his rock nothing more than a replay of so many of the situations that had come his way over the years, all of them Fate's attempts to derail his career. And now, as so often in the past, he had only a matter of seconds in which to make his decision on how to handle this latest assault on his future.

Drum was the closest facility to New York City capable of handling the needs of the moment—with that fact Harris had no argument. National Guard posts like Fort Hamilton in Brooklyn might have been infinitely closer, but they were manned by part-timers, sorely lacking in equipment, not nearly as well trained, and, even worse, situated in the middle of a major metropolitan area. And that, he thought, was his dumb luck at work once more.

This problem had not been dropped in his specific lap; it had been dropped on Drum. There might be nerves out in the world put at ease because he was the commander, but he also realized it was just as likely no one when making the decision to saddle Drum with this particular problem had considered the fact that it would be Major General Mark Harris who would be in charge of the operation.

Don't flatter yourself too much, old man, he told himself. The thought almost made him chuckle, until he added, *That's a real good way to get killed in this job.*

Taking his own advice, the major general returned to pondering his problem. As for being prepared for such an event, Harris had to wonder: What exactly should he do? Lock this thing in a bunker, surround it 24-7 with heavily armed men? And dogs, perhaps? Maybe mount machine guns on the roof, circle the place with tanks? He had plenty of men and guns, more than enough heavy artillery. Even enough dogs.

But, he asked himself, *would any of that have helped that police station? They had men and guns there, too. Doesn't seem to have helped them any.*

The major general was perfectly willing to believe that this Morand character wanted this Dream Thing, needed it for some reason that made some bizarre sort of perfect sense to him and his kind. That meant, most likely, that he or his agents would be on their way soon. To men like Morand, dying in an attempt to acquire this thing was considered as good as, if not better than, succeeding. It was something Harris had learned through bitter experience—you do not underestimate the resolve of a fanatic.

In fact, the part of his brain he had relied upon the heaviest over the years reminded him, *if you're smart, you count on it.*

Pursing his lips, allowing them to make a slight "tsking" sound, the general raised his head slightly so that his eyes were aligned with the FBI agent's once more. Then, giving the man enough of a smile to let him know he was willing to work with him, Harris said;

"So tell me, Mr. Klein, just what kind of sci-fi defenses do you think might help kick this sorry bastard's ass?"

CHAPTER THIRTY-SEVEN

LaRaja's eyes went painfully wide as the specter first enveloped him. He did not seem to notice the fact that the professor had been taken inside the shimmering form as well, was not aware that Knight had gripped his shoulder, that the professor's fingers were digging into his flesh with a force far stronger than any of which he would have imagined the academic capable. No, too much of LaRaja's brain was frozen in primal panic to take note of such things.

Get hold of yourself, you old fool, a sliver of his mind snapped, desperate for him to regain control. *A girl said it was nothing, for Christ's sake—a* girl! *Deal with it!*

Still, the detective's initial fears continued to spiral wildly out of control. Despite the defensive preparations Knight had tried to install within LaRaja's mind, the experience was proving too far beyond the realities the man knew or could understand. It was simply too much for him.

Panic threw itself into the detective's veins, ancestral

terrors pummeling him, screaming to him that he was not dreaming, that he was in contact with exactly that with which he thought he was in contact, and that he should be running as far away as he could as fast as possible. Garbled shrieks of horror filled his mind, clawing at him, ordering, begging, cajoling—slamming the detective with every assault they could find to start him moving and then keep him that way.

But just as the last braces his resolve possessed were beginning to actually crack, at the moment he found his heels starting to rise from the ground, his eyes scanning for the best direction in which to make his retreat, suddenly he felt something that calmed a vital portion of his nerves. Something he understood.

Something familiar.

"J-Jimmy?"

The hue of the glow around LaRaja and the professor shimmered brightly in response to the question, the strongest of the gleaming motes swarming around the detective. LaRaja's eyes went wide as multiple emotions raced through his system. His nerves screeched at him, still wanting him to run. But, deep within the man his instincts began to war among themselves.

It is Jimmy, the back of his mind told him. *Or at least, it's Jimmy's ghost. It has to be!* And then, just as LaRaja blurted;

"Piers—it's Jimmy, back from the dead. It's his ghost, right?"

That was the moment when the cloudless sky roared and a massively thick column of tremendous energy blasted downward, striking the two men and the enveloping spirit of Jimmy Dollins with the force of a crashing jetliner. Once more the ground was split and burned, the grass charred in a reeking circle that rushed to spread twenty yards in every direction. Flames slathered across the faces of the surrounding gravestones, blackening their edges, filling the cut marks of their engraved names and dates with a crackling soot, leaving them scorched and steaming.

"Nooooooooo!"

Bridget's voice shattered the still of the evening with every bit as much force as the lightning blast, its mingled fear and pain equally as piercing as its predecessor. Throwing herself out of the detective's car, she raced forward across the burning grass, uncaring of whatever might befall her.

"Professor," she screamed, clambering up the small hillock, unable to find a trace of either Knight or LaRaja through the acrid smoke. "Where are you?"

"We're here, my dear."

Spinning around, Bridget stopped where she was as she found the professor coming across the cemetery lawn toward her. Behind him, farther back, she could see the detective, whole and hale as Knight, still enshrouded by the spirit of his late partner. Her eyes wide, she stopped before her employer, staring at him, her mind thrown into confusion at the sight of the man unharmed—unscorched, even—as if nothing had happened.

"I, I . . . ," she stammered, her thought processes still not quite capable of explaining with any adequacy what she was seeing, "I don't understand. You were just . . . you were hit—again. But you're all right. The detective . . ."

"We're both fine," said Knight in a quiet voice. The side of his mouth curling into his trademark half smile, he told Bridget gently, "Come now, you didn't think I'd return here, to the same spot, looking to re-create what happened before and not bring along something to assure a different result—did you?" His mouth surrendering to the desire to turn itself into a complete smile, Knight added humorously;

"Ahhhh, youth, you just think everyone over thirty is senile, don't you?"

As the girl simply stared, her mind once again trying to keep pace with things that a few days previous she could never have imagined, the professor reached into his pocket and withdrew a small piece of carved wood. Showing it to her, placing the object in her hand, Knight explained;

"White oak—it's from our good friends the Druids. They knew quite a bit when it came to the manipulation of the forces of nature. As a sect they did not possess any real magic, per se, but they did understand how to use one force to channel another."

"And this, this thing . . ."

"It's a runic symbol, meant to give one control over the staggering might of the storm, specifically high winds and lightning. I filched it from the Dark Ages display earlier today. I had a feeling it would come in handy." As Bridget simply stared, Knight continued his academic drone, telling her;

"It absorbs energy; well, no, it doesn't actually absorb it—more redirects it. Moves it around until it can be harnessed—stored. Of course, it's not as simple to use as just, say, carrying around a rabbit's foot for luck, or something along those lines. I had to make several offerings during the afternoon, actually, a bit of mantra chanting as well. . . . You wouldn't believe what it takes to get a live rabbit delivered to you these days, no questions asked . . . but it all seems to have worked out well. Don't you think?"

"You miserable son of a bitch," Bridget snapped. Giving her employer a harsh glance, she added, "I was worried about you—I thought you were dead! Give a girl a little warning when you pull this kind of crap, why don't you?"

"I'm sorry," the professor whispered, "but I thought if you knew I was preparing defenses against lightning you'd spend the entire day worrying about what would happen. I, I suppose I believed it would be easier on you somehow."

Although Bridget seemed to be holding things together, Knight suddenly realized the inordinate amount of stress the night's events had to be putting her under. Looking directly into her eyes, he told her sincerely; "I'm sorry, my dear. Maybe I shouldn't have brought you along. But if I hadn't, I thought that then I'd just be worried about you, and I knew you would worry if you weren't with me, and . . ." Pausing, the professor sighed deeply, shaking his head sadly as he whispered;

"God. I really have made a mess of things for you, haven't I? You come to New York looking for a new life, a career, and what does meeting me get you? You'd have been better off—"

"No," came Bridget's voice sharply, cutting him off. Her eyes boring into Knight's, she told him, "Don't say it. Don't tell me anything about being 'better off' somewhere else or with someone else."

Deciding to allow Bridget the moment to get things out of her system, Knight merely nodded, allowing her to continue without interruption.

"I'm sorry I got so emotional. I apologize, and don't start in with any nonsense about there being no need to do so. I'm your assistant—I'm supposed to be, anyway. I'm supposed to be a help to you, not a burden. But some of . . ." She paused for a moment, then put her hands out before herself in a gesture of confused futility, adding, ". . . all *this*, all of this insanity I never expected . . . it's just taking me a bit of getting used to it all, if you know what I mean."

Half his mouth returning to a smile, Knight tilted his head and answered the young woman warmly, telling her;

"Yes, my dear. I know exactly what you mean. And as I think over my days and years learning the things I take for granted now, I remember a great number of moments of pure and overwhelming terror that might not have been quite so overwhelming if those acting as my instructors had shown a bit more compassion." Holding out one hand to his assistant, he asked;

"My dear young Bridget, do you think you can forgive me?" Taking his hand, Bridget squeezed it gently, saying;

"I'll think about it, but I'm telling you right now, come September all of this better get me one hell of a reference."

Hearing her make a joke, Knight's smile widened. Once again his assistant was proving to be possessed of a remarkable resilience. Feeling a touch self-conscious still holding Bridget's hand, he released it with an embarrassed suddenness, just about to make a further comment when LaRaja walked up to the pair. Not even acknowledging Bridget's presence, he said to the professor;

"It was him. It was Jimmy."

"I know. I knew it when I was here the other evening, when he approached me. He was trying to tell me something, but I couldn't quite understand what he was attempting to get across to me. And then, like tonight, there was a lightning burst, his essence was dispersed, and I was almost killed."

"And yet," said the detective, "the same thing happened tonight and we're none the worse for wear."

"This time I came prepared. Both to hopefully thwart the possible lightning with this," he said, presenting LaRaja the wooden rune he had shown his assistant a moment earlier, "and to find out what Detective Dollins wanted to tell me, by having available someone he could talk to without any problems whatsoever." The two men stared at each other, neither speaking. After a moment, Knight finally asked;

"So, was I correct? Were you able to decipher his message?"

"Oh yes," responded LaRaja. His eyes boring into the professor's, he said, "That thing in the property room, as Denny fought it, something about a ring you gave him, it allowed him to contain it." The detective stopped to catch his breath, then added excitedly;

"Anyway, I know exactly what we need to do now." To which a disturbingly sinister voice from behind the trio asked;

"Really, do you now? Is that not most fortunate?"

CHAPTER THIRTY-EIGHT

"How's everything coming with the preparations," asked Harris as he studied the map spread out on the table before him. "Especially in grid areas 37 through 48?"

"Everything is moving according to plan, sir."

Klein watched the major general as he worked with his staff, clearly impressed with the officer and his abilities. For the first time in days the FBI man was actually feeling as if he might be able to finally relax. Indeed, despite his bureau-born dread of working with the military, Klein was finding himself more than slightly amazed with the smooth way things had progressed for him so far at Fort Drum. Of course, he told himself, it was not as if he had not had ample reason to be apprehensive. Over the years more than one joint FBI–Armed Forces operation had ended in failure, recriminations, and even fisticuffs.

This is, he thought wryly, working to keep his face passive as he did so, *certainly a new and different experience. And I have to admit, I'm kind of enjoying it.*

Unlike a number of career military men and women circumstances had forced him to collaborate with in the past, Harris had proved to be not only a competent professional but also a man of no little imagination. The FBI agent was certain that the major general suspected more was going on than he was being told, but he also seemed to realize, or at least be willing to believe, that Klein himself did not know anything more than he had related to him. Harris had also shown a marked aptitude for adaptability far beyond that to be found in the other military leaders the agent had met in his time, a thing Klein was finding himself extremely grateful for at that moment.

Thank God this is the guy in charge here, thought the FBI man, watching Harris as he continued to efficiently mobilize his troops. *Not that I'm looking to put a jinx on things, but I'm beginning to believe this may actually turn out okay after all.*

What Klein appreciated most was the fact that the major general did not simply dispatch subordinate officers to get the ball rolling. Harris, of course, realized the necessity of utilizing his chain of command to not only facilitate getting a number of operations started but also keep them moving—he was not the usual micromanaging marionette with no idea how to delegate authority. But beyond that, Harris also seemed to understand the urgency of keeping the Dream Stone safely out of Morand's hands. Thus the officer threw himself completely into every aspect of the defenses being mounted to drive home the urgency of their situation to his men.

"Lead by example," the major general said to Klein in a moment when he noted the FBI man watching him. "You want men to understand something's important, let them see you getting your own hands dirty. They'll get the idea."

"It worked for Patton."

Harris stopped what he was doing for a moment as he considered the obvious compliment. Deciding the FBI man had meant it as such, Harris gave the agent a slight but appreciative nod, answering him with humility, "General Patton had good men."

"And how are your men, sir?"

"They're some of the best."

Klein returned the major general's smile. The fact that the officer did not overly brag about the merits of his command or how he had "made them the men they are," et cetera, impressed the agent greatly, giving him an even more secure feeling that Harris had exactly the kind of competence needed for their situation. The commander had devised a strategy with which the FBI man could find no flaws. Considering that the terrorists had been able to employ whatever this new, hellish weapon they had used against the police station in the middle of a city was, the major general saw no additional safety being offered by placing the Dream Stone within any of his own buildings. Thus he decided on moving the block out onto Drum's extensive testing range.

The fort controlled an incredibly vast spread of open acreage, hilly, twisting land, dotted with trees and trenched with ravines, all of which his troops knew intimately. Setting up three separate defensive points, all several miles apart in a rough triangle, the major general explained to the agent that the target would be placed in one of a trio of similar locked boxes. Thus even the men defending the positions would not know which one actually held the Dream Stone.

"I'm doubting this Morand character of yours can mount overwhelming attacks on three separate positions," Harris told the FBI man. "It's almost assured he'll have to pick a single target and start on it. This way, even if in some manner I can't imagine at this time, he does manage to somehow overwhelm one of our strongholds, those men will have two heavily fortified points to which they can either retreat, or from which they can summon aide."

"And, of course," offered Klein, you have the entire fort from which you can reinforce any of the positions as well."

"You catch on quick, Mr. Klein," offered the major general. Giving the agent a slight nod of approval, Harris added, "I like that. Yes, we already have close to a thousand men on short alert. Gear assembled, weapons to the ready. We can mobilize them in hundred-man units and have them in the field in ten-minute intervals if need be."

"Looks as if everything is under control, sir," answered Klein, unconsciously nodding back as he did so.

"Looks that way to me, too," agreed Harris. "So why is it the hair on the back of my neck is standing at attention?"

"Pardon me, sir?"

"There's a turd somewhere in the punch bowl here," answered the officer. Looking up from his map, he slowly rolled his lips back and forth across his front teeth, then asked, "Don't you think so, Mr. Klein?"

"In all honesty," admitted the FBI man, "I do, sir. But I haven't the slightest idea where it is." The agent paused for a moment, then added;

"I will say, though, sir, that . . . and I beg the major general's pardon for doing so . . . I think there's something weird going on here. Voodoo weird, UFO weird, haunted house, noise-in-the-night, walking-dead weird . . . ah, sir." Harris regarded Klein for a moment, his eyes narrowing as he studied the agent. After only a brief pause, he responded, admitting;

"So do I. And thanks for being honest, Mr. Klein. Trust me, it helps."

The agent nodded, saying nothing in response as Harris turned back to his preparations. It had taken a lot for Klein to reveal his true impression of their assignment. Such statements could end a man's career overnight. He was glad he had done so, however.

The entire affair gave him a sour feeling. Everything connected to the Dream Stone—especially Professor butter-wouldn't-melt-in-his-mouth Piers Knight—gave him a sour feeling. He was relieved to hear that the officer felt the same way he did. Although, as he told himself;

He could just have easily picked up his queasy feeling from us. Meaning you'd better be right about this shit, Martin, my boy, or your career could be headed for the most spectacular Dumpster dive of all time.

Forcing himself to concentrate on the immediate, Klein returned to studying the activity around him. Following the major general's hands, he watched as the officer moved them over the map unrolled on the table before them, pointing out the various stages of what he had planned. Klein found it interesting that despite the fact the command center from which they were operating was equipped with a sophisticated electronics system that would have allowed the officer to simply display the necessary maps on a variety of screens—to then zoom in, do split-screen comparisons and the such—that he preferred to work with paper instead.

What intrigued Klein so was the fact Harris was not an older man. In fact, he seemed to have barely reached an age suitably advanced to have attained the rank he held, let alone to have been entrusted with such a sizable command. Still, there was nothing about the man that indicated he should not hold either his rank or his assigned duty.

Stop worrying about idiot details, Klein told himself. *Better to stay focused on what's heading our way.*

And, oddly enough, as wicked Fate would have it, it was at that precise moment the first alert came streaming in from one of the three defensive outposts. The captain taking the radio call turned to his commander, telling him, "First Post Able, sir—they're under attack."

"Damnation," growled Harris.

"What's wrong?"

"What do you think, Mr. Klein?" The major general snarled, extending his hand to the captain who had fielded the report, demanding the headset in his hand. "Your terrorists are here already, and they somehow picked the right target."

Klein clamped his mouth shut, holding in his own set of curses. Knowing the gathering of intelligence was the most important thing they could do right then, he remained quiet, listening intently as Harris demanded;

"Speak to me, soldier. Just what kind of attack's being mounted out there? Small arms, mortars? What'd those bastards manage to pull together on such short notice?"

"I don't know what to tell you, sir," came the voice on the phone. The major general strained to hear the tone of the man on the other end of the line. Harris could tell the officer in the forward defensive post was more confused than frightened, although he did not know of what. Not pressuring the man, however, Harris allowed him the seconds he seemed to need. After his brief pause, the man swallowed hard, then continued, saying;

"It's not any kind of standard attack, sir. It's, it's . . . it's not like anything I've ever seen before." The captain on the other end of the phone excused himself and started snapping orders to others in his unit. As the major general listened, he could hear commands being given to film whatever constituted the reported attack and to broadcast the feed back to their headquarters. In the background he could hear a continually growing barrage of weapons fire. Finally, after an extended moment, the captain came back on the line, telling Harris;

"Sorry for the delay, sir. We're throwing everything we have at whatever it is, but it's having no effect."

"On what?" The commander paused for a split second, reining

in his temper, then demanded calmly, "What is it they're throwing at you?" And, as he asked the question, an officer at a receiver across the room said;

"We're getting a feed from their video team. We're patching it in now, sir. Monitor A."

All eyes followed the officer's pointing hand to the television screen in question. And as the device quietly warmed, then came into focus, everyone in the room fell silent as their minds tried to comprehend the images coming across the display before them.

"UFOs and voodoo, indeed," muttered Harris. Unable to look away from the monitor, the major general asked;

"Klein, what the hell is that? Is that what did the damage to the police station?"

Agent Martin Klein stared wide-eyed at the screen, in much the same manner as everyone else in the room. Suddenly he understood why the rifle, mortar, and cannon fire he could hear erupting from the room's speakers was having no effect on whatever it was that was approaching Post Able. His mouth hanging open, the FBI man continued to stare at Monitor A, unable to make any comment on what he was seeing whatsoever while the sounds of explosions and hideous screams continued to fill the room all around him.

CHAPTER THIRTY-NINE

"Bakur!" exclaimed Knight, accidentally revealing how completely the terrorist's arrival had caught him off-guard. "What in the devil are you doing here?"

"Making certain that your interference with my plans has come to an end, Piers Knight."

The terrorist walked across the lawn toward Knight, LaRaja, and Bridget slowly, casually, his body language as relaxed as if he were doing nothing more than joining the trio for some sort of midnight picnic. He appeared unarmed—his hands held no weapons, at least. But there was something in his stride, the sauntering deliberateness, the calm measure of it, that sent the nerves of all in the trio racing toward caution. Behind them, the spirit of Jimmy Dollins shifted back and forth, not so much drifting on the breeze as appearing to be phasing in and out of existence. Coming close to the professor, the continually diminishing wraith seemed to disappear altogether.

"*My* interference with your plans?" Knight touched

his chest with his hand, his pose that of one thoroughly confused. Straightening slightly, he added, "And how have I interfered with your plans?"

"By existing, Piers Knight. Worse—by thinking, by believing you have any *right* to exist."

"Well," answered the professor slowly, trying to keep his voice from revealing how truly tense he felt, "that response was certainly both vague and nonsensical. Whatever the case, I did not mean to upset your secret little applecart." Spreading his hands wide, Knight offered;

"Perhaps if I had some idea of what these plans of yours actually were, I'd be better able to avoid interfering with them in the future. You know, in the name of smoother international relations."

Bakur's forward motion ceased then with an odd, robotic-like suddenness. He did not halt normally, like a man deciding to stop because he had gone as far as he wished, because he was suddenly trepidatious about continuing onward, or because of any other reason that might cause a human brain to give the command to cease moving. He simply stopped, fast and cold, freezing in a somewhat stiff position to study the three before him. As he did so, he smiled thinly, his eyes reflecting light from a source none before him could identify.

"I must admit you are a most amusing man, Piers Knight. You are still searching for an answer, are you not? Uselessly continuing to struggle forward toward comprehension, a finned slug, flopping upward onto a nameless beach, hoping for the miracle of mobility."

"Is that bastard just goddamned nuts?" LaRaja's whispered question went unanswered save for a timid shrug from Bridget. The two of them, both instinctively realizing that Bakur's attention was completely focused on Knight, took the moment to take a backward step. Aware that the terrorist had taken no notice of their motions, they both took another.

"My," the professor answered Bakur, his brain racing, "you've certainly become quite the loquacious fellow. But, suddenly wordy or not, I'll admit, yes, I would like to know what's going on—very much so. What has been going on. And, I must admit, I'd certainly like to know how I, a simple museum curator, could possibly be any kind of impediment to a man who commands the kinds of resources that you do."

At first the terrorist remained silent, his eyes continuing to stay focused on Knight. In the far distance one could still hear the sounds of the evening, the noise of the night insects, the rustle of small creatures moving about in the well-manicured brush. But for yards in every direction around the professor and Bakur, a dread and dampening silence lay across the land. No mosquitos buzzed about them; no frogs croaked; no birds or bats dared the air around them.

Taking advantage of the situation, LaRaja used the pair's fascination with each other to keep Bridget moving away from what he sensed was going to be trouble. Part of the detective's mind questioned his actions—saw no sense in them. He was the one who was armed, after all. Bakur might have a weapon hidden on his person, but the officer was certain Knight did not. By rights he was the one who should be confronting the terrorist.

Yeah, thought LaRaja, his hand now around Bridget's arm, moving her along at an even retreat, *Knight brings us out here to talk to ghosts, then keeps us from being fried by lightning. And then this certified creep shows up. I'm sure that's all the freaky shit we're going to see here tonight.*

The detective felt no shame in retreating. His main concern was to be able to move Bridget to his car, to give her his keys along with a chance to escape to safety. After that he could turn back to see if there was anything he could do.

Whatever goddamned little that might be.

The thought chilled LaRaja. What, he wondered, what could he actually do? And about what? What exactly was going to happen next? What could happen? For all intents and purposes, the scene from which he was retreating was just two men standing on a lawn. What in the name of God, the surface levels of his mind screamed at him, was he so worried about?

But that was the rational part of his brain, the cop, the everyday fellow who still liked John Wayne movies, the tea drinker, the piece of him that still believed a two and another two could be reasonably assembled into a four no matter what. The part of him that was almost always in control, that had steered the ship of his actions nearly every second of his life.

What had him so worried, he knew, was that there were more voices within his head than that one guiding force. And after what he had seen that evening, those other voices were stirring, flooding his mind with dread warnings and whispered possibilities, most of them beyond his immediate comprehension. Normally he could dismiss such thoughts easily, locking them back in their cells where they belonged.

That night, however, his nerves screamed at him to listen to them. His entire body seemed to be teaming up with that part of his brain. Although he was striving to remain in control, sweat was beading on his brow, running down his spine, gathering in his armpits, behind his elbows and knees, around his ankles. His back was chilled, his neck tightening. His breathing was coming faster; his eyes had stopped blinking.

"There are ghosts in the world, Denny," the new voice whispered. "You *know* it's true now. And, just as surely as you know that, you *know* there is something completely, terribly wrong with this whole scene."

LaRaja, his shoulders beginning to shake, the muscles in his knees trembling, signaling their desire to collapse, to throw him to the ground, caught hold of himself with a violent, internal scream. Still moving toward his car, his hand still clutching Bridget's arm, he hurried forward, ignoring all the sounds within his mind. He would reach his car, give it to the girl, send her on her way.

Then, he told himself, then he would figure out what he was going to do next.

AT THE SAME TIME AS THE DETECTIVE'S RETREAT, KNIGHT AND HIS adversary had begun to move slowly, eyes locked, circling one another. Their movements were not threatening; they were not crouching, ready to pounce at the first sign of weakness. It was more a need to move, to stay in motion, to simply not remain stationary.

"You surprised my people at the museum," Bakur said, his tone thick and dark. "They were not expecting interference. Especially not anything so effective."

"We do what we can," answered Knight. "So it was you that sent the thieves. Makes sense. But tell me, if you would, why? The museum would certainly have granted full access to the Dream Stone to Ungari. Why steal it?"

"Access." Bakur laughed at the word, the noise of him a snarling bark. "And what good would that be to one such as I? Oh, may we touch your stolen rock? Might we breathe the air surrounding it? Your generosity is boundless, Piers Knight."

"I'm certain you could have taken the piece back to Syria in time. The museum has worked with many governments to—"

"I am no *government*, you *fool*!"

The professor stumbled slightly in reaction to Bakur's sudden outburst. The man screamed his words, spittle flying from his lips, the bizarre light in his eyes intensifying. As Knight continued to stare, the terrorist bent his neck at an odd angle, tilting his head until his eyes were practically perpendicular. Opening his mouth wide, two lines of drool sliding down over his cheek, he allowed another dark sound to rumble upward from within, then bellowed;

"I am not interested in the workings of your world. I have no concern for babbling rules, idiot regulations. I am come to take all that I desire—and the first thing I want, the event I cherish at this moment, Piers Knight, is your *death*!"

And with those words, Bakur snapped his head in the opposite direction. Standing suddenly straight, he threw his arms directly out before him and sent a dazzling blast of flaming, searing power in an unavoidably straight line at the professor.

CHAPTER FORTY

"Keep firing! For Christ's sake, pour it on!"

The captain's orders did not go unheeded, but the following of them accomplished little. First Post Able was about to be overrun and there was absolutely nothing that could be done about it.

"What the hell is that thing, Captain?"

"You tell me, soldier, and we'll both know."

That the fifty men assigned to defend Post Able could react at all in the face of the thing approaching them was a testament to their training and their commander. Large it was, gigantic, but formless for the most part as well. The tanks that had been sent out to meet it had pumped shell after shell into it with no effect. The rounds had passed through the shape, exploding against whatever they finally struck that stopped their progress.

The gunners had known their missiles were on-target. Their line-of-sight weapons utilized heat-seeking technology, which made it impossible to miss their target, for the thing at which they hurled their shells was completely made of fire. It was akin to the horror sent into the precinct house basement with which Jimmy Dollins had done battle, but a thousand times larger.

"What's happening there, Captain?" Major General Harris' voice boomed through the officer's earpiece.

"Aren't you receiving our video feed, sir?"

"Negative. We're getting something, but there must be some sort of interference. The images we're receiving are too unclear for us to make anything out. Repeat, what's happening there? What are you up against?"

"I, I don't know, sir," answered the captain. "It's gigantic, twenty, thirty stories. I don't know exactly; it keeps changing size."

"Changing size?"

"Yes, sir." The captain closed his eyes, straining to keep the terror he was feeling out of his voice. The man was a well-trained soldier. He had no overwhelming fear of dying. That was his duty and he was ready to give his all. "I don't think it's actually alive, sir. I don't know how else to say this, sir, but this . . . *thing*, it's like it's made of fire."

But this was different. This enemy was not here to capture territory, to seize plunder or make some sort of political statement. The captain knew—could feel it in his bones—this thing had come to suck away souls, and nowhere in his indoctrination did anyone mention the possibility of that.

"Fire?"

"Yes, sir—fire. It's walking flames. Sometimes you can make out a kind of body, but it, it shifts, sir. It just . . . changes. Our shells either pass right through it or they explode from the heat. When they do explode, they kind of spread the fire around, but they can't put it out. Nothing can put it out. It just . . . keeps coming. It just . . . keeps *coming*!"

"Get that damn hunk of rock out of there, Captain. Move it to Post Baker, now!"

"Already done, sir. We . . ."

And then, the captain's voice faded from Harris' receiver. Try as he might, the officer could not speak. His mind had become riveted, focused entirely on the sight spread out before him. The thing seemed to have become enraged—the officer could think of no other word—at the attacking tanks. So far its speed had appeared ponderous, clumsy. But now, suddenly the walking fire simply threw itself at one of the Abrams, enveloping it in flame. Screams filled the air as the men inside the tank were roasted, their uniforms burned from their bodies, their flesh melted to their seats. Then, the molten force swirling within the war wagon finally reached a sufficient temperature to ignite its ammunition. The tank disintegrated from the force of the explosion.

"Oh God, oh my—"

Before the captain could complete his prayer, the shambling horror turned its attention to more of the tanks. Having found a way to rid itself of the petty annoyances, it hurled itself from one to another. Traveling at practically the speed of light, it burned its way into each of them, incinerating their crews, then either causing them to explode or melting them into slag. After watching some twenty such attacks, the captain finally managed to shout into his microphone;

"Sir, don't send out any more Abrams. It, it's destroying them all—one by one. It can't be stopped, sir."

"Captain, listen to me—can you hear me, soldier?"

"Oh dear God, it can't be stopped. It can't be *stopped*!"

"Captain . . ."

Harris tried to halt his officer's apparent mental breakdown, worked at focusing the captain's attention on performing his duty, but it was too late. The man was no longer capable of responding to orders. His men, those he had not sent to remove the Dream

Stone to the next post in the chain of command, were running across the fields, screaming in terror. They were not in retreat, nor were they deserting their duty station. Either would have taken the ability to make rational decisions, and none of them was capable of such at the moment.

"Captain . . ."

None of them could explain what they were witnessing. They had been told they might be facing some manner of new offensive technology, but this their minds knew was no man-made weapon. This thing coming toward them was some terrible, malevolent evil thrust forth from one ancient hell or another to lay waste to everything in its path.

"Goddamn it, *Captain* . . . come in . . . answer me, soldier."

As the officer stood transfixed in his command bunker, he watched as one after another of his men were barbecued, the flaming monstrosity launching small napalm blasts at the running figures as if spitting at mice. Several score spots of the countryside were now ablaze, each of them with a flaming war machine or fallen soldier burning in its center.

"Captain," Harris growled, his voice terse but still crackling with authority. Refusing to give up, he snapped, "Pull yourself together. Get yourself out of there. Do you hear me, soldier?"

"Too late," came the captain's feeble whisper after a moment. His voice low and frightened, reduced to that of a man stripped of any sense that the future still lay before him, he whimpered, "Too late . . . sir."

The captain's voice broke into a momentary sob, after which came a terrible rumbling. Before any could question the sound, tremors rattled the room—walls cracked; light fixtures fell. Then, as the room flooded with darkness, Major General Harris' earpiece was filled with the sound of rushing flames, a terrible scream, and then a cold and horrible silence.

CHAPTER FORTY-ONE

"You are, I must admit, a very resilient human being, Piers Knight."

The words flowing from Bakur were not an understatement. The scorching power he had released from his body had been more than enough to overturn an eighteen-wheel truck, to send it rolling end over end. Yet the professor had only been forced back several feet, and then it had been but the force sliding his hard-soled shoes across the close-cropped cemetery lawn. Knight had, of course, utilized his white-oak rune to divert the energy blast. The defense had taken every bit of his concentration, and the effort had left him quite drained. But the effort had also left him alive and unscathed, and his opponent a trifle confused.

"Well, you know," the professor answered, breathing heavily, desperately stalling for time, "in my profession you have to be somewhat hearty. All that sorting through files, flipping page after page, and . . . oh my goodness, the card catalogs—don't get me started—"

When Knight had scattered Bakur's life force, he had also managed to study it. As the power passed over his protective shield, he allowed the barest contact between it and his own aura so he might identify his enemy's energy source. What the professor had felt startled him greatly. So greatly, in fact, he began to scrutinize the terrorist more closely, trying to determine exactly what had happened to the man.

"Are you babbling out of fear, Piers Knight, or are you attempting to waste my time?"

Watching Bakur closely, the professor realized the words he was hearing were not being spoken, were not emanating from the terrorist's larynx, were not being formed by his tongue and teeth. Nor, Knight finally concluded, was he hearing them within his ears as he would other sounds. What he was hearing was being created within his brain, a fact that terrified the academic deeply. Summoning what little courage he could find left within him, Knight answered;

"Well, since you're not laughing, I suppose I was wasting your time, after all. But all right, if it's going to be nothing but work, work, work with you, perhaps we should get down to business. So, here's a question. . . . I'm not actually conversing with Hamid Bakur, am I?"

"Of course not, Piers Knight. That creature gave itself over to me long ago. At first I could only make suggestions to it, guide it, and then only where our mutual interests crossed. But it did not take long before this shell you see was merely my puppet, an extension of my will in your dimension."

The professor clamped down upon his nerves as harshly as he could, desperate to not show what he was feeling. His system screamed in rebellion, desperate to shake, to thrash. His knees flared with pain, hoping to force him to the ground. Every part of him that was human, the primal mammalian instincts of him, were all rolling one over the other within his mind in unimaginable terror, overloading his neural pathways with commands to run, to crawl, to beg—to faint.

"Well, it's not actually my dimension, you know."

The part of Knight that was more than animal rallied around his ability to still toss off a joke. Minuscule and unfunny as it might have been, it was still a sign of defiance, one thrown at both his foe as well as at those parts of his mind bellowing for him to surrender. More frightened at his own human weakness than at whatever had sunk its ethereal claws into Bakur, the professor followed up his answer with a question;

"Look, let's make this easy on ourselves. You want something. I'm insignificant. You have power; all humans want power. Surely there must be some basis for mutual cooperation where we can work something out here."

The body of Hamid Bakur continued to stand in the same robotic pose it had taken when first it had begun to converse with Knight. Nothing about its stance changed—its mouth did not twitch, eyes did not move. And yet, despite any of the normal clues one might look for to determine what was happening within the mind of another, the professor knew he was being studied, that his words were being considered.

Perhaps it's the fact we're in mental communication, he thought. *It must not be able to read my mind. If it could, if nothing else, it would have known about the white oak, would have made some different attack. Or would have kept attacking.*

Knight gave off watching the unmoving figure. Searching for human cues was useless, for Bakur was no longer human. He had been taken over, possessed—but by what?

Come on, curator, the professor snarled at himself within his mind. *Think. You're so damn proud of this brain of yours*—use it, *goddamn it! What is this thing? Where does it come from? What does it want?*

Deciding the entity within Bakur was not going to speak again without further prompting, Knight decided on the direct approach. Summoning all of his diminished courage into one lump, he squeezed it as tightly as he could, praying his voice would not crack as he asked;

"So, this dimension of yours, where is it exactly? Why have you come here? What is it you want?"

"You question me?"

Knight froze slightly. For the first time, the Bakur thing managed to throw tone into its communication. Darker, angry, the words crackled with warning within the professor's mind. Straining to remain jovial, the curator answered;

"Again, my fine new friend, I can't help you if I don't know where you're from, or what you want. I mean, are you something that's come this way before? What we might think of as, oh, I don't know . . . the Christian Devil? An Iblis, Ahriman, or Shaitan from the Middle East? Maybe the Teutonic Nixie, the Huldrefolk of Norway, Australia's Bunyip . . . we've had so many extradimensional visitors here. If you would just—"

Silence!

The single word rang within Knight's mind, shattering his concentration, forcing his mounting fear once more to the surface. His nerve endings tingling, teeth close to chattering, the professor searched desperately for a next move when suddenly the Bakur thing obliged him by revealing all he had wanted to know.

"I am none of the petty mites your tiny monkey brain can comprehend. But do not know fear, Piers Knight. I will reveal to you all you wish to know, and then you will do all that I command!"

The professor heard the horror's words in his mind, and for a moment his soul sparked with hope. Once he understood, once he had a handle on what was happening, he prayed, then he might plan a strategy; then he might be able to cobble together some kind of defense. For one brief split second, optimism flooded the curator's brain with assurance.

Then, the Bakur thing seared his mind with all the information he desired, and Piers Knight responded by falling to his knees and screaming into the night.

CHAPTER FORTY-TWO

"Get those men out of there," shouted Harris. Waving his arms at his subordinates in the command center, he told them, "Do it. Get everyone out of the field. Pull them back—*now, goddamn it!*"

The major general did not fault those around him for being stunned—for momentarily freezing in helpless silence. The fantastic horrors they all had witnessed, the screaming terror they had heard, it had shocked him into immobility for a moment as well. Scores of his men dead, hundreds of thousands of dollars of equipment destroyed, in only a matter of minutes. He had never before experienced such losses, never had a command so utterly routed—so completely destroyed. Worse than all that had happened so far, however, was the fact that none of them still had even the slightest idea what they were up against.

What in all the hells is that thing, wondered Harris, his mind swirling, grasping at straws. It was one thing to dutifully trot off to services every Sunday, to drone prayers along with the rest of the congregation, mouthing homilies as he had done since childhood. Where he was at that instant in time was something completely different—something for which he was not prepared. Now he was faced with what appeared to be exactly what he had been praying about all that time, and he had no idea what he was supposed to do.

Dear Jesus in Heaven, he thought. *Is this it?* Staring at the one monitor someone in the room had managed to get working once more, the major general studied the moving images they had chosen to replay. Once more watching the shambling monstrosity blaze its way across his domain with impunity, he wondered;

Is it . . . that thing *. . . is it a demon, some kind of devil—the Devil?*

And then the absurdity of what Harris had just said reminded the commander of an old *Weekly World News* cover. It had featured a diabolical face superimposed over a cloud above the Chernobyl nuclear reactor. The headline had read: *Satan Escapes from Hell.*

It couldn't be, he thought to himself, worked hard to believe. *But if it's not, then what? What is it?*

A blazing, silent beast striding the earth, destroying the faithful, obliterating his men with ease, wiping all he had been charged to keep whole from the face of the planet. Merciless, monstrous—evil incarnate.

Is it? the major general continued to wonder. *Could it be? Could it actually* be?

A second series of tremendous quakes rattled the command post at that moment, overturning tables and chairs, throwing people to the ground, disrupting the ever so recently reestablished power. Lights flickered once more; computer screens phased in and out of operation. The new, major tremors were followed by a series of lesser ones, then another massive blast that rattled the entire building, violently shaking the roof and showering the interior with the dust of decades. As he staggered back to his feet, Harris demanded;

"What in the name of God is going on?"

"I'm on the line with Charlie command, sir!" shouted an officer who had already managed to regain his footing. "That, that thing—whatever it is—it's blasting the ground. It's not even trying to hit anything. They say it's just firing randomly, into the sky, burning the hills. It's throwing energy in every direction. . . . It's not even looking for targets anymore."

The soldier seemed ready to say more, then stopped suddenly. Realizing the officer was receiving further updates through his com link, Harris held his mounting questions, giving his subordinate a moment to not only finish listening to whatever message was coming in but to compose himself. Listening to the nervous edge in the man's voice a moment earlier, the major general had been afraid the officer was about to lose control.

"Sir," Harris let go a silent sigh of relief at the renewed vigor in the officer's tone. The commander could tell from the single word that somehow the soldier had pulled himself together even though what he had to report was worse news. "The . . . the thing . . ."

The major general understood the officer's hesitation. It had dawned on Harris suddenly that by using the word "thing" that he was describing the force they were struggling against as some sort of actual, possibly even *living* being. The major general nodded to the man, a motion giving the officer silent approval to continue. Swallowing hard, the soldier added;

"It's moving again, sir. It appears the moment the objective was delivered to Post Baker, the thing started on a direct path toward that post."

"Sir," interrupted Klein, dusting himself off. "If I might make a suggestion?"

"Right now I'm open to even civilian opinions."

The FBI man took an extra second to make certain of his footing, then hurried across the room, saying, "We're out of the city, out in the country. They worry about fires everywhere, but out here, where there isn't a fire hydrant every forty feet, they have to have different options—right?" Not being slow on the uptake, Harris saw instantly where Klein was trying to lead him;

"You're talking forest-fire equipment, helicopters outfitted with water-drop bags, chemical foam bombs—that kind of thing. Right?"

"That was my thought, sir."

Immediately the major general sprang into action. Signaling his communications officer, he ordered the man to mobilize the fort's own firefighting teams. Then, as soon as that was accomplished, he was to pull together a team as quickly as possible and to get them working on finding any additional firefighting equipment that might be available in the area.

"Put no more than five minutes into each call," Harris ordered. "And if they don't volunteer their services, send a detachment at top speed to confiscate everything they have." As the soldier snapped off a salute, then turned to start putting those he picked to work, the major general called out to another of his aides;

"Captain, I'm willing to gamble that damn Hell thing is in tune with our Dream Stone. That it somehow knows where it is at all times."

"Yes, sir."

"Get in touch with Post Baker. Grab a Jeep and get out there in person if the phones are out. That damned monster thing, whatever it is, it's obviously attracted to Mr. Klein's Dream Stone. All right, fine, if that's the case, then I want that thing stuffed into something light and fast, and I want it in motion."

"Sir . . . ?"

"Get it in a truck and get it moving. We want to keep that thing in the area and we want to keep it busy."

And, with those words, all across the command center the faces of men and women began to light up as they regained their confidence. Their leader had a plan. Something for them to focus upon, to work toward. Brushing at the dust covering his head, Harris stared into the face of the FBI man standing next to him and said;

"We'll knock this thing down a peg yet, what do you think, Mr. Klein?"

"Goddamn it, sir," responded the agent, crossing his fingers as the entire command center suddenly shook once more, "but you just might be right."

Then, Klein closed his eyes for a moment and offered up a prayer in the Hebrew that he had not used for a very long time.

CHAPTER FORTY-THREE

"Foolish mortal . . ."

Professor Piers Knight lay on the ground, panting, steam rising from his pain-wracked body. The part of his brain that had managed to regain control over at least some of its functions was desperately struggling to get him moving once more with little success.

"Your pitiful resistance . . ."

With a Homeric effort the professor managed to flip himself over, his back coming away from the ground, his hands bracing for the inevitable impact. Catching himself a split second before the action would have driven his face into the cemetery lawn, Knight fought the urge to simply collapse.

"Do you understand now, human, how useless such actions are?"

The professor nodded weakly, struggling to give off an outward appearance of weak compliance while his brain raced to make use of the information it had acquired.

He now understood that the man known as Hamid Bakur was long gone, that he had been completely replaced by the horror sneering within Knight's own mind. The thing living within the terrorist's former shell was burning it away at a rapid pace, using its life force at a tremendous rate. The professor had also learned that the thing was indeed from another dimension. And that within its home plane of existence it was known as the A'ademir.

"You've been here before," gasped Knight, stalling for time. Releasing his words as slowly as possible, using each of them as a desperate bid to regain his strength, he said, "Thousands of years ago. You came to this world. You devoured Memak'tori."

In his mind, during the burning moment of agony in which he and the A'ademir had shared consciousness, the professor had witnessed the entire affair. Nearly ten thousand years in the past, the world's first great metropolis had grown too fast, become too cosmopolitan too quickly. Within its boundaries, possessed by the arrogance of the naive, its citizens believed all truly intelligent beings had to be benevolent.

"Its inhabitants . . . their minds, their souls," Knight gasped audibly, more for dramatic purposes than to capture breath. Forcing his knees to bend, his arms to slowly push his body upward, he continued to stall, asking, "The freshness of their ideas, the purity of the ideals . . . that's what attracted you here. That . . . that's why you're here again—isn't it?"

"You are a wonderfully clever little bug, Piers Knight. I am certain you will prove to be one of the tastiest morsels to be found when I return."

"Yes, that's the key, isn't it?" Lifting his hands from the ground, his feet finally planted firmly beneath himself once more, the professor stood slowly, then turned to face the horror from beyond. Coughing, not surprised to taste blood as he did so, Knight wiped at his mouth as he asked;

"That's why you haven't been able to simply reach out and suck away my life essence, or anyone else's. You're not actually here yet, are you?"

The Bakur thing stood unmoving for a moment, then raised its hands until they were at the level of the puppet's waist. The horror paused for another few seconds and then, with mocking slowness, applauded Knight's answer. Forcing a smile onto its face, the shambler said;

"So exceptionally clever. You are correct, Piers Knight. I do not touch at this moment, in any sense in which you understand the physical planes of existence, touch your world—no. Not yet. But I shall soon. As soon as the mite which I have dispatched to retrieve the beacon completes its task."

"The Dream Stone," gasped Knight. Finally standing erect once more, honestly swaying slightly from the exertion, the professor took a moment to steady himself before he ended up falling back to the ground. Then, panting, he wiped at his mouth, again, telling the thing before him, "Its form, its carvings, that's got nothing to do with its value to you. You simply need it returned to Memak'tori. You can't find your way back here without it being there—can you?"

"Immensely correct you are," answered the A'ademir smugly. "But that idea shall be fact in but a handful of breaths. And then I shall flash across the face of your world consuming all in my path."

The professor did not bother himself with trying to understand the insane geometry of it all. Why the horror could not find a location in which, in at least one sense, at least some part of it already existed was an academic puzzle that could be solved later. Right now, it gave Knight the answer he needed. Pointing at the Bakur thing, he spat;

"You, you were invited by the Memak'torians. They thought

you some manner of great benefactor, some all-knowing Godhead. They imagined that interaction with you would make them gods themselves, didn't they?"

"Always so very true. I have devoured trillions of such helplessly infantile races. Their minds, so childishly foolish, believing all advancement leads to the same destination. Last time I passed by close enough to taste your universe, it was but one small patch of you that had cluttered their minds with such gibberish—"

"But," interrupted Knight, his breathing nearly under his control once more, "it was enough to guide you here."

"It was. They beseeched the Heavens for such as me, and I came to them. Now, not enough of you truly believe in anything to light the way of my coming, but it matters not. Once the stone is returned to Memak'tori, that will be light enough. My Bakur puppet has welcomed me in. When his city is whole once more, I shall reap your souls by the billions."

Knight, sweat pouring down his forehead, the taste of blood still foul in his mouth, took a long, deep breath. Gulping it down, he twisted the ring newly restored to his hand, then hissed;

"Well then, I guess we'd better remove your puppet before you can help him recover his stone."

And, so saying, the professor threw up his hands and released the spirit of Detective James Dollins, which had been hiding within him for so long, sending it directly into the A'ademir!

CHAPTER FORTY-FOUR

On the burning plains of Fort Drum, firefighters emptied their hoses and released their chemical foam at the shambling horror still lighting the night sky. The monstrosity had been reduced in both size and power by their continual bombardment, but not to the point where anyone felt it might be dealt with safely. A helicopter rigged with a tremendous scoop had successfully dumped thousands of gallons of water from a nearby lake twice upon the blazing behemoth, only to then be blasted from the night sky.

"It appears we're having an effect, sir."

Staring through his binoculars, Major General Harris agreed with his subordinate's estimation of the battle, but he was in no way satisfied. The commander was convinced the only reason for the limited progress they had made thus far against the burning thing was that it was in no way concerned with their struggle. Its only concern seemed to be the capture of the Dream Stone, and its single-minded aggression in that area kept it too focused on its prize to mount more than the occasional defense.

"But it's too damn little, and it may end up being too damn late." Lowering his binoculars, Harris shouted, "What's the word on those bombs? Are they even anywhere nearby yet?"

"Yes, sir," answered a lieutenant with one ear pressed firmly against a headset. "They've just reported in with the airfield. They're already in our airspace, and they've got the target sighted." The officer stopped speaking for a moment, obviously listening once more, then added;

"They estimate sixty seconds to target."

All eyes in the command center turned toward the battlefield. All duties were forgotten for the moment, all hope pouring out toward the pair of unseen bombers everyone present knew were somewhere in the dark sky above them.

"Fifty-five seconds . . ."

Once used for dropping explosive or fiery payloads on enemy troops, they had been converted decades earlier for use in combating forest fires in the mountains of upstate New York.

"Fifty seconds . . ."

Outfitted with warheads that released an oxygen-smothering foam, the airships once thought to have been rendered useless by the advancing technology of war had gained a new lease on life by becoming engines of mercy. Bulky, and ponderously slow, they were completely unfit for the wars of the modern world but perfectly suited for combating the fires that ravaged it. They did possess one glaring defect, however, considering the use to which they were about to be put.

"Forty-five seconds . . ."

They were hideously noisy.

"Sir!" shouted Klein, a frightening thought suddenly filling his mind. "Can you hear bombers, their engines, I mean? Can you hear them coming?" When Harris admitted that he could, the FBI man added;

"Do you think that thing can hear them?"

"Forty seconds . . ."

Instantly understanding Klein's implication, the major general turned to his second-in-command, barking orders. The fort's tanks and cannons, silent for so long during the battle, were now all to open fire upon the blazing monster once again.

"Thirty-five seconds . . ."

From some two score points around the battlefield, from far-off cannon emplacements as well as from tanks scattered all about the area, shells began to rain down on the burning monstrosity.

"Thirty seconds . . ."

As before, the continual explosions had little effect on the oddly lumbering creature—

"Twenty-five seconds . . ."

But they did manage to capture its attention once more.

"Fifteen seconds . . ."

So heavy was the sudden fire that the single-minded beast could not help but notice. Its primitive mind enraged, the horror turned from its pursuit of the truck holding the Dream Stone, directing its heated fury against the shells flooding the air, tearing up the ground beneath it, their explosions sending worrisome ripples through its less-than-substantial form.

"Ten seconds . . ."

Harris clamped his teeth fast against each other, grinding them in cold fury as the blazing shambler turned its power anew against his men and machines. Searing blasts of intense flame tore through the night once more, exploding tanks, disintegrating men.

"How many more," wondered Harris, watching his troops being burned to cinders, a part of his mind agonizing over each death while the rest of it maintained the calm every still-living member of his command desperately needed from him.

"Five seconds . . ."

Two more Abrams were destroyed in a furious blast spewed forth from the near-formless mass.

"Four . . ."

Shells exploding all about it, tremendous hunks of the Earth being launched through its ever-changing shape, the thing lashed out in a dozen directions at once, the single volley obliterating five more of the great war machines and their crews.

"Three . . ."

And then, suddenly the burning terror returned its attention to the Dream Stone. Perhaps its primitive instincts had redirected it; perhaps its target was reaching the boundaries of its ability to track it. Whatever the case, the monstrosity's attention fell away completely from the continual barrage chipping away at its form, preparing one final, massive release of power.

"Two . . ."

Its pseudoarms raised on high, the telltale glow signaling another energy release began to build. Unerringly pointing through the darkness at the fleeing vehicle, the horror prepared its last assault—

"One!"

And then, the landscape burst in an explosion of scorching white and flying cinders.

CHAPTER FORTY-FIVE

The Bakur thing, caught completely off-guard, had been splattered—knocked end over end by Knight's assault. Yes, the puppet had been aware of the instance earlier when the spirit of Dollins had entered the professor's body. It had realized the wraith meant to add its strength to Knight's abilities, but it had seen no reason to worry over the fact. One human plus one ghost meant simply the power of two human souls turned against it.

Such feeble odds did not concern a power as overwhelming as that of the A'ademir.

Walking stiffly across the cemetery lawn to where Bakur's steaming body lay, Knight offered several mental prayers pleading that the puppet had been destroyed. The professor had thrown all his remaining tricks into one final basket, a desperate gamble that had left him with barely the strength to stand. If he had not triumphed by that point, he feared he would never be able to do so. Nudging the body before him with his foot, he croaked;

"Well, are you dead, you miserable bastard?"

"Oh, that shell is quite dead."

Groaning internally, Knight turned as quickly as he could to confront the unexpected form of Dr. Ashur Ungari. Dropping his chin to his chest in weary exasperation, the professor whispered;

"Oh, damn the fools who plague me so . . . what are you doing here?"

"Nothing, I am afraid, my old friend, of which I think you are going to approve."

Knight's shoulders sagged heavily, dropping as far as they could without actually leaving their sockets. If only he knew what Agent Klein was thinking. If he knew the Dream Stone was safe, that bit of knowledge might have given him the hope to go on. But the FBI man's thoughts, along with those of all the others present that day when Knight had spiked their water, had completely ceased within his head half a day earlier.

Now the professor stared at the approaching Ungari, unable to comprehend what the doctor was doing there in the cemetery, cut off from all sources of information. Helpless and alone. And worse, as best his senses could tell, the archaeologist was not under the control of the A'ademir as his assistant had been—was not merely another extension of the extradimensional plunderer's will.

But, wondered Knight, *if he's not, then why is he here in Green-Wood? And why, if not controlled by the A'ademir, does he stink of the damn thing's power?*

"Both excellent questions, Piers. But," asked the doctor, "are you certain you would really like the answers?"

And at that moment, Knight froze in his tracks. He had said nothing, and yet Ungari had heard him, had heard his thoughts—

something even the Bakur puppet had not been able to do. Responding in a tired, defeated tone, the professor said;

"As greatly as I might fear whatever it is you have to say, I'm afraid that yes—I must hear it."

"Very well," answered the doctor, his smile somehow hard yet benevolent. "I will tell you all I know, that you might understand. First, allow me to congratulate your efforts. I never really thought any of you would be able to stop the—"

Ungari paused, fumbling for a word. After a moment, he finally shrugged, his smile widening as he admitted;

"The fiery beasts, there is no name for them. They are not native to our world. The A'ademir sent me a . . . how best to describe it? Ummm, a formula—yes. A recipe, as it were, for creating them. The one I sent upstate, to recover the Dream Stone, can you believe it? Destroyed by mere mortal troops."

Knight's heart surged.

The Dream Stone was safe.

Klein had upheld his part of the bargain. It was a miracle.

Now, the professor's brain hissed at him, *if we can only manufacture our own miracle . . .*

"And the detective," Ungari continued, seemingly oblivious to the effect of his news on Knight's flagging spirit, "containing one of them. It just proves the indomitable will of the human soul, my friend."

"How do you mean?"

The professor asked his question out of true curiosity. Yes, he meant to stall his former friend, needing every second he could to cobble together his fatigued strength. But yes again, a part of him realized that Ungari's answer was of extreme importance. Something was going on Knight could not yet comprehend, but which he knew he desperately needed to understand.

"I know you're stalling for time, but that is all right. You must come to see why I am doing as I am."

"I say this in all honesty, Ashur," Knight responded truthfully. "I certainly want to."

"I know you do, and thus I shall explain. You destroyed Bakur with the combined power of this remarkable detective person—"

"Dollins." When the doctor stared, uncomprehending, Knight explained, "His name was Jimmy Dollins."

"Ahhh, I see, yes—of course. Your Mr. Dollins must have been a remarkable man. He had the assistance of your magical trinket, but still, in his dying moments to not try to flee, to go to his death willingly as long as he could take the beast with him, ahh, as I said, remarkable."

Knight nodded his head in agreement, sucking down deep breaths one after another as he listened to the doctor. As Ungari continued, he almost seemed unaware of the professor's presence. Returning to the subject of Dollins' sacrifice, he said;

"This man, he saves all his fellows, and manages to contain the beast by sheer force of will. To do this, of course, he has to doom himself to an existence of roaming the world as a wraith. I send lightning to free my beast, thinking he will take this moment to pass on, and he manages to pull himself back together and contain my pet once more. Finally, he gives his soul over to you to destroy Bakur. Such nobility. And, it is for men like him that I do what I do."

Hopelessly lost, not having the slightest idea what Ungari was talking about, the professor closed his eyes, pulling down one final deep breath at the same time to cleanse his system. Then, reopening his eyes, he asked;

"And what exactly is it you are doing?"

"Saving the world, of course. No, I misspeak. I am saving humanity."

"From this A'ademir?"

"No, Piers—from itself." When Knight showed no further comprehension, Ungari began again, using the tone he would if trying to explain geometry to a child.

"We have pushed this planet to the brink of our own extinction. While the politicians lie and wrangle over the facts of global warming, greedily searching for their own temporary benefits, they doom their children to famine, misery, and death."

"Ashur—"

"Listen to me, Piers, old man: The facts are in; they are incontrovertible. The polar ice caps are disappearing. The deserts of the world are shifting. The Sahara is sweeping northward into Europe. In only thirty years it will be pushing its way through the Black Forest of Bavaria. The Sahara, extending into the heart of Germany—an incontrovertible fact. Do you not understand what this means? The human race is doomed, and there is nothing that can be done."

"Surely—"

"Nothing, my friend. If all greenhouse emissions were ceased this very night, it would not be enough. There were only three billion people on the face of the planet in the 1960s. Now the number is spinning toward seven billion. Human beings give off carbon dioxide when they breathe. Piers, the collective governments of the world could agree to slaughter two-thirds of their populations and it would not help. Rotting bodies also give off carbon dioxide. No, it is too late now, my friend, for any solution other than my own."

And then, in one frightening moment of clarity, Piers Knight suddenly understood what Ungari was trying to explain, and his blood froze within his veins.

CHAPTER FORTY-SIX

"You, you can't mean . . ."

"Ahhh." The light behind Ungari's eyes sparkled. "You understand at last. Of course I mean it. Just as the people of Memak'tori were swept from the face of the earth, so shall I save humanity by opening our world to the A'ademir."

Knight stood for a moment, transfixed, unable to move, to speak—even to blink. The monstrous truth of his one-time friend's admission had stunned him utterly, throwing his mind into a turmoil. He had just been told the sacrificial destruction of billions of human beings was but seconds away. Standing in the darkened cemetery, the early summer night's chill invading his bones, the professor wrestled with the magnitude of Ungari's proposal.

Was there, he wondered, something to it?

If the human race was doomed to massive starvation, to plague and food riots, to a reversion to tribal gang wars, ever-shrinking pockets of people slaughtering one another over ever-dwindling resources, might there not be something to the doctor's solution? It was severe, cold-hearted—but then, so was amputating a young man's leg to protect him from gangrene.

If there's really no other way to save the human race from extinction, thought Knight, *could the ends justify the means?*

"Understand me, Piers," came Ungari's voice in a whisper. "I'm not doing this to become king of the world. To allow the A'ademir access to this world, I will have to offer my own body as its passageway. I would be the first consumed." And with those words, the doctor turned Knight from any consideration of his ideals. His eyes narrowing to hard slits, fingers curling into fists, the professor responded;

"You almost had me convinced."

"You do not believe me?"

"Oh, I believe you, Ashur. That's the problem. Like all self-made martyrs, you think that passing by the rewards of those you consider villains makes you noble. But the prize you're chasing is adoration. 'He gave his life for humanity. Oh, how we love him.' Your problem is you're afraid to be here when the rising tides have swamped the coasts. You're terrified of the idea of sand dunes spreading across the base of the Eiffel Tower. You're a coward—but the thing that annoys me is, for a minute there . . . you almost turned me into one, too."

The doctor's body went coldly rigid. His teeth grinding down firm, he blinked, and suddenly the light behind his eyes flashed forward with a menacing glow. His hands rising, fingertips meeting, pressing against one another before his face, Ungari growled;

"I wanted you to understand what I was doing, Piers. To join me. To welcome the A'ademir."

"What, as they did in Memak'tori? Tell me, 'old friend,' did your precious A'ademir leave anyone behind ten thousand years ago when it dropped in for lunch? For God's sake, man, what makes you think it's going to this time?"

Without answering, without warning, Ungari turned his palms toward the professor and unleashed a bolt of pure force, one far more focused than the lightning he had used previously. Expecting such treachery, however, Knight was ready with his white-oak rune held firm in the same hand wearing the ring returned to him that evening. Deflecting the shot, knowing he could not survive many more, the professor turned and ran into the cemetery, desperate to gain some time. Shaking his head slightly, sadly, Ungari marched forward at a steady pace, calling out;

"Do not waste our time, Piers. You cannot escape me. You cannot defeat me."

Ignoring the doctor's comments, Knight raced through the cemetery, his mind desperately attempting to concoct some sort of plan.

"You are a competent, minor magician, Piers!" shouted Ungari. "I grant you that. But the tiny grams of power you might be able to pull out of this place are nothing compared to that which I hold. Let us make this easy upon ourselves."

Crashing wildly along through the poorly lit graveyard, the professor tried to remember the way to one particular spot. Ungari was correct about his magical abilities. As he had explained to Bridget only the other night, he was capable of extracting the stored energy in objects. But what object, anywhere within Green-Wood, could possibly hold enough energy to withstand the power granted the doctor by his extradimensional accomplice?

Hoping he knew, Knight pushed himself to the limit, throwing himself through hedges, slipping on the dew-soaked grass, while all along Ungari followed him slowly but steadily.

Finally, when the doctor caught up to Knight, he found the

professor sprawled in front of a slightly larger than life-size statue of one goddess or another. Walking forward, the doctor reached down and then jerked Knight roughly to his feet. Holding him aloft, he said in a chiding voice;

"Piers, foolish little Piers. This is your answer, your means of defeating me? A statue of Minerva? How much energy did you think you would find stored here? It has been nearly two thousand years since she was worshiped with any regularity by the *pontifex maximus.* Since I don't believe this edifice was erected that long ago, who do you think has been leaving any emotional energy here?" Throwing the professor back against the statue, Ungari laughed as he added;

"Here, old man, take what you want from your relic. Take your best shot. Then I shall get along with the business of saving mankind."

Clutching the statue, licking at the blood leaking from his cracked lips, dribbling down from his broken nose, Knight slowly began to drag himself upward as he explained;

"You're right; it is a statue of Minerva. She was the Roman goddess of war, as I'm certain you remember."

"I do."

"Well, the funny thing about history, Ashur, is that it's hard to know all of it. For instance, Charles Higgins, the man who built this mausoleum for himself, christened this piece *Minerva and the Altar of Liberty.* Can you guess why?" When Ungari merely shrugged, Knight, his hands still gripping the statue hard as he continued to struggle back to his feet, told him;

"It was meant to commemorate the Revolutionary War's Battle of Brooklyn. Higgins built his resting place here, on this hill, because it was the site of one of the bloodiest battles of that conflict. Lot of blood spilled here, lot of mourning—still, you're right, even with nearly a hundred years of visitors to this site to see this piece, there couldn't be enough energy for me to gather to stop the A'ademir." The professor paused for a moment, then added softly;

"Or at least, there wouldn't be, if it weren't for one little thing."

"And what is that?"

"To leave behind a piece of one's soul, to mark a site with one's own ectoplasmic residue, one must be moved. The soul must be stirred. You were right about Minerva. In this day and age she does not elicit much in the way of human response anymore. But . . . she makes an excellent receptacle for a lady who does."

So saying, Knight pointed forward off to some faraway point in the gloomy distance. Still unworried over Knight or his abilities, the doctor turned around to see at what his former friend was pointing. As he did so, Ungari caught sight of something far off in the waters beyond the distant shore. As he tried to make it out in the gloom, the professor told him;

"If you haven't heard, we call her the Statue of Liberty. And unlike Minerva, the sight of her does stir the souls of men."

And, so saying, Piers Knight reached into Higgins' monument and unleashed in one overwhelming flash the stored awe and respect of millions for the great bronze lady in the harbor beyond.

For close to a century, visitors had been following Minerva's hand as it pointed through the always carefully trimmed trees to her counterpart beyond. Goddess of war, Mistress of Liberty, the effect of seeing the one hailing the other had moved hundreds upon hundreds of thousands to tears. Now, Knight gathered every iota of that raw emotion unto himself and used it to defend all of mankind.

The power slammed into Ungari with the force of a runaway truck. The doctor was smashed into the ground, flipped head over heels, then driven harshly into the earth. Despite the power granted to him by his extradimensional benefactor, Ungari's bones were cracked, his nervous system set afire, his blood boiled within his organs and veins and heart.

The doctor struggled to turn back toward Knight, to defend himself, to protect his dream. He could not. His eyes roasted, steam falling away from his body, drifting on the breeze, he attempted to take a step toward the professor, only to fall over suddenly. His back slamming against a small tombstone, Ungari felt his spine shatter. He gasped as the additional pain tore through his nervous system. Then, just when Knight had no more energy to throw against him, the doctor slumped over and slid to the ground. Beaten.

Destroyed.

Hoping his work might finally be over, the professor allowed his straining legs to collapse underneath himself. Somewhere on the trip to the ground he closed his eyes, never actually feeling the moment of impact.

EPILOGUE

It was several hours before Piers Knight woke up. When he did so, he found himself stretched out upon his own living room couch. Sitting in one of the chairs on the other side of the room he found Denny LaRaja, quietly sipping a cup of tea. As the professor stirred, the detective said;

"Hmmm, well, look at you, all awake and everything. Welcome back to the land of the living."

"Thank you. Glad to be back. Where's Bridget?"

"In the kitchen, making more tea. Shall we get you a cup?" Forcing himself up upon his elbows, Knight replied;

"I think I'd like that—yes."

Over the next forty-some minutes, the three caught each other up-to-date. Word from Fort Drum was that a terrorist attack had been averted at a great cost of American life and property. Hints were made about some sort of terrible new weapon, but there had been no mention of fire demons. As for Bakur and Ungari, LaRaja had called in an "anonymous" tip, alerting the authorities as to where they might find the bodies. Charred, broken, partially disintegrated, the uncovering of what had happened to them would be left to the federal authorities, along with the mystery of the disappearance of the FBI agents who had been keeping tabs on the two men.

Most likely, Knight thought, *it will simply be decided they fell victim to the same weapon that was unleashed at Drum. Bureaucrats do like to tie things up neatly.*

It was agreed upon that if as simple a thing as keeping the Dream Stone from being returned to Syria could forestall the A'ademir from entering the Middle East, then it would be best if the artifact was destroyed. Considering the world already believed that was the case anyway, the professor had suggested to Klein while they were updating each other that the agent take care of that small problem. The FBI man assured Knight such would give him immense satisfaction.

"So that's it," asked the detective. "This whole thing is over now?"

"As best I can tell," answered Knight honestly. "I mean, until a few hours ago, we didn't even know what it was about. And once we did, it was finished. Thanks to Detective Dollins more than anyone else, I think. He was a brave man, and he sacrificed more than possibly any other man ever has to safeguard us all. Your friend was a real hero."

"He was a New York City cop," answered LaRaja quietly. Taking a last sip from his tea, he started to speak once more, but was forced to stop for a moment, obviously overcome by emotion. Then, after his brief pause, he added, "And he was a cop I'm going to miss."

"What will you do now," asked Bridget.

"I could write a book on dark forces in the Big Apple, I suppose," responded the detective. "But I doubt anyone would believe me."

"I've tried to tell some of what I've seen over the years," admitted Knight, "but to be honest, people only seem to want to hear about things like this when they can still believe it's all myths. Once you make it real for them, they usually start talking burning stakes and pillory wheels."

"Better than castigation from the tongues of the so-called Moral Majority," joked the detective. Knight thought to correct him, then let the comment slide, simply gracing the officer with a half smile.

LaRaja stayed for only a short while longer. Making an admission of his own, that he needed to spend some time thinking as to whether or not he finally wanted to take his retirement, he finished his tea and then excused himself. Although he had not said so, he left the professor's home having made it quite clear he would not be saying anything to anyone else about the nature of the extraordinary events he had witnessed.

After the detective had exited, Knight and his assistant sat in the living room for quite a few long minutes without speaking. They busied themselves with their tea, as well as the biscuits and cookies Bridget had brought out, but words failed them. The professor chose not to speak for two reasons. The first was simply that he was tired and had been given much to think upon. The second was that he could tell the young redhead sitting on the other end of the couch was troubled by something.

Give her some time, he thought. *If she wants you to know something, she'll tell you.* And then no sooner had he given himself that piece of advice, she said;

"Professor, do you think we're all done with monsters and ghosts and lightning bolts and the like? At least for a moment?" When he assured her he thought it most likely, Bridget asked, "Then I'd like to tell you something."

"I think at this point, my dear, you've earned the right to say whatever you'd like to me."

Bridget gave herself a moment. Then, she turned herself bodily, lifting one leg onto the couch and tucking it under herself so that she was facing Knight directly. Realizing whatever she wanted to say must be important to her, the professor turned himself likewise.

"I'm not a virgin."

"Well," answered Knight, slightly taken aback but trying not to show it, "commendable. Good for you."

"You've been treating me since I met you as if I were made of Dresden china. I just wanted to . . ." She paused for a second, blushing, then said, "To make sure you knew I was actually a woman."

As Bridget paused once more, her head dropping slightly for a moment, Knight reached forward, setting his teacup on the table in front of the couch. When she looked back up, her eyes locked with the professor's as she explained;

"Granted, I'm not usually such a forward woman, but—"

And then, as Knight's eyes suddenly went slightly wide, Bridget realized that it had taken him that long to realize what she had been implying. Blushing harder, she did not notice the professor blushing as well as she said;

"Okay, now that I've made a complete fool out of myself, I think I'd, I mean—"

Bridget began to stand, but the jerkiness to the way in which she was moving indicated she had no idea in which direction she should go. Upstairs, outside—where? Before she could pick one, however, the professor reached across the couch, touching her gently on the wrist. As she turned to him, a slightly flustered Knight offered;

"You know there isn't a red-blooded man on the face of this planet who would turn down such an offer. You, ah . . . you were making an—"

"Yes," she cut him off, half-ready to laugh, half-ready to cry, "I was throwing myself at you. . . ."

"Please." The professor said the word softly, his tone as tender as human speech could render the word. "Please sit down. Don't make an old fool feel even more foolish." Bridget sat again, unable to look at Knight. Moving his hand down to where he could envelop her fingers with his, the professor said;

"First, allow me to apologize. Since we had earlier so thoroughly dismissed the idea of my, how shall I phrase it, 'making advances' toward you, I have to admit I really was quite caught off-guard at the idea of you doing so toward me." Giving the back of Bridget's head a half smile, he added;

"Devilish unfair of you, teasing the elderly so."

"I wasn't teasing," she answered, still not turning around. Sighing at the dismal reception his feeble attempt at humor had garnered, the professor admitted;

"I know you weren't. But really, my dear, are you certain you've quite thought this through?" Not allowing Bridget the chance to answer, he continued, saying;

"You've had a rather exciting introduction to our fair city, and I, for one, am quite certain that you deserve a bit of time to think about this, I have to say, quite wonderful idea of yours, a bit later, say when the sky isn't literally falling in on us."

"Are you saying I don't know my own mind, Professor?"

"No, not at all." As Bridget finally turned back toward Knight, their eyes met once more as he told her gently, "I'm telling you that I think a great deal of you. And that we have months together ahead of us." Locking his eyes with hers, he then added;

"I'm saying I think we both need to spend a little time contemplating such a thing. I mean, after all, I want you to still respect me in the morning."

"I think I would," Bridget answered, her tone a trifle hurt.

"You know," answered Knight with a grin, "I think you would, too. But, let's be certain. Besides . . ." His eyes suddenly filling with merriment, the professor released his assistant's hand as he exclaimed;

"Bless all the tiny monkeys, I know what we need!" Hustling Bridget up off the couch and toward the door to his garage, he said;

"I know an all-night diner, the Del Rio, wonderful place, one of Brooklyn's finest—no more than fifteen minutes from here. They serve a full menu, but they're only good for two things, burgers and breakfast."

Jumping down the three stairs leading into the garage, Knight circled to the driver's side of the car, calling out;

"We'll order family-style—pancakes and sausages, home fries and toast, juice and eggs, three different types. And bacon. What do you say, my dear? If we're going to sin this early in our relationship, let's start with nitrates."

Throwing the professor a grin that signaled the acceptance of her defeat, Bridget leaped down into the garage, heading for the passenger-side door.

Why not? she told herself. *I like bacon as much as the next girl. And besides, as far as you and I are concerned, Professor Piers Knight . . .*

Smiling, she slid into her seat.

I've got all summer.